THE MAN WHO CALLED HIMSELF POE

THE MAN
WHO CALLED
HIMSELF POE

Edited by Sam Moskowitz

Doubleday & Company, Inc., Garden City, New York

ACKNOWLEDGMENTS

Thomas Ollive Mabbott, in *The Reader's Encyclopedia of American Literature*, by Max J. Herzberg. Copyright © 1962 by Thomas Y. Crowell Company, New York, publishers.

In Which an Author and His Character Are Well Met, Copyright 1928 by Doubleday, Doran & Company, Inc., for *Seaports in the Moon* by Vincent Starrett. Reprinted by permission of the author.

When It Was Moonlight by Manly Wade Wellman. Copyright 1940 by Street & Smith Publications, Inc., for *Unknown*, February 1940. Reprinted by permission of the copyright owner, The Condé Nast Publications, Inc.

The Man Who Collected Poe by Robert Bloch. Copyright 1951 by Popular Publications, Inc., for *Famous Fantastic Mysteries*, October 1951. Reprinted by permission of the author and the author's agent, Harry Altshuler.

The Man Who Thought He Was Poe by Michael Avallone, *Tales of the Frightened*, August 1957. Copyright 1957 by Republic Features Syndicate, Inc. Reprinted by permission of the author.

The Dark Brotherhood by H. P. Lovecraft and August W. Derleth. Copyright 1966 by August Derleth for *The Dark Brotherhood and Other Pieces by H. P. Lovecraft & Divers Hands*, Arkham House, Suak City, Wisconsin. Reprinted by permission of the copyright owner.

Manuscript Found in a Drawer by Charles Norman. Copyright 1968 by Charles Norman.

Castaway by Edmond Hamilton. Copyright 1968 by Edmond Hamilton. Published by permission of the author and the author's agents, Scott Meredith Literary Agency, Inc.

The Lighthouse by Edgar Allan Poe and Robert Bloch. Copyright 1952 by Ziff-Davis Publishing Co. for *Fantastic*, January-February 1953. Reprinted by permission of the author and the author's agent, Harry Altshuler.

Edgar Allan Poe by Adolphe de Castro, published in the May 1937 *Weird Tales* magazine. Copyright © 1937 by the Popular Fiction Company. Reprinted by permission of the copyright owners.

Providence: Two Gentlemen Meet at Midnight by August W. Derleth. Published in *The Arkham Sampler*, Autumn 1948. Copyright 1948 by August Derleth. Reprinted by permission of the copyright owner.

Baltimore, October 3rd by Robert A. W. Lowndes. Copyright 1968 by Robert A. W. Lowndes.

To Madeline Haycock
Who has always possessed a real interest
in Edgar Allan Poe
the man and his works

Contents

Fiction by Poe (?)

Introduction

By Sam Moskowitz

If the life of any American author can be said to be making a transition from fact to folklore, it is that of Edgar Allan Poe. He stands unique among American authors, a strange and tragic figure, a victim of his times and of his temperament, striking chords of originality that marked him a multifaceted literary genius. He is revered by devotees of the detective and mystery story as the true father of the genre. He flawlessly designed the basic principles of the modern science fiction story, which through Jules Verne created the field as we know it today. He presaged the effectiveness of the psychological in tales of terror.

In poetry, he had an absolute pitch for the cadence of words, supreme and unsurpassed in the art. Quite practically, he was the first important literary critic on the American scene, and as an editor, except for his own poorly financed venture, he was dramatically effective.

He appeals to a wide range of readers, many of whom evince a considerable interest in his background, philosophy, and times. The result has been a substantial number of biographies and literary critiques that reflect considerable research and information.

First editions of some of his books command among the highest prices for works produced upon American presses. His original letters and manuscripts are sought after by wealthy men and well-financed institutions, the only ones who can afford them.

As a result, much is known about the life of the man and a substantial amount of what is known has received widespread circulation not only among the literary but also among the general public.

At least one biography, substantially buttressed with original scholarship, was a best seller—*Israfel* by Hervey Allen (1924)—and other scholars have never forgiven him his success. The biography generally acknowledged to be the most satisfactory, Arthur Hobson Quinn's *Edgar Allan Poe*, has gone into six printings since its publication in 1941. The foregoing, and the considerable number of other biographies, have contributed to building the Poe mystique.

Literary critics and historians referring to the "mystery" of Edgar Allan Poe the man infuriated Arthur Hobson Quinn, who though he was probably that author's leading biographer, was also his apologist.

"Most of the problems have arisen from the deliberate perversion of facts by his biographers, beginning with himself, or by the invention of theories concerning his nature which reveal not his impotency but that of his critics," Quinn stormed in his *American Fiction* (1936). "There is no mystery about the real Poe, the hard working man of letters, proud as a demon, yet, in order to make a living, descending to many of the tricks he despised."

He was railing against such critics and literary historians as Fred Lewis Pattee, who in *The First Century of American Literature, 1770–1870* (1935), after conceding Poe no virtue but "genius," then justifies his undiminished literary reputation across the generations by concluding: "To read him with fullest effect, however, one must be conscious at every moment of Edgar Allan Poe. He has been kept alive these two generations or three not because of his work but because of himself. And the mystery has become a myth, the shadow of which lengthens with the years."

It would seem that Pattee's logic had flip-flopped. He was correct when he stated that a delicious note of mystery increasingly surrounded the name of Edgar Allan Poe. He was wrong when he attributed the longevity of the works to the interest in the man. It is only because the stories and poems are unlike any other in literature; because they are cast in formats superlative to any of their predecessors; because they deal with subject matter remarkable in originality and bizarreness; because they are written in rhythms and arrangements flashed through with genius; *that the public is interested in the man.*

How did he come to create masterpieces which stand so uniquely alone? What was he prevented from writing and what did he plan to do had he lived?

Speculation on the life of Poe is impelled by the same unbridled curiosity that causes people to read science fiction. Up until the dawn of the space age, astronomy had revealed to mankind that the sky was filled with myriad worlds, and concerning some of them it uncovered tantalizing hints and absorbing mysteries. To the truly imaginative the point where astronomical knowledge ended was one of maddening frustration. Beyond this point writers of science fiction were called upon to astound the reader with intriguing speculations and to parade the planets like fashion models through the pages of pulp magazines, clad in the garments of the firmament, as a palliative for a curiosity that had grown to the proportions of lust.

The cult that has formed with fascination around the unelaborated inferences and minutia of Sherlock Holmes bears close resemblance to the attitudes of the more rabid science fiction readers. What started out as a "don't take yourself so serious" joke from friend to friend when Robert Barr, writing under the name of Luke Sharp, published *The Adventures of Sherlaw Kombs* in the April 1892 issue of *The Idler* has achieved the proportions of a separate literary genre. The field of Sherlock Holmes research, pastiche writing, and errata has developed lead writers, second stringers, and hacks. Pieces concerning "the sacred writings" appear in leading national publications; specialized periodicals are issued by its devotees, and not a year passes when there are not at least a couple of hard covers adding to the legend.

If you want a Who's Who of all characters in Sherlock Holmes stories, a plot outline of each of the stories, a generous selection of quotations concerning the Great Detective, a dossier on Holmes' biographer Watson and a brief one on A. Conan Doyle, read *The Sherlock Holmes Companion* by Michael and Mollie Hardwick (John Murray, 1962). Lest there is any doubt concerning the authenticity of the locale of the Sherlock Holmes stories, they will be mitigated by *In the Footsteps of Sherlock Holmes* by Michael Harrison (Cassell & Company, 1958), which substantiates them all thoroughly. If a lingering question still remains that Sherlock Holmes was anything but a real person, it will be eliminated by William S. Baring-Gould's *Sherlock Holmes of Baker Street* (Clarkson N. Potter, 1962), which fills in all the gaps in Holmes' "life" and joins together his cases in an incredibly believable scholarly and literary achievement. The foregoing are but a sample selection of an entire literature on the subject of Sherlock Holmes.

As can be seen, the efforts of the Baker Street Irregulars has been dedicated to turning a fictional character into a real person. Only one readership phenomenon in literary history can be compared to it and that is the attempts of the admirers of Edgar Allan Poe to turn his life into fiction!

The more people read Poe, the more absorbed they become in the man himself. Few lives are as thoroughly documented as that of Edgar Allan Poe, yet his admirers are not satisfied. They are sure there is more, much more, to the life of Poe than has yet been told, particularly since Poe deliberately spread fanciful stories about himself. As strange as Poe's life was, it does not adequately supply them with the feeling that they know why he wrote as he did.

This book is dedicated to assisting those thousands of readers all over the world who are determined to turn the real Edgar Allan Poe into a fictional character in order to assuage their curiosity concerning him.

It collects for the first time in literary history the best stories in which Edgar Allan Poe appears as an integral character. It is intended to serve the same purpose that science fiction offers to the young student of astronomy—conjecture of what is beyond the sight of the telescope. Like all good science fiction, each story begins from a factual premise, some basic and valid information about Edgar Allan Poe, and proceeds from there. Yet only a few of these stories are science fiction, for quite logically they tend to cover the gamut of Poe's own genius: the detective story, murder mystery, horror tale, supernatural, humor, bittersweet remembrance, and even verse.

This volume goes one step further and includes rarely seen Poe marginalia, tipping the book in the direction of scholarship. Though the intent is entertainment, the method is serious and the tongue is not in the cheek.

This compilation leads off with a biographical sketch of Edgar Allan Poe by the late Thomas Ollive Mabbott, who was widely regarded during his lifetime as the greatest authority on that author. Before his death, Professor Mabbott had completed preparation on the *definitive* edition of the works of Edgar Allan Poe, to be published by Harvard, containing 20 per cent more material than any previous assemblage and running into a number of volumes. The purpose of his biographical sketch of Poe here is to supply a jumping-off-place for the readers of the fiction. Supplied are the facts of Poe's life set down by the man best qualified to tell them. The biography should be read first, and as the reader relates the truth to the events described in the fiction, enjoyment will be greatly enhanced.

Perhaps the most remarkable item in this collection is "The Valley of Unrest" by Douglass Sherley. This novelette with its two introductions by the author actually comprised an entire book originally printed in 1884 and reprinted here in its entirety. It is virtually unknown to Poe scholars, Professor Mabbott asserting he had never previously seen or heard of it, and is the one selection which may be more than fiction, for mixed in with facts about Poe's school days known to be true there are others which might be and have not been verified or disproved. It should provide an entertaining exercise for Poe scholars to separate fact from fiction in this one with the conceivable result of adding a few footnotes of interest to the life of Poe.

Julian Hawthorne, the son of Nathaniel Hawthorne, was one of those to whom the facts of Poe's life were not enough. He delves into psychology in "My Adventure with Edgar Allan Poe," in which the author is brought back to life and given a chance for a new start.

Perhaps the best-known short story featuring Edgar Allan Poe is the work of the deservedly popular literary critic Vincent Starrett, "In Which an Author and His Character Are Well Met," from his book *Seaports in the Moon* (Doubleday, 1928). The last days of Edgar Allan Poe provide the basis of a beautifully told fantasy.

Manly Wade Wellman, highly regarded as a writer of mystery, science fiction, and the supernatural, appropriately combines all three elements in "When It Was Moonlight" to conjecture on how at least three of Poe's stories came to be written.

The influence of Poe upon the reader is the subject of "The Man Who Thought He Was Poe," a murder mystery with an Alfred Hitchcock-like twist by the talented creator of the Ed Noon private-eye series, Michael Avallone.

The name most frequently linked with Poe in this generation is that of H. P. Lovecraft. "The Dark Brotherhood" is based on one of his dreams, set to fiction by August W.

Derleth. Quite typically of Lovecraft, multiple Poes are linked to a menace from outer space.

Two stories involving Poe make their first appearance in print in this anthology. "Manuscript Found in a Drawer" by the distinguished biographer and mystery story writer Charles Norman sets out to tell a story in the Poe tradition and in so doing also shows the impact of its happenings on the life of Poe. "Castaway" was commissioned especially for this volume and deals with the brief period during Poe's life when he was publisher of his own magazine. Its author, Edmond Hamilton, as one of the leading science fiction writers, has cast it in the format most natural to him.

Regarded as the modern master of psychological terror is Robert Bloch, who wrote the book upon which the film *Psycho* was based. Many have brooded upon what Poe might have written had he lived a little longer, and Bloch seeks to answer that question, incorporating actual passages from Poe's work in "The Man Who Collected Poe" to heighten the realism.

How can there be a book of Poe without something by Poe?

Before he died, Poe wrote a 600-word fragment of a tale he planned to call "The Lighthouse." This fragment is not included in his collected works and appears here finished by Robert Bloch as a truly effective terror tale that does Poe no dishonor.

Among those things which Poe authorities have seriously considered as possibly his under a pen name is the Utopian satire "The Atlantis," a novel-length work originally published in 1838–39. A five-thousand-word segment, with the most Poe-esque flavor, is reprinted for the first time since its original appearance so that the Poe specialists can form their own opinion.

Were this book about anyone but Poe, verse might be considered an affectation. To omit it, considering Poe was one of the greatest stylists ever to rhyme a line, would be an affront. The poetry selections are not only highly unusual but are in keeping with the motif of the volume. Three sonnets by three poets, H. P. Lovecraft, R. H. Barlow, and Adolphe de Castro, written in a Providence graveyard where once Poe walked, are presented as a trinity. They inspired an extraordinarily appropriate narrative in verse in which the shades of H. P. Lovecraft and Edgar Allan Poe meet in that very graveyard, penned by August W. Derleth.

A rarely seen and unusual item, a valentine poem written to her husband by Poe's dying wife Virginia, is also included.

The book is appropriately closed by a narrative poem of Poe's last days composed especially for this volume by Robert A. W. Lowndes, editor of *The Magazine of Horror,* a publication for which Poe would have felt an affinity.

Every piece in the book is prefaced by introductory notes of various lengths by the editor, to put them in proper perspective for reader understanding and enjoyment.

The Mystery Writers of America annually award coveted busts of Edgar Allan Poe, called "Edgars," for the best mystery stories of the year, and have a special award appropriately known as "The Raven." With that impetus the great danger of this book is that it will start a cult calling themselves "The Ravens," who will meet in a loft called "The House of Usher" and publish as their official organ "The Stylus."

THE MAN WHO CALLED HIMSELF POE

Before his death, Thomas Ollive Mabbott had completed the summation of his life's work: a definitive compilation of the writings of Edgar Allan Poe, with approximately 20 per cent more wordage than had ever previously been collected or published. The early volumes have been ready for publication since 1962 and Harvard is to undertake the project.

Few books on the life of Poe have appeared in the last 40 years without some reference, if not direct acknowledgment, to the researches of Professor Mabbott. His books on Poe include *Poe's Politan* (1923), *Selected Poems of Poe* (1928), *Poe's Doings of Gotham* (1929), *Poe's Tamerlane* (1941), and *Selections From Poe* (1951), among others. When Mabbott's definitive edition of Poe appears, it will not only incorporate a very substantial amount of previously uncollected criticism but also some newly discovered poems.

Poe was by no means Mabbott's only literary interest. He had written works on Walt Whitman and William Cullen Bryant, actively collected H. P. Lovecraft, and had admitted to an unrepentant fondness for the sword and sorcery sagas of Robert E. Howard.

No fiction based on the life of Poe could be adequately enjoyed without a ready reference to the key events in which that author was involved. The following essay, a little under five thousand words, is perhaps the most excellent brief condensation of the life and criticism of the works of Edgar Allan Poe ever set down on paper, prepared by a ranking scholar who utilized primary sources in gathering and verifying the bulk of his information.

Edgar Allan Poe: A Biography in Brief

By Thomas Ollive Mabbott

Born: Boston, January 19, 1809   Died: October 7, 1849

Edgar Allan Poe was born the son of a talented actress, Elizabeth Arnold, and her second husband, David Poe, Jr., an actor and the son of a prominent officer in the Revolution. Orphaned in Richmond late in 1811, Poe was taken into the home of John Allan, a wealthy merchant. Allan, who regarded the boy as a genius, apparently became his godfather but did not formally adopt him.

The Allan family visited Scotland, and went to England in 1815, where Poe attended the classical academy of Dr. John Bransby at Stoke Newington. In the summer of 1820 the family returned to Richmond, where the boy entered the school of Joseph H. Clarke, and composed a number of verses in honor of local schoolgirls. These are lost, but a satire, written when Poe was enrolled at the school of William Burke in 1823 and 1824 has survived.

Poe fell in love with Elmira Royster and was secretly engaged when he went to the University of Virginia in February 1826; however, the engagement came to nothing, for Miss Royster's family intercepted the letters of the pair, and shortly thereafter arranged for her engagement to Alexander Barret Shelton of Richmond. At the university Poe stood high in Greek, Latin, French, Italian, and Spanish, but remained only one term; apparently Allan had refused Poe spending money, and the young man gambled in hopes of raising funds. When he acquired only debts, Allan withdrew his godson from the university. Tales of Poe's heavy drinking at that time are probably exaggerated; however, Poe was constitutionally unable to tolerate liquor, and even small amounts often had disastrous effects upon him.

On his return to Richmond Poe quarreled with his godfather and ran away to Baltimore and then to Boston, where he arranged for his first volume, *Tamerlane and Other Poems* (1827), to be published anonymously. Some of the poems concerned his unhappy love affair with Miss Royster; the best one, "The Lake," is about the legends told of the Lake of the Dismal Swamp, near Norfolk. Poe was unable to find employment, and, in desperate financial straits, enlisted in the army under the name of "Edgar A. Perry";

he was sent to Fort Moultrie on Sullivan's Island, the scene of his later story, "The Gold Bug." He wrote to Allan, asking him to help secure his release from the army, but Allan refused until the death of his wife, who pleaded Poe's cause on her deathbed. Allan sent for Poe on the condition that Poe would enter West Point, and the two were at least temporarily reconciled.

Poe published another volume, *Al Aaraaf, Tamerlane, and Minor Poems,* in Baltimore in 1829. Included is "Fairyland," an archly humorous poem owing something to *A Midsummer Night's Dream* and entirely unlike anything else Poe wrote. He returned to Richmond and quarreled again with John Allan before entering West Point in the summer of 1830. When Allan remarried in October of that year, it was apparent to Poe that he could expect little further aid from that quarter; shortly thereafter Allan disowned him because of a disparaging remark made by Poe in a letter that reached Allan's hands. With no immediate financial resources and no hope of any from the Allan family, Poe set about getting himself expelled from West Point.

Poe came to New York, where he published *Poems* (1831). The preface to this volume shows he took an interest in Coleridge's critical theories, by which some critics feel Poe was influenced. Others find in Poe a kinship to Byron, Moore, and Shelley alone among the great romantics. The influence of the Baltimore lyrist, Edward Coote Pinckney, also seems sure. But Poe was already very much his own man, as is evidenced in the great brief lyric "To Helen," in "Israfel," and in "The Sleeper," a macabre poem of which its author was curiously fond. The two strange landscapes, "The City in the Sea," which describes the ruins of Gomorrah, and "The Valley of Unrest," about the Hebrides, show great originality.

Poe went to Baltimore and began to write short stories. Some of these, submitted in a prize contest, were published in the Philadelphia *Saturday Courier* in 1832. In 1833 the

"Ms. Found in a Bottle" won a fifty-dollar prize from the Baltimore *Saturday Visiter* and brought Poe some national recognition. He went to work on a play, *Politan*, which he never finished. Through the novelist John P. Kennedy he established a connection with the *Southern Literary Messenger* of Richmond; he became its assistant editor and then, in December 1835, its editor. He urged high literary standards, and during his editorship the *Messenger's* subscription list increased from 500 to over 3500. However, his castigations of unimportant books led to literary quarrels from which he was never to be free thereafter. Meanwhile Poe's aunt, Mrs. Maria Poe Clemm, with whom he had resided in Baltimore, arranged a marriage there in September between Poe and her daughter Virginia, who was then only thirteen years old. The couple lived for two years as brother and sister, but the marriage led to some social disapproval. Virginia was a devoted and sometimes a tolerant wife, but "never read half" of her husband's poetry. During her life Poe addressed no poems to her. He was apparently very much attached to Mrs. Clemm, who was the mainstay of the family during their long bouts of poverty and Virginia's illness; Poe wrote for her his charming sonnet "To My Mother" (1849).

For the *Messenger* Poe wrote "Berenice" and "Morella," as well as *Hans Pfaal*, a comic tale of a voyage to the moon. Two poems, "Bridal Ballad" and "To Zante," may have related to a meeting with his first love, Elmira Royster, now Mrs. Shelton. Poe also began a serial, "Arthur Gordon Pym," installments of which appeared in January and February of 1837; however, he then resigned from the *Messenger* and came to New York, where he published the complete serial as a book in 1838. An account of sea adventures based on fact, *The Narrative* is a grotesque and imaginative tale that ends in wildly incredible scenes near the South Pole. It was greatly admired by Charles Baudelaire, though Poe himself called it a silly book.

In the summer of 1838 Poe was in Philadelphia, helping a Professor Thomas Wyatt bring out two books on natural history. Finally he became an editor of *Burton's Gentleman's Magazine* in May 1839. The magazine was owned by the comedian William E. Burton, with whom Poe remained until they quarreled in June of 1840. Poe had plans for a magazine of his own to be called, punningly, *The Penn,* and later *The Stylus.* Beyond several prospectuses, the last in 1848, nothing came of it. He also solved ciphers in a paper called *Alexander's Weekly Messenger,* and wrote miscellaneous papers, including a few news articles. In *The Saturday Evening Post* for May 1, 1841, Poe predicted the ending of Dickens' *Barnaby Rudge* from the first chapters.

George R. Graham bought Burton out and established *Graham's Magazine* in December of 1840. Poe became an editor in charge of reviews with the April issue, and remained until May 1842. As had been the case with the *Southern Literary Messenger,* the circulation of the magazine increased dramatically while Poe was associated with it.

Although *Tales of the Grotesque and Arabesque* (1840), containing twenty-five pieces, sold badly, Poe was busy with short stories, and produced some of his masterpieces. "The Murders in the Rue Morgue" was in *Graham's* for April 1841; if not the first detective story, it was certainly that which set the form. Poe was also to invent almost all the species of the genus; he made an attempt (not wholly successful) to solve a real crime in "The Mystery of Marie Rogêt" in 1842; he dismissed the crime itself as of no interest in "The Purloined Letter" (1844); and in the same year he wrote "Thou Art the Man," the first story in which the criminal is at first undetected because he looks like a wholly respectable person. Other notable stories written between 1838 and 1843 include "Ligeia," "The Fall of the House of Usher," "William Wilson," the enigmatic "Eleonora," "The Masque of the Red Death," "The Tell-Tale Heart," "The

Black Cat," "The Premature Burial," and the most popular of all, "The Gold Bug," perhaps the greatest of all tales of buried treasure.

Misfortune struck the Poe household in January of 1842 when Virginia broke a blood vessel in singing. Her life was despaired of, and although she recovered somewhat, her health continued to be poor until her death from tuberculosis five years later.

Poe met Charles Dickens in Philadelphia in 1842 and hoped, vainly, to form some connections in England through him. Poe was also in correspondence with James Russell Lowell; they met in 1845, and did not like each other.

In April of 1844 Poe, with Virginia, Mrs. Clemm, and the celebrated pet, Cat-erina, came to New York. He sold his "Balloon-Hoax" to the New York *Sun*, and went to work on the genial Major Mordecai M. Noah's paper, the *Sunday Times*. In October he joined N. P. Willis and General George P. Morris on the new "paper for the upper ten thousand," the *Evening Mirror*. He lived for a time "in the country" (near what is now Eighty-fourth Street and Broadway), and there wrote a final draft of "The Raven." After it was rejected by Graham, it was sold to George H. Colton for pseudonymous publication in the February issue of a new magazine, the *American Review*. Willis saw it in proof and published it in the *Evening Mirror* on January 29, 1845, with an enthusiastic introduction and the author's name. Success was instantaneous; "Mr. Poe the poet" was to be world-famous, permanently.

He became an editor of a weekly paper, the *Broadway Journal*, and published a series of papers on Longfellow's "plagiarisms"—although Poe meant only that Longfellow was a derivative poet. He lectured on poetry at the Society Library. He met Mrs. Frances Sargent Osgood (temporarily separated, though not publicly, from her husband), and fell in love with her—perhaps platonically, and in any case with Virginia's approval. He also frequented the salon of the beautiful Anne Charlotte Lynch, later Mrs. Botta. And he was pursued by Mrs. Elizabeth F. Ellet, a woman of bad character—vain, ambitious only of reputation, and given to writing anonymous letters. This all led to complicated quarrels which may be left to the major biographers. He published *The Raven and Other Poems* and a selection of a dozen of his *Tales*. He went to Boston to lecture, became drunk, and read his poem "Al Aaraaf," which the audience found baffling, although T. W. Higginson testified to its beauty. He became the sole proprietor of the *Broadway Journal*, in which he published revised versions of most of his stories. But the paper collapsed with the last issue of January 3, 1846.

At the advice of the eccentric though melodious poet Dr. Thomas Holley Chivers, he moved again from the city to the cottage at Fordham, his last home. He published "The Philosophy of Composition" in *Graham's Magazine* in April of 1846. For *Godey's Lady's Book* he wrote a series of papers called *The Literati of New York*, most of which were innocuous; but, one on Dr. Thomas Dunn English, with whom Poe had had a fist fight (remotely connected with Mrs. Ellet and Mrs. Osgood), led to bitter controversy. Poe ultimately sued for libel and won his case, but at the expense of all reputation for sobriety or reliability. Godey gave up *The Literati* series, but printed "The Cask of Amontillado," a story of revenge now thought to be in part inspired by the author's own bitter quarrels. The story is ironic—a villain murders his enemy and is not found out; but at the end he realizes that the victim has rested in peace, while he has not.

Early in 1847 Virginia died. Poe was also very ill, and was nursed by Mrs. Clemm and Mrs. Marie Louise Shew; the latter was the daughter of a physician and had been trained as one at home. To her Poe wrote several poems; one, "The Beloved Physician," of some length, is lost save for ten lines. She is supposed to have suggested "The Bells" to him. Mrs. Shew consulted the famous Dr. Valentine Mott about her patient; she was told Poe had had a brain lesion in youth and would not live long. The lesion is thought to have produced manic and depressive periods, which might account for some of Poe's wild freaks and for occasional references to his being kept under sedation. All medical men who knew the poet or have studied his case agree that he did not use drugs habitually. Poe's one important work of 1847 was "Ulalume," composed for an elocutionist, Cotesworth P. Bronson.

Early in 1848 Poe gave a lecture on the universe, which was revised as a book, *Eureka*. In September he went to Providence and became engaged to the local poetess, Sarah Helen Whitman, to whom he had written a second "To Helen" (now sometimes called "To Helen Whitman") before their meeting. This affair produced a number of impassioned and very literary letters, but soon ended. Poe had visited Lowell, Massachusetts, in July and lectured on the "Poetic Principle"; while in Lowell he first met Mrs. Annie Richmond, with whom he fell in love. In 1849 he addressed to her a long poem, "For Annie," ascribing his recovery from illness to the thought of the beloved lady's presence.

Poe began to write for the Boston *Flag of Our Union,* a cheap paper that paid well. To it he sent his last horror story, "Hop-Frog," his sonnet "To My Mother," and the short poem "Eldorado," which is about a search for beauty rather than gold. Poe also found a patron, Sarah (or Estelle) Anna Lewis, who employed him as her press agent. Poe and Mrs. Clemm spent a good deal of time visiting the Lewis home in Brooklyn.

Late in June of 1849, after having composed a final version of "The Bells" and "Annabel Lee," Poe went south. He had a horrible spree in Philadelphia, but was rescued by C. Chauncey Burr, a minor writer, and John Sartain, the engraver who now ran the *Union Magazine.* They sent the poet to Richmond, where he had a happy summer, becoming engaged again to the sweetheart of his youth, the widowed Elmira Royster Shelton. He was also received in society, and enjoyed the friendship of the very young poetess Susan Archer Talley, later Mrs. Weiss. Poe lectured both in Richmond and Norfolk. He went on two sprees, however, and on August 27 joined the Sons of Temperance.

Late in September he started for the north by boat and arrived in Baltimore probably on the twenty-eighth. There, according to Bishop O. P. Fitzgerald, he attended a birthday party, pledged his hostess in wine, and went on a spree. His whereabouts are unknown from then until October 3, an election day, when he was found in great distress by a compositor, Joseph W. Walker. The story that he had been taken, drunken or drugged, to polling places by "repeaters," though widely related, is a hoax. Friends brought him to the Washington Hospital where, under the care of Dr. John J. Moran (who later published overcolored reminiscences), he died without ever becoming completely conscious. The last words attributed to him, "Lord, help my poor soul," seem to be authentic. He was buried in what is now Westminster Churchyard on October 8, 1849, where a monument to him was erected in 1875. Mrs. Clemm and her daughter now rest beside him.

Poe was primarily and by choice a poet. He held three important ideas besides his insistence on brevity: that poetry is close to music, that beauty is the chief aim of poetry, and that a poem may be composed logically (see "The Philosophy of Composition"). He was deeply interested in prosody and other technical aspects of verse, and published on the subject *The Rationale of Verse* (October and November 1848, in issues of the *Southern Literary Messenger*).

For reasons of economic necessity, Poe wrote little verse between 1831 and 1845, concentrating instead on the tales. Nevertheless, "The Haunted Palace," an allegory of madness, and "The Conqueror Worm," the most pessimistic yet the most powerful of all his poems, belong to this period. With the sudden recognition brought by the publication of

"The Raven" in 1845, he turned more to poetry. In the last years of his life he wrote "The Bells," which had been begun by Mrs. Shew; "For Annie," the simplest of his ballads; the courageous brief lyric "Eldorado"; and the touching ballad "Annabel Lee."

Poe cared less for his tales than for his poems. Nevertheless, he had a firm and workable theory about the short story, which he expounded in his famous review (*Graham's Magazine*, April–May 1842) of Hawthorne's *Twice-Told Tales*. A skillful literary artist, said Poe, does not fashion his thoughts to accommodate his incidents, "but having conceived, with deliberate care, a certain unique or single *effect* to be wrought out, he then invents such incidents—he then combines such events as may best aid him in establishing this preconceived effect. . . . In the whole composition there should be no word written, of which the tendency, direct or indirect, is not to the one pre-established design." He insisted on unity of mood as well as of time, space, and action. Poe is credited with the invention of the modern detective story with its amateur sleuth. He was similarly original in his version of the treasure hunt, "The Gold Bug," particularly in his introduction of a cryptogram.

Although Poe fancied his humorous work, the best of it is too much taken up with the faults and foibles of the world around him. "Some Words with a Mummy," for instance, deals with a brief American fad for Egyptology, and "The Literary Life of *Thingum* Bob," the best of the humorous tales, was a satire on the magazines of his day. Both are too dated to give pleasure to any but a few students of the period. He also wrote a gentle love story, "Three Sundays in a Week," but his great stories, beyond any doubt, are the tales of horror, ratiocination, or pure beauty.

The style of Poe's stories progressed from one highly decorated and elaborate, as in "The Assignation," to one of straightforward simplicity, as in "The Imp of the Perverse" and "Hop-Frog." He said that the stories of pure beauty, most notably "The Domain of Arnheim," had in them much of his soul. Toward the end of his life he remarked that he thought he had accomplished his purpose in poetry, but that he saw new possibilities in prose.

Besides the books of criticism mentioned above, there is a great deal extant of Poe's work as a day-to-day critic. Much of it is about works that came unchosen to a reviewer's table. It often contains keen remarks of great significance, but too much of it is devoted to the examination of flies in amber.

Poe had a tremendous influence abroad. His special kind of poetry was echoed by Tennyson, Swinburne, and Rossetti; his stories influenced Stevenson, Conan Doyle, Jules Verne, Huysmans, and many others. It was in France that Poe's influence attained its widest range, largely owing to the deep respect of Charles Baudelaire for Poe's poems, stories, and aesthetic theories. Between 1856 and 1864 Baudelaire wrote three articles on Poe and translated, with singular felicity, several of his works. Lois and Francis E. Hyslop, Jr., translated and edited *Baudelaire on Poe* (1952), which contains Baudelaire's three major essays and various prefaces and notes. Mallarmé, Valéry, and Rimbaud, as well as the whole flock of Parnassians, symbolists, and surrealists, exhibit the influence of Poe. Covering the entire range of "influences" is a volume on *Poe in Foreign Lands and Tongues* (1941), edited by John C. French.

Poe was given to telling romantic stories of himself, and the construction of an accurate biography has been fraught with the greatest difficulties. The first formal biographer, R. W. Griswold, published in the *Works* a memoir (1850) which was bitterly unfriendly to the poet, but which cannot be wholly neglected. In 1859 Sarah Helen Whitman published *Edgar Poe and His Critics,* the first full-length defense of her fiancé. John H. Ingram, an Englishman, wrote many biographical articles and a full-length book, *Edgar Allan Poe* (1880). He had access to many friends of Poe, espe-

cially ladies, but in his zeal to defend Poe's memory he sometimes disregarded facts. Most of Ingram's papers are now at
the University of Virginia; an annotated check list (1960) of
them by John C. Miller is of great value. In 1885 appeared
George Edward Woodberry's very valuable *Edgar Allan
Poe* (rev. ed., 2 vols., 1909). The biography (1902) by
James A. Harrison was highly favorable to Poe; it contained
much new information, but is in some ways superficial. In
1926 Hervey Allen published *Israfel,* the most widely read of
Poe's biographies, but it was begun as a novel, and the author never completely eliminated all fictional passages. In
the same year appeared *Edgar Allan Poe the Man* by Mary
E. Phillips, which, though uncritical and prejudiced, contains a repository of stories and pictures that, if used dis-
cerningly, is of great value. One of the most controversial
of all books on Poe was Joseph Wood Krutch's *Edgar Allan
Poe: A Study in Genius* (1926). Krutch found the key to Poe's
morbidity in the fact that his stories were marked by a "complete sexlessness." Killis Campbell wrote often and signifi-
cantly on Poe. His most important book is *The Mind of Poe
and Other Studies* (1933). His title essay is an invaluable
summing up. Particularly important is Campbell's evidence
on Poe's use of contemporary life in America. Campbell
also produced a valuable edition of *The Poems of Edgar
Allan Poe* (1917).

The best single life of Poe is Arthur Hobson Quinn's *Edgar Allan Poe* (1941), though it is too much for the defense
to be wholly satisfactory.

Most of the many editions of Poe's works are founded
on Griswold's (1849–56). Ingram's edition (1874–75) made
a few additions to the canon, as did that of Stedman and
Woodberry (1895). The only edition that even approached
completeness was the seventeen-volume work (1902) of
James A. Harrison. Harvard Press promises a new edition
under the general editorship of T. O. Mabbott to contain
much new material, mostly in criticism.

Other important books on various aspects of Poe and his works include: N. Bryllion Fagin, *The Histrionic Mr. Poe* (1949); Haldeen Braddy, *Glorious Incense* (1953); Patrick H. Quinn, *The French Face of Edgar Poe* (1957); Vincent Buranelli, *Edgar Allan Poe* (1961); and Edward Wagenknecht, *Edgar Allan Poe* (1963).

FICTION ABOUT POE

"The Valley of Unrest" is much more than the title of one of Edgar Allan Poe's poems, it also is the inspiration of one of the strangest "books" ever published, known in its entirety as *The Valley of Unrest, A Book Without a Woman, Edgar Allan Poe, An Old Oddity Paper,* Edited by Douglass Sherley. The copy at hand was published in New York by White, Stokes, and Allen in 1884 (though the book is copyrighted 1883 by Douglass Sherley). The volume is twelve and a half inches high and nine and three fourths inches wide, printed on hundred-pound *orange* book paper, with covers of the same reinforced paper stock one sixteenth of an inch thick. It has five holes punched through the sixty-five pages (which are bulked to five-eighths-of-an-inch thickness) and the book is bound with strong brown *cord*, looped horizontally around the spine as well as vertically upward. The text is printed on one side of the paper with f's serving as s's throughout.

The volume's dedication page bears the legend: "A book without a woman dedicated to a woman." There are two introductions, both by Douglass Sherley. The first purports that the book is written by someone else, who had spent most of his life traveling about the world as the consequence of "an awful crime," yet previously that man had been responsible for a "rare, brilliant" deed which brought him "the applause of an hour." Most important, ". . . these pages tell the tale of other people's lives, and not of his own. They tell something of that strange man, Edgar Allan Poe, who was an intimate college friend." They purport to tell the origin of the poem "The Valley of Unrest."

Edgar Allan Poe is a major figure in the story that is related, and the discussions of his status at the University of Richmond, his personal habits, and early literary efforts harmonize so closely with anecdotes told by various schoolmates of Poe that one has the very sure feeling that the story may contribute some elaboration on existing material if not a few new facts. Its version of the origin of the poem "The Valley of Unrest" was quite unacceptable to Thomas Ollive Mabbott, who had established to his personal satisfaction that the work referred to a location in Scotland.

The closeness of the style of the introductions to that of the story leads one to believe that the entire work is not only edited by but also written by Douglass Sherley. Though the early portion is believably factual, the latter part of the story would seem to be fiction.

Just who was Douglass Sherley, and is there the slightest basis for believing that he could have come into possession of some information concerning Poe that was not previously published?

George Douglass Sherley was born in 1857, quite possibly in the area of Louisville, Kentucky. That would make him only twenty-six at the time he wrote *The Valley of Unrest*, which appears to be his first published book. Three other titles are known: *Love Perpetuated; The Story of a Dagger* (1884), *A Few Short Sketches* (1893), and *The Inner Sisterhood; A Social Study in High Colors* (no date). All books were initially published by J. P. Morton & Co., Louisville, Kentucky, and all are outsize, printed on strange-color stock and relatively short in length. It is quite conceivable that the printing of *The Valley of Unrest* by White, Stokes, and Allen is a second edition, though this is not stated. All the books seem to have been privately published. George E. Woodberry in his *Edgar Allan Poe* (1885) specifically states that Douglass Sherley was in correspondence with Thomas Goode Tucker and that some of that correspondence exists. Thomas Goode Tucker was one of Poe's closest schoolmates at Virginia University. Douglass Sherley included material from two letters by Thomas Goode Tucker in two pieces titled *Old Oddity Papers* which appeared in the *Virginia University Magazine* for March and April 1880. Douglass Sherley is referred to as "a student of the (Virginia) University" by Floyd Stovall in his article *Edgar Allan Poe and the University of Virginia* (*The Virginia Quarterly Review*, Spring 1967).

It is not inconceivable that the mention of Poe's various companions in *The Valley of Unrest* may have had something to do with another of Poe's Virginia University schoolmates, W. M. "Billie" Burwell, writing his remembrances in the New Orleans *Times-Democrat* of May 18, 1884.

The Valley of Unrest is a very strange book, unquestionably extremely rare and not likely to be easily found by students of Poe. For that reason the *entire* contents follow. They include the two introductions by Douglass Sherley, the poem from which the book derives its title, and, of course, the entire text of the story itself, complete with the original footnotes. The f's have been changed to s's for easy reading, otherwise no alterations of any nature, not even of outdated punctuation or eccentricities of word separation or conjunction, were made in the text.

Despite a certain ornateness of style, this narrative is one of the most effective pieces yet contrived in which Edgar Allan Poe is a major character and central to the theme of the story. It deserves to be preserved on its own merits regardless of its possible historical value.

INTRODUCTION—I

This book does not begin with an apology for its appearance. I, the editor, have none to offer. But it begins instead with what I am sure will be an unsatisfactory statement. I have neither the right nor the inclination to make public the knowledge which, by a mere accident, I chance to possess, concerning the author of the following pages.

This much I feel at liberty to state: He was well born, well reared, eccentric. He passed through life bearing the burden of some particular grievance of which the world did not know. His education was of his own curious making. His writings, a trifle weird, bear more plainly the marks of a peculiar originality than they do of erudition.

He was the only son, the hope and the pride of a proud man full of bitterness and world-hate. Between this father and child there was but little love, and absolutely no sympathy. A roving spirit early developed, and a fondness for studying human nature *direct*, rather than through the oftentimes more tedious medium of books, soon dissipated the hope and soon broke the pride of this over-ambitious and too exacting father. Young, erratic, with only the uncertain memory of a good mother, long dead, to keep him pure—without guile—he drifted beyond the line that sharply defines the difference between the right and the wrong.

Then there came a time when he was allowed to gratify the one passionate desire of his early youth—travel, travel, constant, world-wide travel. Those many years of restless wandering gained for him a unique and rich experience. Fortunate, indeed, were those who listened to his talk. He was a fanciful, magnetic man, full of strange conceits. He was a tragedy. His life was a rugged, tragic poem.

One act of his full-primed manhood—rare, brilliant—brought him the applause of an hour. Yet it was an act so rare, so brilliant, that it deserved better things. If I could mention his name, there are those now living who would recall to mind the matter and the man. Later on in life, embittered, scorned by those who by nature and by right ought to have been every thing to him, he committed an awful crime. Each detail thereof was coldly, calculatingly planned. And each detail was even more coldly, more calculatingly executed. But it was a crime with the criminal unknown. That guilty one, now dead, speaks to those who may listen from the printed pages of this book. But these pages tell the tale of other people's lives, and not of his own. They tell something of that strange man, Edgar Allan Poe, who was an intimate college friend. They tell something that may chance to lend a fresh interest and a new charm to the always interesting and to the always charming study of—to quote from the following pages—That mysterious human fantasy.

Autumn, 1883   The Editor.

INTRODUCTION—II

Whatever an idle fancy may chance to term this *Valley of Unrest,* it is woven, as may be seen, in and around about a poem, a mere fragment, seldom read, written by Edgar Allan Poe.

The Valley of Unrest is the name of the poem, and *The Valley of Unrest* is the name of the book.

It is a book without a woman. She does not find her subtle accustomed places in this valley of unrest. She seems to be absent in both the body and the spirit. It is an Eden without an Eve: but it is not a paradise without a serpent.

Harmony long ago fled the bounds of this strange unhappy valley, but she was not driven forth by woman.

Discord in greedy haste found a foothold in the dell, once a land of sweet and quiet rest. But discord was not brought thereto by woman's call or by woman's art.

Now, let the Valley of Unrest and the dwellers therein speak for themselves.

Midsummer, 1883   Douglass Sherley.

THE VALLEY OF UNREST

By Edgar Allan Poe

Once it smiled a silent dell
Where the people did not dwell;
They had gone unto the wars,
Trusting to the mild-eyed stars,
Nightly, from their azure towers,
To keep watch above the flowers,
In the midst of which all day
The red sun-light lazily lay.
Now each visitor shall confess
The sad valley's restlessness.
Nothing there is motionless—
Nothing save the airs that brood
Over the magic solitude.
Ah, by no wind are stirred those trees
That palpitate like the chill seas
Around the misty Hebrides!
Ah, by no wind those clouds are driven
That rustle through the unquiet Heaven
Uneasily, from morn till even,
Over the violets there that lie
In myriad types of the human eye—
Over the lilies there that wave
And weep above a nameless grave!
They wave:—from out their fragrant tops
Eternal dews come down in drops.
They weep:—from off their delicate stems
Perennial tears descend in gems.

The Valley of Unrest

(By Douglass Sherley)

There are moments in the lives of all men when the fragrance of some one flower, or the brief snatch of some favorite love-song, or the sound of some familiar voice, will instantly charm the mind with a strange and subtle witchery.

Mysterious moments, that bring back again the banished or forgotten things. Peculiar association of ideas that reproduce the once vivid pictures which have vanished from the canvas of life.

So it was to-night.

Here, in my den of old oddities, nothing pleased me. I put aside the yellow sheets of a German manuscript, a curious mass of erudition. It had failed to furnish solace to my lonely hour. I was possessed by a spirit of restlessness. I passed over to the square hole under the deep slant eaves that answers the purpose of a window. I thrust back the darkened unpainted shutter. It creaked dismally on its one rusty hinge. I looked out into the blackness of the night. A snow storm was raging. I could feel the soft white flakes falling against my withered face. And I thought of the snow storm of life that was beating in upon my full wintered years.

From below, far down the turn of the road, there came a sound of many voices, and the musical ring of jingling sleigh-bells, and then all was silent.

That was hours ago, early in the night. Yet the sound of

those musical bells has somehow, by the charm of that strange subtle witchery, brought back from out of the past a mysterious human fantasy, which in those other and far-off years gave a coloring to my life that has not faded out, and never will.

A glance, a hand-clasp, and a word. Three potent factors that won my home-sick heart, on the afternoon of my first day at Virginia University. Edgar Allan Poe was the winner thereof. I had stood aloof, a lonely sixteen-year-old boy, on the outer edge of an unsympathetic crowd. His eye met mine. He came forward, offered me his hand, and said, "I like you. I want to know you." From that moment dated our friendship. From that day I was recognized as the most intimate friend of Poe while he remained at the University.

Now, in truth, he was indeed a mysterious human fantasy.

To-day, even after all these years of diligent investigation, there is so little actually known of the inner life of this strange man.

Several periods bear so heavy a mist of uncertainty and false report that we are forced to content ourselves with the barest outline.

Somewhere there is told a legend of a man, who did for sake of gold sell his shadow. But this, our human fantasy, must have parted with his substance, and passed through life only a shadow in dalliance with an immortal soul.

In that part fanciful, part biographical sketch of his own life, "William Wilson," thus does he speak of those years spent in the Manor-House School at Stoke Newington, England: "My earliest recollections of a school are connected with a large, rambling Elizabethan house in a misty looking village of England, where were a vast number of gigantic and gnarled trees, and where all the houses were excessively ancient.

"In truth it was a dream-like and spirit-soothing place, that venerable old town.

"At this moment, in fancy, I feel the refreshing chilliness of its deeply shadowed avenues, inhale the fragrance of its thousand shrubberies and thrill anew with indefinable delight at the deep hollow note of the church bell, breaking each hour with sudden and sullen roar upon the stillness of the dusky atmosphere in which the fretted Gothic steeple lay embedded and asleep."

Many a time, while we walked arm and arm beneath those now crumbling arcades at the Virginia University, Poe has talked by the hour of that old Manor-House School, long before he had even thought of formulating William Wilson. He would often thrill my boyish fancy with his world of romance and dreams without wakenings. The other day, a lengthening street of the English metropolis stretched itself over the leveled ruins of that ancient Manor House.

His life at the University has always been buried deep in a mass of obscurity. Much has been written about him, but little has been written and less is known about his University career.

With this one period of his life I am familiar, for he was then my only friend, and I knew him well.

Now in those days, a spirit of dissipation prevailed among the students of the University. While men like unto Gessner Harrison, Henry Tutwiler, and Phil. Cooke abstained from the midnight revel and strictly obeyed each obligation placed upon them by the faculty, we, a gay rollicking set, with Poe for our leader, were much given to a non-attendance at the daily lecture, and to a freedom from all regulations and restraints imposed by those high in authority. Yet somehow we managed to spend a large portion of our time in the University library; seated side by side, in one of those curious and now musty alcoves, we read the histories of Lingard and Hume.

Poe was passionately fond of French literature. Often have

I made pause in my own reading and listened to his musically whispered translation from some old French play, until Wertenbaker, the ancient librarian appointed by Jefferson, and who died only a little while ago, would place a warning finger on his closed lips. Of late years I have often made search for those particular passages in the old French dramas; but I have not found them. And now this is my thought: he would more frequently weave the alleged translation from his own imaginative brain than from the printed page; for he knew that my knowledge of French was limited, and that I would not be able to discover the charming fraud. The French drama is an old and pleasant story to me now. But it has never yielded the pleasure found in that library alcove, listening to those fraudulent translations, dreading the approach of Wertenbaker bidding us to be silent or leave the library.

We were familiar with the whole field of English poetry from Chaucer to Scott. There was not a passage of singular beauty in either that Poe could not instantly recall. And so it was with intermediate writers. He declared Shakespeare to be a magnificent whirlpool, into which he constantly desired to fling away the best that was in him. Once he said to me, "Shakespeare fascinates me with an evil fascination. He stirs up within me the demon-side of my nature. I have for him a passionate love-hate."

Halcyon indeed were those days of my youth, when Poe was my friend, aye, the other half of my soul. Ah, there is a grim philosophy in the old saying, that we are never young but once!

Those weird tales and musical poems of the after years are but the crystallization of his thoughts and his fancies which so often found an echo in my heart, or that made echo up and down *The Valley of Unrest* that lies buried deep in the Ragged Mountains of Virginia.

My Lord Beachonfield's portraiture of his remarkable father, Isaac Disraeli, bears a strong likeness to young Poe, "indicating by the whole carriage of his life that he was of a different order from those among whom he lived; timid, susceptible, lost in revery, fond of solitude, or seeking no better company than a book, the years had stolen on till he had arrived at the mournful period of boyhood *when eccentricities excite attention and command no sympathy.*

Poe, unlike Isaac Disraeli, could at times completely yield himself to the gay companionship of reckless young fellows. But down in his heart he cared nothing for that wild dissipation that so often characterized his actions. It was but an effort, an unsuccessful effort, to make himself like unto others. Eccentricity is often a curse, and always a crime —a crime perpetrated against the ignorance of willfully common-place people; people who live according to rule; people who erect a standard, and who would have all live up, or rather down to it, and woe unto the man who departs therefrom.

Edgar Allan Poe, when first I knew him, was seventeen years of age, rather short of stature, thick and somewhat compactly set. He was strong of arm and swift of foot—for he was an expert in athletic and gymnastic arts. A more beautiful face on man or woman I have never seen. It was the beauty of the soul, always near the surface, always in a glow of strange, unearthly passion. His walk was rapid, and his movement quick and nervous. He had about him the air of a native-born Frenchman, and a mercurial disposition deliciously unstable. He was fond of cards. Seven-up and loo were his favorite games. He played like a mad-man. He drank like a mad-man. He did both under a sudden impulse. Something always seemed to drive him on. Unseen forces played havoc with his reason. He would seize the glass that he actually loathed, yet always seemed to love, and without the least apparent pleasure swallow the contents, quickly draining the last drop. One glass, and his whole nervous nature ran riot within its highly tortured self. Then

followed a flow of wild talk which enchained each fortunate
listener with a syren-like power.

It is curious to follow the subsequent lives of those men
who were his constant companions around the card-table,
and who filled, from out of the same punch-bowl, their
never-empty glasses with the same *peach and honey.*

Peach and honey, that drink once so popular, long years
ago, with the Virginia and Carolina gentlemen of the old
school.

There was Thomas S. Gholson, and of all the set there
was not one more reckless. He was afterward a pious judge
of some distinction and of great integrity.

Upton Beale, who always held the winning card, became
an Episcopal Minister. He was stationed for years, in fact
until his death, at Norfolk, Virginia, and he was beloved
by the people of his parish.

Philip Slaughter, Poe's most intimate *card-friend,* is still
living. He, too, a minister of the gospel. I am told that he is
an excellent God-fearing man. I wonder if he remembers
those wayward days of his youth, when he and Poe were
partners at cards, and held between them a common
treasury.

I have lost sight of Nat. Dunn and Wm. A. Creighton. In
all likelihood they have gone unto that other land.

Billie Burwell, a rare genius of that old set, has suffered
many changes of fortune. He is neither judge nor minister;
unlike the rest, he has never been able to finish sowing his
wild oats. When last I heard of him he was living in New
Orleans. He was still assiduously cultivating the refined
society of kings and queens, and he was still a large dealer
in diamonds and clubs. And there was yet another one,
Thos. Goode Tucker, of North Carolina. He was a great-
hearted fellow. He was handsome, bold, and reckless. He
was a warm friend and a bitter enemy, and he was passionately devoted to young Poe. This same Tucker was a great
fox hunter. Poe and he were the constant terror of that

Piedmont country. Whenever the farmers of Albemarle found their fences down, their fields of small grain trampled and all but ruined, they would roundly swear those infernal young rascals—Poe and Tucker—were the guilty ones, out on the chase again. And those farmers were right.

Tucker is now, like unto myself, an old man; yet he wrote me the other day, "Come with me for the sake of those old times, let us follow the hounds once more."

A strong, linked intimacy existed between Tucker and Poe. Tucker was not only intimate with the dissipated side of his nature, but with that other and better side known to only a few, principally women. It was a side which good and pure women were so sure to find out, appreciate, and defend, when others were so ready to blame. Whatever Poe may have been in after years, he was, when I knew him at the University of Virginia, as honest a friend as the sometimes waywardness of his otherwise noble nature would allow. There was then not the least touch of insincerity, and never the slightest indication of that maliciously fickle disposition which in after times was so often brought up against him in life, and against his memory in death.

Marked peculiarities do not elicit sympathy from the common run of people—the great majority. They place the unhappy possessor in a most undesirable position. Misunderstandings constantly arise, and they can not often be explained, even if explanation be sought. Therefore it is not a matter of much surprise that Edgar Poe did not have many intimate friends. For he was indeed, even when I knew him —a mere boy—a man of strongly marked peculiarities. These peculiarities constantly led him into trouble. He made enemies out of those who should have been his friends. And of this he was more oftentimes unaware. For his enemies at the university were of that most dangerous, most contemptible order—*secret enemies*—fellows ready to give the stab from behind, and under cover of darkness. A band of envious cowards outskirt the ways of all such men as Poe.

And always must eccentric greatness pay a penalty; nay, not one, but numberless ones to the clamoring, commonplace fool and the silent, envious knave.

Yet Poe was a power when he cared to try his strength. He was full of adaptability. He could play cards and drink *peach and honey* hour after hour, and day in and day out, with those who merely chanced to be thrown in his way. But a genuine friendship asks for something more and better than ordinary conviviality and a shuffling, each in turn, the same pack of cards. Other ties than those must be found to bring two souls together in a life-long attachment.

There was a curious magnetic sympathy existing not only between our hearts but even between our minds. In the silent watches of the night I have often closed the book before me, no matter how interesting, risen from my seat and, moving under the guidance of an irresistible impulse, gone out beneath the arcade, so full of strange shadows, and started toward the room near by, occupied by Poe, and have met him in his own doorway, coming to me, actuated by the *same irresistible impulse.* Not once, twice, or thrice, but again and again has this happened. And often in those silent watches of the night did he read to me the early productions of his youth. They were not published—not one of them— because unspared by his critical hand. His sensitive nature oftentimes made him a ruthless destroyer of much that was good. He could not brook the idle, laughing censure of his comrades. On several occasions I persuaded him to give his own small circle of intimate friends the rare privilege of listening to him read his own weird writings.

Those men—now all dead but Tucker and myself—who were so fortunate as to hear those impromptu readings could never forget them. In their old age their fireside stories were all the better for that memory. From out of the past, clear and strongly outlined, rise those readings. It is the memory of one especial night. The hour is late—after twelve.

On West Range one midnight lamp is burning. It is the room of Edgar Allan Poe—No. 13. Our small circle is complete. By accident we have gathered there. It is a rare meeting, unmarred by the presence of uncongenial souls. Each a kindred spirit, each in sympathy with the other. There is a short, impressive silence. Then, spell-bound, barely breathing, we listen to a story, weird and wonderfully strange, which Poe has just written—the ink not yet dry on the last page.

He reads with his whole soul thrown into every action and into each musical intonation of his well-toned voice. Now loud and rapid, like the mad rush of many waters; now low and slow, like the trickling of a stream in a hollow cavern. Then sinking into a whispered sentence of incantations and mad curses; then into a softly murmured, yet passionate vow of some ardent, hopeless lover, and—the story is told, the reading over. Ah, it was indeed a privilege to be there!

Once he wrote and read to us a long story full of quaint humor. Unlike the most of his stories, it was free from that usual somber coloring and those sad conclusions merged in a mist of impenetrable gloom that we so often find in his published writings. In a spirit of idle jest and not of adverse criticism, some one of our number spoke lightly of the story. This produced within him a fit of nervous anger, and he flung every sheet behind the blaze on his hearth. And thus was lost a story of excellent parts. "Gaffy," the name of his hero, furnished a name for the story. He was often thereafter good humoredly called "Gaffy" Poe, which was a name that he did not like.

Now, in those early days of the University of Virginia, a pernicious practice prevailed among the students at large. It was gambling at cards and for money. This vice was then prevalent among the best of Southern people. But Thomas Jefferson did not propose to tolerate its dangerous presence in his well-planned institution of learning. He found that it needed a speedy and effectual check. This, the year before his death, he promptly attempted to give; and while he may not have been entirely successful, yet, as one of the results of that effort, we were driven into The Valley of Unrest, which lies hidden in the wooded heart of the Ragged Mountains.

Mr. Jefferson, after much anxious deliberation with the University Board of Directors and others, decided upon a plan to eradicate the baleful habit of playing cards for sake of gold and silver coin. He consulted with the civil authorities. He found out the names of the most noted young gamblers, and he gave instructions that they should be indicted in due form and brought before the next grand jury. So, one bright morning in the early spring, the sheriff, with a goodly posse, suddenly appeared within the doorway of our lecture-room during the Latin hour. The staid old professor was calling the roll. That servant of the law stood in readiness to serve his writs on certain ones as the professor should mention the names of each guilty party. But gay young rascals are not to be so easily ensnared within the toils of the eager enemy. We needed no word of warning. The shadow across the doorway, and a gang of men behind, told its own story. With Edgar Allan Poe for our leader, we scattered in every direction—some through the window, and some through an opposite door.

Sheriff, posse, and professor were left in full possession of the lecture-room. Once on the outside, under the guidance of Poe—our master spirit in all times of danger—we marshaled our scattered forces. Then, the hot pursuit. But those whom they wanted the most, the ringleaders—our own set— had made a successful escape, not to our rooms, for there we would not have been safe, but off to the wild Ragged Mountains, a jagged spur of the Blue Ridge, over an almost untrodden path.

But it was a hidden way well known to Poe, over which, always alone, he had often traveled. With ruling passion, strong even in hasty flight, some of the party had managed to arm themselves with a deck of cards and a goodly portion of *peach and honey*. This, in order that the hours of our self-imposed banishment might not hang heavy upon our idle hands.

Our place of concealment was The Valley of Unrest. It was a beautiful dell, high up in the mountains, almost inaccessible, and far away from the beaten path. It was the favorite haunt of Edgar Allan Poe. When almost overpowered by those strange spells of mental depression, approaching near unto the border-land of insanity, thither would he go, and alone. There for hours he would often linger, buried deep in the bitter-sweets of melancholy; and there, environed by low-sweeping pines, murmuring perpetual dirges, his active brain became strongly imbued with those wild, fanciful ideas which are so realistic even in their unreality; for, out of the dark-green, needle-pointed foliage of those low-sweeping pines there forever actually seemed to ooze a dreary somberness that permeated all the atmosphere with a gloom which hung like an uncanny mist over the beautiful dell.

It was a mysterious place. Something seemed to hush our voices and to muffle each footfall. If the spirit of adventure had not within each one of us been driven up to fever heat by the excitement of the moment, there could have been no human power able to detain us in that place of mystery. Surely it was this haunt of his youth that Poe did in after years so cunningly picture in exquisite verse, and fittingly termed *The Valley of Unrest*.

It must indeed be true that Poe was filled with the memory of that lonely dell, which lies so deeply buried in the great wooded heart of the Ragged Mountains, when he wrote that beautiful poem. And in that lonely dell, for the better part of three days and nights, we did conceal ourselves from the search of the sheriff and his posse in that long ago springtime.

Each day it was our custom to play cards and drink

peach and honey. Each night we would light our torches, kindle a fire of pine fagots to dispel the chill night airs of early spring, then each in turn tell his story. After midnight we would go in single file and in silence down the mountain side. On the outskirts of the University we would find a little knot of anxious friends ready to supply us with provisions and *peach and honey.*

Before the coming of the dawn we would find ourselves back again within the shadows of that lonely dell, The Valley of Unrest.

Two lines that occur in the poem—

> *"Over the lilies there that wave*
> *And weep above a nameless grave"* °

were uttered by Edgar Allan Poe while he told his story on the last night of our banishment in the Ragged Mountains; and it was the last story told on that night. Each time Poe's tale was the last; and while he talked we would forget to replenish the fire, forget every thing but the intricate plot which he might chance to unroll before us. When he finished we would, shivering, rise to our feet, and hastily depart from the spot and pass away from under its uncanny shadows, but not from the memory thereof. All of these years have not brought me a forgetfulness of those springtime nights and of that one last night.

On the afternoon of the third day the glad news came that we had been forgiven. Poe, our ringleader, was the only unhappy one of the party. He thought it so tame an ending for our flight, he was half unwilling to return again. That afternoon and night he was exceedingly gloomy and held aloof.

For the last time we lighted the torches and kindled the fire; for the last time we, each in turn, told our stories. Poe alone had not spoken. We had left him to himself.

° *See the Poem*

Thomas Goode Tucker had just finished a tale of a sweet and tender nature. The old story of two lovers—a grievous misunderstanding, a cruel separation, a happy reconciliation. It was a restful bit of human nature, a trifle commonplace, but so restfully, charmingly told as to gain a forgiveness for its evident touch of everyday life. During the little pause that follows the telling of any good story, Poe, still full of gloom, strode in from out of the shadows and stood in our midst with folded arms, and told *his* story.

To-night the recollection of those burning words, slow and distinctly uttered, rise before me in all of their original freshness and in all of their original horror. On the day after, I alone of that little party expressed a willingness to return some day to that spot in the Ragged Mountains where we had listened to that strange story, so wonderfully and strangely told.

His first words, delivered in a slow, monotonous tone, were those mysterious lines found in the poem—

> "Over the lilies there that wave
> And weep above a *nameless grave*."

He paused, then pointed to a little clump of early spring lilies. They were just coming into bloom. They were growing into beauty beneath the shadows of a large hemlock, on the inner edge of the firelight glow, plainly in the sight of all. Somehow, instantaneously, came the thought to each one of us, how like a grave-mound those clustered lilies had shaped themselves as they grew.

"No; you are wrong," he said, seeming to divine our very thought; the shape of yonder bed of fair lilies is but a fore-shadowing of a grave yet to be there—a grave that shall be forever *nameless*. No one now lies beneath the purity of those blossoms. Their fragrance and their liveliness are not stolen from any human mold slowly decaying beneath the dark, rich soil. Out in the blackness of the night, beyond the flare of your torch and in the light of your fire, a company of ill-boding spirits have gathered. In their center three Demons of the Darkness. They are dancing. It is the Death-Dance. They stop. And now they are, each in turn, whispering to me. But you can neither hear nor see them. As they whisper to me I will repeat the words to you."

Bending forward in the attitude of an eager listener, and as if straining to catch the words of some one whispering, Poe slowly uttered the strange sentences of his wild story. The deception—if deception it was—was indeed most perfect. Each one of our number was ready to believe that Poe was actually hearing and repeating words spoken to him by some invisible person. The action was so wonderfully natural that it created the most absorbing effect. For a brief while I could scarcely believe my own identity. It was, in truth, some time before I could rid myself of the impression that Poe was in actual and direct communication with evil spirits. Tucker afterwards told me that several members of the party—otherwise sensible fellows—were never able entirely to rid themselves of this impression.

It is useless to even attempt a reproduction of that story. The bare outline—at best feeble—is all that I dare trust myself to give. Those three Demons are supposed to be the narrators using Poe as a mouthpiece. Consequently the story is divided into three parts.

I

Two young men start out in life together. They have been unto one another more like brothers than like friends. Their hearts are drawn together by the tenderest ties that can bind two unselfish souls. Manhood finds them living a peaceful, harmonious life. Thus far without the shadows. But a curse yet unfulfilled hangs over them—some iniquity of the fathers that must be visited on the children of the third and fourth generation.

Discord, and then the horrors of civil war invade the peaceful land. The execution of the curse is near. There is a great issue at stake, and those young men differ about the merits of the cause. It is their first difference. They go on the battle-field and on opposite sides. In an evil hour, in the bitterness of a hand-to-hand conflict, they meet, each unknown to the other. Their weapons cross, a deadly thrust, and one lies dying. Then the cruel agony of a too-late recognition. While the dying man breathes away his life, young, and so like a flower, on the bosom of his comrade, full of wretchedness, a voice:—"Your soul has expiated the curse of your race; peace abide with you." He is dead. But other voices, harsh and penetrating, ring out upon the ear of the grief-stricken survivor, "Your curse has barely begun its baleful course; you are to go about the world a homeless, friendless wanderer; and when the end does come, you are to lie in a grave forever *nameless.*"

II

A storm. Night falls about, drawn on before its time. Out of the darkness of a distant valley a man full of years toils up the mountain side. But a human shadow. He trembles with fatigue and fright. The storm sweeps along the mountain. He seeks protection from its raging, unpent fury beneath the branches of a wide-spreading hemlock. It is where you are seated to-night. Years hence will mark his coming to this lonely dell in the heart of the Ragged Mountains. The shadows will steal away his power of action, and the shadows will close in and around about him, and from this spot he will not again depart.

III

This human shadow, shut in by a troop of Demon-sent shadows, labors day by day at some mysterious task. Never man worked at so strange a labor. It is the slow making of a grave—*and his own*. Day after day the work goes on. Then there comes a pause. His labors are ended. And there, at the foot of a beautiful bed of lilies, an open grave. And now he sleeps in that grave, made by the painful toil of his weak and shriveled hands.

And Edgar Allan Poe, in conclusion, "The fitfulness of his life goes out into a perpetual darkness. *The Angel of Death* forever calms the trouble heart. And in those days when my three now powerful Demons shall have lost their high and most evil estate, and when other and better spirits shall have gathered here to hold high carnival in their stead, then the song of the midnight elfin shall be—

> 'Over the lilies there that wave
> And weep above a *nameless grave.*'"

His story was ended. Those last words were said in a whisper. Then there was a long and painful silence. Not a word, not a movement, only the crackling sound of pine fagots almost burned out. We made effort to shake off the gloom settling down upon us. It was useless. Then we were startled to our feet by the sound of a retreating footfall. It came from the tangled mountain growth that enclosed our open space around the camp-fire.

Poe, with a wild expression on his face, lighted by the glare of the torch and fire, stood erect in our midst. With a mocking laugh that chilled every heart, he made this cry: —"Be still, my brave comrades; it is only the retreating footfall of my last Demon. He is gone! Come, scatter the dying embers. Bid farewell to our safe retreat. Now let us go, and in peace, down the mountain side, and again return to the University."

It is indeed a mystery how, on that night, we reached our deserted rooms; for it was the darkest night that I have ever known. And our souls too were filled with the darkness—a troop of grim terrors. Present in every mind the picture of that *nameless grave*. It was a picture with a ghoulish background of human Shadows and Death-Dancing Demons.

Now this which I have told is the bare outline—an incomplete synopsis—of that strange tale. It would take the touch of a master hand to render full justice to a story told by that master spirit, Edgar Allan Poe.

The days which followed thereafter almost drifted us into the belief that we had somewhere and somehow dreamed away the period of our hiding in the Ragged Mountains—a delicious slumber ruffled by the shadowy presence of a whispering phantom and a *nameless grave*—yet to be—far up in the wooded heart of that spur of the Blue Ridge.

The following December ended my term and my stay at the Virginia University. Poe left at the same time. Our lines of life stretched out in directions widely different, and they never crossed again. Our old friendship was never renewed. But our parting that December night was exceeding sad, full of tenderness and—pardon the weakness, for we were hardly more than boys—tears, hot, impulsive tears of deep regret. "I will never see you again," he said. His words were indeed prophetic. And perhaps it was better so, yet— But no; I will leave untold that which would only gratify an idle curiosity and open to public gaze an unsuspected heart-wound.

There is a sequel to that story of the *nameless grave*, as it was told to us by the boy Poe on that spring-time night in The Valley of Unrest.

About five years ago, after a long period of wandering in many strange and out-of-the-way places, I found myself in an old Italian town. There was a charm about the place. It was ancient, crude and interesting. To gratify an idle fancy— a mere whim—I had taken for the winter an old Ducal Palace, long ago given over to the chance tenant and—ruin.

There came a holiday; then a night of the Carnival. I stood on the carved stone balcony of my own Ducal Palace and watched the motley throng passing down the crowded

street. They pelted me where I stood, and laughed to see a
face so full of sober thought in so gay a time.

Something—perhaps the odor of some flower, or, as it was
to-night, the sound of some voice, rich, suggestive—something
brought the desire to come back again to this, my native
land. It had been for me the scene of much unhappiness,
but a new generation of haste-lovers had risen, and I thought
to go again to the home of my fathers. Vacant all the rest of
that winter was my Ducal Palace. And the people said that
I was driven out by the ill-resting spirit of some Duke foully
murdered in the long ago. So I left that uneasy shade in the
full possession of that Ducal Palace, rich in tarnished gild-
ings and faded colorings.

On my return, familiar places claimed my attention. Many
of those whom I had known and loved were dead, and many
changes marked the town of my birth. I turned from them
all. I was disappointed. Only one place had not changed.
Only one of those old places satisfied me. It was the University of Virginia. There everything seemed the same. True,
a new set of Professors filled the chairs of those whom I
had known, and men with unfamiliar faces frequented
Rotunda, Porch, Arcade, and Lawn. Yet the place itself—its
walls and its groves consecrated to knowlege—was just as
I had left it.

One thought absorbed my attention. It was a foolish notion that would not down, and was yet ill-defined. Perhaps,
by a mere accident, some one might have been buried in
The Valley of Unrest and in a *nameless grave*. So it was,
filled with this almost belief, that I determined to go and
see for myself.

But to find that lonely dell far up in the wooded heart of
the Ragged Mountains was not an easy task.

While a student I had often rambled over the University
Range of Mountains. I had often gathered flowers and ferns
from the scattered ruins of the old observatory.* I had often

* Now a new and beautiful Observatory stands on the old site.

stood on the summit of Lewis Mountain and looked down upon the Pantheon-modeled Dome of the old Rotunda. I had often watched the afternoon sunlight slowly creeping beneath the Arcades of Range and Lawn. And I had often looked down upon the town of Charlottesville, with glittering spire and gleaming roof, softened into a suggestion of something picturesque by distance and sunshine. But I had never but that once—those three days of hiding—explored the Ragged Mountains. From the time that I first saw them looking then as they always did, the embodiment of dense and somber loneliness, they had for me a charm. This charm was enhanced by our self-imposed banishment and the tale told by Edgar Allan Poe on that spring-time night beneath the shadows of those low-sweeping pines and in the glare of torch and camp-fire.

That memory, after all of those years, had brought me again within the reach of The Valley of Unrest.

It was the spring-time. And it was early one bright morning when I started up the mountain-side to find again that beautiful dell. But in vain I wandered up and down the length and breadth of the Ragged Mountains. The old path was overgrown and forgotten. I was wearied with much and fruitless searching. I stretched out beneath a huge pine, on a bed of dry moss, and closed my eyes, but not in slumber. A bunch of new-blown lilies growing on a *nameless grave* was my one and troubled thought. It was about the hour of noon. Suddenly I grew conscious that some one was near, looking down into my face, studying its features. It was that peculiar and unmistakable feeling of a *nearness* to a human being. Out of mere perverseness I remained still and as if asleep. My ear, on the alert for the slightest sound, caught the better part of these sentences: "Yes, yes, I am sure he is one of their number. True, he is greatly changed; but in spite of his long white hair and his heavily bearded face, I know him."

Breaking away from the capricious control of that perverse spirit, I arose and stood before a man as old, if not older than myself. He was a tall, angular, raw-boned mountaineer. His manner was calm, collected. His eye was bright and full of the fires of life, not yet burned out by the hoary encroachments of many years.

"Stranger," said he, in a voice somewhat low, and full of earnestness, "I have seen you before. But you have never seen me. You were about these parts now nigh on to fifty years ago. You were with a crowd of students from the University who came hither to hide from the county sheriff. Now come, stranger, and behold the fulfillment of a strange prediction that you and I and all the rest of us heard on the third and last night of your stay in the Ragged Mountains."

I had no answer. I was full of ill-concealed wonder. In silence I followed the man who had just spoken. We penetrated deep into the dense gloom of the forest. We neared an open spot. It was a lonely dell, and I was sure that once again, after all the years, I stood within the shadows of that Valley of Unrest.

Instantly came to mind those words placed in the mouth of Bedloe, in Edgar Allan Poe's "Tale of the Ragged Mountains": "The scenery which presented itself on all sides had about it an indescribable and to me a delicious aspect of dreary desolation. The solitude seemed absolutely virgin. I could not help believing that the green sods and the gray rocks upon which I trod had been trodden never before by the foot of human being."

"Do you remember," said the old man, "the tale that was told to us on that last spring-time night? See," and in the same tone, low and earnest, he repeated those familiar lines—

> "Over the lilies there that wave
> And weep above a *nameless grave*."

Slowly I turned, as he pointed, toward the center of the dell, and there my eyes fastened upon a green mound of earth, grave-shaped, without a stone, only a bunch of lilies at the head, just coming into bloom. In truth, I had found it, and there it was before me, the *nameless grave*.

There, seated beneath the same low-sweeping pines that had sheltered our party nearly fifty years before, and within sight of that grave-mound crowned with its early spring lilies, I listened to the plain and straightforward story of that ancient mountaineer, Gasper Conrad:

"Five miles from this place, just on the other side of the mountain-top, I was born. During the early years of my life I was a wood-cutter, full of ignorance and stupid happiness. Three times a week I hauled a load of wood into Charlottesville. And that was all. It was my life. One morning about this time of the year I was chopping wood, just over yonder to the left of this spot. I heard a voice, loud, and then low. I rested on my ax and listened. In those days it was a rare thing to see or hear any body but our neighbors, rough, ignorant mountain people like myself. I came over this way and looked in through the wild undergrowth of the mountain. I saw a young man about eighteen or twenty years old walking rapidly up and down the open space. He walked in a hurried, jerky manner, repeating words clearly and distinctly, but words that I could not understand. I was rooted to the spot. My morning work was entirely forgotten. My heart while I listened seemed to beat with a new life and I seemed to hear a promise of better things. Suddenly he wheeled about and quickly disappeared. After that he often came, and always alone; frequently several times a week. I always managed to be near by. There was in the mere sound of his voice a new charm to me. It was a charm that I could not resist. One day, bold with desire to hear every word, I ventured too near. He saw me. My eagerness and my delight gained for me a ready forgiveness, and it gained for me something besides—his deep and generous interest. For to him I owe all of the little knowledge I now possess. From that time on, which was early in the

spring, until late in the following December, he came almost
daily to this lonely valley up here in the mountains. Each
time he would bring a bundle of books for me to read.
Each time he would patiently explain away that which I did
not understand and gladly remove every difficulty. This
opened up to me a new life full of hitherto unknown riches.
My chief delight was to listen while he read poetry and
stories which he had just written, often the very night before. I never knew his name. Once I asked him. He said
for his answer that he was a University student, and more
than that it was neither well nor necessary for me to know.
Each time he came alone, except when he brought your
crowd of young fellows, to find a safe hiding place from the
search of the county sheriff. That was about the time when
I first knew him. I remember each detail of your stay in the
mountain. Throughout the day you played your cards and
drank your *peach and honey*. But with the coming of night
you gathered around your bright fire, lit your torches, and,
half laughing, half in earnest, told such queer things about
Witches, Wizards, and Goblins. So passed away your time.
It was on the last night that my friend told his story—and it
was the last one told—of that *nameless grave*. Do you remember how you were startled to your feet, in the after-still-
ness, when the story was ended? Do you remember the sound
of retreating footsteps on the outer edge of your company?
They were mine. I had been concealed in the tangled undergrowth. I had heard the story. He alone, as he told his now
prophetic tale, discovered me in my place of hiding. You
know how well he used my hasty retreat to make you *feel*,
even if you did not *believe*, that it was the departure of his
last Demon. He came here for the last time on a raw
December day. He bade me a tender, reluctant farewell.
'On the morrow,' he said, 'I leave forever this haunt of my
youth. I will have no desire again to return. Solemnly,
faithfully promise that you will not leave the mountains, and
go down into that Valley of Human Wretchedness, that

world about which you have read so much. Heaven knows it must be far better to read about it—aye, to even think and dream about it—than it is to know it, and alas! to *love it,* as I do. Stay here always. Do what good you may among your neighbors. Forget all that which I have taught you. Be ignorant; be happy. But remember, dear Gasper, some day,' he said, pointing to what was then only a clump of new lilies in the early bloom, 'the clouds above will rapidly drift, unmoved by any wind,

> "Over the lilies there that wave
> And weep above a *nameless grave.*" '

"Ah, stranger, well may you look with wonder on that lily-crowned grave. Two people have known the manner of its making—my good wife and myself. But she is dead. I alone can give report of that grave-maker—the maker of his own grave, who lies at last in peace, I trust, beneath the evergreen sod of that *nameless grave.*

"In the autumn of 1835, near the close of the day, and in the midst of a frightful storm, there came about these parts a stranger. He was some fifty-five or six years of age. He sought shelter beneath my roof. He expressed to me while there the intention of building a small hut in which he intended to pass the winter. I liked the man. I liked his manner and his talk. So I tried to prevail upon him to live with us—share our poor quarters—because I knew they were far better than any he could provide for himself. He was kindly disposed toward me from the start. But he refused absolutely to have any thing to do with my neighbors. He would not accept from them a single offer of assistance, and would not even answer their questions. He was first regarded by the mountain people as a rough, surly fellow, and finally he was held in absolute dread—this partly on account of his manner toward them, and partly on account of his strange, uncouth appearance. He wore a great heavy beard,

and his long coarse, gray hair was always in a mass of ugly
tangles. He was known by the somewhat appropriate name
of Old Shaggy. The bare mention of his name was all-
sufficient to quiet the noisy child or make the older and unruly ones creep off to their beds of straw in the low-swinging
loft. Old women by the fireside told many a story of
midnight murder and broad, open daylight crime. Old
Shaggy was said to be, in each instance, the murderer or the
criminal. If a child died suddenly, it was supposed that the
curse of Old Shaggy rested on its little head. Even the death
of our beasts of burden, our oxen and our few horses, was
laid at the door of Old Shaggy. He was the terror of all this
country side for twenty miles around. My continued intimacy with the man cost me the love and the good will of
many of these honest people. They believed that he was an
Evil Spirit in flesh, and blood, sent to torture the few inhabitants of the Ragged Mountains for some wrong-doing, the
nature of which they did not know. When I passed among
them they would draw aside, and, whispering, point after
me: 'Gasper Conrad, poor fellow; Old Shaggy has sorely be-
witched him, and his wife too. We 'uns will have nothin'
mo' to do wid 'em.'

"They faithfully kept their word for many years, even
after Old Shaggy had mysteriously disappeared from among
them. To this day there is not one, even those of a new generation, no matter how brave, who will draw near this fatal
place. For yonder, on the edge of this clearing, used to
stand the little hut of Old Shaggy.

"He was a man of much information. He had rubbed up
against the world and gotten from it much that was good
and more that was bad. Yet it was all of the most intense
interest, both the good and the bad. He had been every-
where, in every known part of the world. He once told me
that he had been a steady traveler for about twenty years;
that he did not remain long in any one place; and that now,
weary of the life, he had returned here in order that he

might die not far away from the place of his birth. For he said that he was born somewhere in Albemarle County, near the little town of Milton; that he was of a good family, always wayward, latterly profligate. His people thought him dead years before, killed in a drunken brawl; so they were told. He did not care for them to think otherwise, for he was indeed worse than dead to them.

"He parted from me one night with these words: 'And furthermore, dear Gasper, I know to the day, and even to the hour, the time appointed for my death. Years ago I determined that my grave should be in some unfrequented dell in the Ragged Mountains. For I love their lonely hollows and their wooded peaks. Hereabouts I have so often wandered in the days of my boyhood with dog and gun. Some day I will sleep in peace beneath its perpetual shadows, and in a grave that shall be forever *nameless*.'

"Those words filled my soul with terror. Back with a new force and a new meaning came the lines—

> 'Over the lilies there that wave
> And weep above a *nameless grave*.'

But I was silent. My emotion did not betray me. After that he more frequently spoke of himself and of his eventful life. Yet he never told me any thing of his actual history. That he was filled with a remorse of some kind for some crime or wrong-doing, I am sure. It seemed to be a remorse unsatisfied, relentless.

"A short while before his death he told me that he had been with Aaron Burr during his famous expedition, and that Burr was a brilliant man, fascinating, powerful, and that he had been the indirect cause of the one great evil in his miserable life. Somehow, stranger, I have always thought that evil was a foul but unintentional murder. I have gathered the idea more from the manner of Old Shaggy than from his guarded words.

"It was after dark, on the night of September 14, 1836. There was a loud knock at my door. Old Shaggy stood outside in the darkness; he refused to come in. 'No, no,' he said; 'there is not a moment to lose; every thing is ready; come, and come quickly!' I made a fresh torch, and followed after his rapid strides into the lonely valley. I felt that I was with a madman. I made no question. I was alone with Old Shaggy and with the Silence and the Shadows. By the light of the torch I discovered that he had torn down his hut, and cut the rough boards into short pieces, and placed them in a regular pile on the edge of an open grave. 'Made with my own hands,' he said. It was ten or twelve feet deep, and there was in the broad bottom a rough-made coffin; an ill-shaped lid near by on the outside. Without any emotion in either his manner or his voice, he turned to me and said: 'It is about over now, this ugly dream called life. I am grateful to you for all your kindness. Do not let it fail me now, when I need it the most and for the last time.' Speechless, powerless, I stood by his side. He turned away and flipped down into the grave. He deliberately placed himself in the coffin which he had made. He closed his eyes. He folded his strong arms across his great breast. One moment thus. Then he sprang up into a sitting posture, and in a loud voice, full of pitiful entreaty, exclaimed: 'Don't! don't! I am *Albert Pike Carr!*' He fell back into the coffin exhausted, as I thought, after this strange and unusual excitement. But it was the exhaustion that only death itself can bring.

"I made new torches and worked until the early dawn and afterward. The sunlight found the valley just as it used to be before the coming of Old Shaggy. For I had buried everything with him, even the rough boards of his hut. Nothing remained.

"But here in the center was the grave. And it was then, and even now is, as our friend predicted and as Old Shaggy wished it to be—*nameless.*

"Stranger, you have heard the story of that mount with

its pretty lilies. I have told you all that I know about the man who lies beneath. I do not think his name was *Albert Pike Carr*. That must have been the name of the man he murdered. And Old Shaggy died with the same words on his own lips that formed the death-cry of his victim—'Don't! don't! I am *Albert Pike Carr!*'"

The old man's story was ended. He was weary and out of breath. Yet he was full of nervous excitement. "Look!" and he seized my hand; "there is not a breath of wind, yet the trees are trembling as if in a storm, and the clouds overhead rush madly through the heavens.

> "Over the lilies there that wave
> And weep above a *nameless grave*."

I left the old man standing by that lonely grave in that lonely dell. I reluctantly passed down the mountain-side. The evening wind, new risen, from out of those low-sweeping and mournful pines, made echo—laughing, mocking echo—"*nameless grave, nameless grave*."

Thereafter, a short time, and while still at the University, a bundle of old family letters was placed at my disposal. They were written by a Virginia woman. She was the rarest wit of her day. I had known and liked her while a student. So each letter was to me full of interest; each page brought back a memory. Several sentences in a letter to her brother, a prominent Richmond lawyer, instantly attracted my attention. This was the excerpt:

"By the way, have you heard the latest news? I am told that one of the *Carrs*—Albert, I think; at all events the one inclined to be wild, and who is a lover of the venturesome— has run away from home, and in company with a *dissolute companion* gone to join that dreadful expedition of Col. Aaron Burr. The name of his comrade is unknown."

That was all—a mere dainty bit of a fair maiden's gossip. But it is enough to furnish the missing point in that story of the *nameless grave*. Now, given a number of facts, and a certain conclusion is inevitable. With the facts already brought forth, this is *my* theory—*my* conclusion:

Young Carr and his *dissolute companion* together go forth to join the expedition of the brilliant Burr. One of their number weakens in his devotion. Something must be done. Burr sends for this *dissolute companion*. "He will be on duty near the marsh to-night; do it quickly! do it well!" said Col. Burr. But the sides of a tent, like the walls of a house, have ears. Somebody crouching near, lost in the darkness.

"I am sick to-night; take my place on duty near the marsh; won't you, please?" said a soldier to young Carr. And "I will" was the brief and generous answer.

Later on, a man hurries across the corner of the marsh and goes far beyond the camp. He is a deserter, and he had made good his escape. Brave young Carr stands watchful duty in his place *near the marsh*. A footstep. "Who goes there?" cries out the valiant Carr. A sharp sword-thrust from behind. He turns, recognizes the man he loves, and conscious that it is the result of some cruel mistake, quickly exclaims: "Don't! don't! I am *Albert Pike Carr*."

But the recognition and words are too late. The moon had risen, but her tardy light was a mockery.

Years of remorse and constant wandering. The *dissolute companion* returns once again to his native place. By a curious coincidence he falls upon a dell, almost inaccessible, far up into the heart of the Ragged Mountains—The Valley of Unrest. He reaches the spot in the midst of a frightful storm, and he does not again leave the place. But with the skill and cunning of a madman he brings his life to a close by poison, or like means, on that 14th day of September, 1836—the deathday of Aaron Burr—another curious coincidence or strange fatality. Which?

It is not more than passing strange that a man run mad by the thought of a crime committed, double in its nature, should determine to end his life in some one particular spot and in some one particular way. Any clever madman might have brought about a death and a burial just as unique in its character. This signifies nothing. Yet it does seem strange indeed to find him in that one particular spot above all others—The Valley of Unrest. And stranger still, that he should have so strongly desired what is actually the case, and that which had been predicted by Edgar Allan Poe—a *nameless grave*. That he should chance to die on the same day, perhaps the very same hour, with Aaron Burr, who was the cause of his lifelong remorse—the cold-blooded instigator of his crime—is, in truth, a remarkable element in this tangle of human destinies. Unnatural and most improbable sounds the entire story. If true, it is—of course by accident—the perfect fulfillment of a most peculiar prediction. If not true—only the garrulous mutterings of old age—then it is a curious, close-woven line of unaccountable things. But it is the plain and simple truth, this story as told by Gasper Conrad, the honest mountaineer.

Now this much I know to be a fact and beyond all doubt: There is in the Ragged Mountains of Virginia a certain lonely dell which does contain the grave of some man whose name is unknown. The mountaineers thereabout know by tradition the presence of that grave; consequently no power on earth can induce any one of them to enter that dell. And they know—also by tradition—the story of Old Shaggy, but not of his death and the strange manner thereof.

I also know it to be a fact, because told to me by Poe himself, that he constantly frequented that dell in the Ragged Mountains. I know that it was there that he guided us into a safe retreat from the pursuit of the county sheriff, and it was there I heard the story of the *nameless grave,* and it was there I heard him slowly, distinctly repeat those lines,

> "Over the lilies there that wave
> And weep above a *nameless grave*"—

not once only, but twice; at the opening and at the close
of his mysterious prophetic tale. This—both the story and
the lines—must have been heard by Gasper Conrad. How
else could he have caught the oft-repeated refrain?

That Edgar Allan Poe must surely have meant this lonely
dell when he wrote *The Valley of Unrest*, needs no proof.
Read the Poem. It makes most excellent answer to any
denial, no matter how idle or how earnest it may chance
to be.

After reading those words in the old letter of that dead
Beauty-Wit, I determined to go back into The Valley of
Unrest, find Gasper Conrad, and question him more closely.
Now, one Bishop keeps a little grocery and notion-store
near the University Post-office, and there I had occasion to
stop on my way out to the mountains and overheard this
conversation, which made my intention useless: "So you say
old Gasper Conrad is dead, do you?" I heard some one
exclaim, and then add, "When did he die?"

"Night 'fore last," answered a gruff, rough-looking fellow.
He was evidently one of the Ragged Mountain people.
There was a long, rusty piece of limp crape hanging on his
left arm. It bore signs of frequent use.

A man idling near the door, leaning against an empty
box, whittling a stick, said in a lazy, drawling tone, "Is that
the same old fellow was all the time acting curious-like, and
talking about graves and lilies, or some kind of flowers
growing somewhere up there on the mountains?"

"The very same 'un," shortly answered the mountaineer,
and then he strode out of the store and out of sight, with his
heavy, stupid face turned toward his humble home.

"He was the old man's nevy, he was," said a melancholy
bystander.

Dr. McKennie, who keeps the University Bookstore° established during my time by his excellent father, told me

° The University Bookstore is now in other hands. But Dr. West is still
living. His address—University of Virginia, Albemarle Co., Va.

that he had for many years known and respected this rather remarkable mountaineer, Gasper Conrad. To use the words of the good Doctor: "He was honest, quiet, sensible; but to me a continual surprise. He had cultivated not only a taste, but an actual thirst for reading, and of a certain kind —always books of travel and adventure."

Filled with a desire to give a glimpse of Edgar Allan Poe, his inner life, while a student at the Virginia University, I have unreservedly written that which has gone before. I do not know into whose hands it may fall. I do not know if the great world will ever hear the burden of my song. Yet it was on my heart to write, and I have written. I have added something—if only a little something—to the much which has been said and written about this my Mysterious Human Fantasy. That much I have done, and something else. I have shown the curious juxtaposition of circumstances bringing about the complete fulfillment of a prediction made in a moment of midnight revel in the heart of the Ragged Mountains and by Edgar Allan Poe. It has about it at least the coloring, the strong coloring of a perfected prophecy.

Now the talk of the night is finished, and the night has gone. Again, far down the turn of the road I hear the musical ring of jingling sleigh-bells which hours ago rang up the memory of that Mysterious Human Fantasy, like unto the Witch of Endor bringing back a dead Samuel to a living and troubled Saul. Again, I hear the gladsome sound of merry voices—that same gay party which I heard so early in the night, returning now, at the break of another winter day, from the county dance.

They are gone.

Again, I lean out of the square hole under the deep, slanting eaves.

The cold gray lights creep into my den of Old Oddities. They chill my heart.

The sun will shine to-day.

But will it bring brightness and warmth into my life?

Again, and from out of the cold, misty depths of the early dawn rises before me that Mysterious Human Fantasy.

It floats away with the dark humors of the night.

It teaches the first rising wind of this new-born day to whisper,

> "Over the lilies there that wave
> And weep above a *nameless grave*."

Julian Hawthorne was the son of the great American writer Nathaniel Hawthorne. As early as 1874 he had succeeded in placing novels with the book publishers and both novels and short story collections appeared regularly until well into the twentieth century. Like his father, Julian loved to work with the terrors of the psychological and the accouterments of science. It may accurately be said that most of his material fell within those fields.

It can also be said that his inspiration derived not only from his father, but from Edgar Allan Poe. "My Adventure with Edgar Allan Poe" is a fantasy that deals with the question: What might Poe have written had his life been uneventful, average, and "normal"? Julian Hawthorne's weakness was never that he lacked imagination but that his style was ordinary and that, as he grew older, he did not modernize it to acclimate to changing modes. Yet this story, which appeared in *Lippincott's Monthly Magazine* for August 1891, when Julian Hawthorne was forty-five years old, is not only polished, but reveals a high degree of sophistication. It will strike students of Poe's life with considerable force and cogency.

Julian Hawthorne died at the age of eighty-eight in 1934. As he grew older his imagination became more unrestrained, though his style became increasingly Victorian. *The Cosmic Courtship, An Inter-Planetary Romance,* a three-part novel begun in the November 24, 1917, *All-Story Weekly,* takes place in the year 2001 when a method of transferring disembodied intelligences to the planet Saturn has been conceived. The novel becomes a morality story with echoes of *The Scarlet Letter,* as the hero apparently sees his beloved voluntarily give herself to the sexual advances of a man from another world. A series of stories narrated by Martha Klemm, believed to be the reincarnation of a Salem woman hanged for witchcraft, started with "Absolute Evil" in the April 13, 1918, *All-Story Weekly* and culminated with a five-part novel, *Sarah Was Judith,* beginning in the May 1, 1920, issue, telling of the spirit of a dead daughter that takes possession of her mother's body. Each of the stories combined the supernatural with scenes suggestive of passion and lust on the part of one of the woman characters concerned, but the style belonged to another age and another manner.

Yet at least one short story of the supernatural written by Julian Hawthorne is a true masterpiece in the genre and unjustly neglected. That story is "The Delusion of Ralph Penwyn" (*Cosmopolitan Magazine*, February 1909), one of the most exquisitely polished tales ever to appear on the theme of mortal man unknowingly courting the gray lady of death.

Julian Hawthorne, true to the spirit of Poe all of his life, great exploiter of reincarnation and the theme of "possession," was certainly qualified to bring Poe back to life, as he has admirably done in this tale.

My Adventure with Edgar Allan Poe

By Julian Hawthorne

There is in Philadelphia a small restaurant, known to a limited circle, and situated in a narrow street off one of the busiest thoroughfares. The house is kept by a German widow of respectable aspect and unimpeachable character, who establishes relations of personal amity with her guests. On entering, you find yourself in a barroom, where beer and cheap German wines can be drunk, in the American fashion, standing; beyond, there is an inner room, furnished with three tables, one large enough to seat twenty persons, the other two much smaller. The attendants are a couple of German youths, occasionally assisted by the widow herself. At noon, a *table d'hôte* is served in this inner room, garnished with a rough but palatable red wine at twenty-five cents a pint. Most of the patrons of this dinner are German tradesmen, who are extremely sociable among themselves, and, after the wine or the beer has circulated a few times, not a little loquacious and noisy also. Their conversation, so far as I can report it, is upon topics of social and political science, interspersed with illustrations, occasionally humorous, sometimes sentimental, from real life. In addition to this regular contingent (who sit at the large table), I am in the habit of meeting there two or three journalists and other literary friends; and we grow eloquent and jovial together over the vegetable soup, the cheese sandwiches, and the rough red wine.

The other day I had it in mind to take my lunch there, but I was delayed by a series of accidents, and did not arrive until more than an hour after the appointed time. As I entered the barroom, the widow greeted me with a smile and a shake of the head. "Are the gentlemen gone, then?" I asked.

"*Schon längst!*" she replied. "But I save some soup for you. *Treten Sie nur hinein! Sie werden wohl alles bequem finden!*"

In accordance with her invitation, I stepped inside, and found everything comfortable. The room was empty, except for the presence of one gentleman, who was seated at the farther of the two small tables, with his back to the wall, and his face toward me. He had a cup of coffee and a cheese sandwich in front of him, and held in his right hand a book, in which he seemed to be a good deal interested. As I took my seat at the small table opposite his, I could not help noticing that the volume) which was of a tasteful, dull-green hue) bore on its left-hand cover, in gold lettering, the legend *Letters to Dead Authors*.

As Mr. Andrew Lang's *spirituelle* little work is a favorite of my own, I was naturally led to regard its reader with favorable attention. He was a man of slight build, with sloping and rather narrow shoulders; but his head was large, and of magnificent proportions: I know not that I have ever beheld a forehead promising such intellectual power. His hair was black, wavy, and rather long; his eyes were black, deeply set under level and finely sculptured brows. The nose was rather large; the mouth, sensitive and delicate, was decorated with a short moustache. But for the moustache, I should have taken him to be either an actor or a clergyman: his black broadcloth coat, buttoned up nearly to the chin, gave him a somewhat clerical air. Looking at him with more consideration, however, I was slow to believe that a face like his had ever gazed across the cushions of a pulpit. It was too poetical, too strange, too shy: it was the face of a man prone to dark musings and incommunicable thoughts—of a man who might passionately crave human sympathy, but was either too proud, or too separate in nature, to ask it or to win it. A transparent shadow seemed to rest upon the pale, reserved, handsome countenance; but, though transparent, it removed him from ordinary human approach. And yet, methought, a beautiful and emotional woman, or a broad-minded, genial friend, might overcome his reticence, and discover, behind it, a passionate and wayward impulse to reveal even more than man commonly reveals to his fellow.

I suppose the gentleman must have felt my look; for he suddenly raised his eyes from his book and fixed them upon me. I was embarrassed at having been detected in a discourtesy; but the next moment the conviction came over me that I had somewhere seen him before. Yes, I recognized every lineament of his face, and even his figure, attire, and bearing. Where could I have met him? Was it at the theater? Was it at some public dinner? Had I traveled with him in a railway-train? Wherever it was, it was no mere passing glimpse that I had had of him; I was minutely familiar with those features; I recalled distinctly the marked difference between the two sides of the face—the right side being much stronger and more regular than the left, and the mouth having a perceptible "lift" at the left corner, producing somewhat the effect of a sneer. Certainly I knew this man, and, on the impulse of the moment, I bowed to him slightly.

He returned the courtesy, but said, in a low and pleasantly modulated voice, "Pardon me, sir; I believe you have the advantage of me."

"Really," returned I, feeling unpleasantly like a confidence-operator in the act of entrapping his victim, "I don't know whether I have or not. There is something in your appearance that is very familiar to me; and yet I can't give you your name."

"You can, perhaps, give me yours?" was his quiet answer.

"With pleasure!" said I; and I mentioned it.

"Ah!" he said; "the novelist? I have read—indeed, I have reviewed—your writings; but that was over fifty years—I would say they could hardly have been yours. You are too young a man."

"I should be surprised if I were not older than you," said I, with a smile. He certainly could not have been over forty.

"Your impression is a natural one," he replied; "But the circumstances happen to be peculiar. I was born in 1809."

"In 1849, you mean!" exclaimed I.

He shook his head. "Oddly enough," he remarked, "you have named the year in which (according to the general belief) I died. I need hardly add," he continued, with a faint smile, "that the belief is a mistaken one. I did not die, and I am not an insubstantial specter. And yet, perhaps, I am hardly justified in calling myself eighty-two years old. The truth is, sir—though this is a matter to which, for reasons you will appreciate, I am not accustomed to refer— the truth is, I have been the subject of a very unusual experience, and, what is more, of one which I had myself in some sort foreshadowed. It is possible you may have happened to read a little fancy of mine called 'The Premature Burial'—"

"Pardon me for interrupting you," said I at this point, "but I think I must be misinterpreting your meaning. The only story called 'The Premature Burial' that I am acquainted with was written by—"

"By Edgar Allan Poe. And that, sir, is my name."

At this juncture the widow brought in my lunch, and this diversion, together with the extremity of my stupefaction, which had an outwardly composing effect, prevented my saying anything for several moments. If I were describing an imaginary incident, I should say that my first impulse was to regard the man as a lunatic; for between the alternatives of believing either him or myself insane, I would naturally select the least distressing. Edgar Allan Poe was dead and buried forty-two years ago; that was certain. This man was alive and in the flesh, and was not more than forty years of age. And yet he asserted he was the great author. Of course he must be out of his mind.

I am not aware of being a particularly credulous man; but the simple truth is that, in the face of the above considerations, I believed on the spot that Edgar Allan Poe sat before me. In the first place, the manner with which he made the statement was convincing. His voice was quiet, distinct, and grave, his countenance serious, and his glance direct. He was not mad, nor was he jesting; he was a gentleman, making a statement to another. But he was also Poe in every contour of his face and line of his figure. I now understood how I had come to think that I had seen him before. There was in my possession an engraving from a daguerreotype of the poet, taken, I believe, about 1846. I had often studied this portrait, which had a singular fascination for me, and I had completely familiarized myself with it. The man before me did not merely bear a resemblance to the picture; he was the original of it. I should have known it without his assistance, but that one does not spontaneously invite a miracle.

"It is a great pleasure to me to meet you, Mr. Poe," I said, at length. "I suppose I needn't add that it is an unexpected one."

"My return to this life was as unexpected to myself as it could have been to any one else," was his reply. "I ought, perhaps, to say that you are the first person to whom I have spoken of the affair, and that I should not like it to go further. I have taken the name of Arnold, which was that of my mother's family. It is my intention, for obvious reasons, to preserve the incognito. I am not disposed to let my new

life be disturbed by constant efforts to establish my identity, or to become the cynosure of fools should the attempt
succeed. I have laid out a course of existence for myself,
and I purpose to pursue it, quietly and unobtrusively, so
long as destiny may permit."

"And when—that is—how long is it since your new career
began?" I inquired.

"It is about a week since I obtained a position as private
secretary to a gentleman in the banking business here," he
replied. "My handwriting attracted him—as it did my friend
Kennedy when, in 1833, I competed for a literary prize
offered by the *Saturday Visiter*. An interview satisfied him
as to my other qualifications, and he engaged me at a
salary which—according to my ideas—is a generous one.
Outside of office-hours I am master of my own time. I do
not go into society, and I see no one. I spend my time in
reading, and I am well content. I was just glancing over this
little *jeu d'esprit* by Mr. Andrew Lang. He writes well. He
has treated me with great consideration. But I am amused
to learn, from his 'letter,' as he calls it, that the animosi-
ties aroused by my critical divagations, a generation and a
half ago, are not forgotten, nor forgiven, yet."

"Mr. Lang is an Englishman, and perhaps exaggerates
the American sentiment on that subject," I said. "For my
own part, I have always found your genius recognized as
unique and unapproachable. But did I understand you to
say that it is only a week since you returned to this world?"

"No: that event took place some three months ago, as
near as I can recollect," he answered. "To be frank, my
impressions as to the details of my resuscitation are a trifle
hazy. As you may be aware—I was not myself aware of it
until quite recently—I was interred in the graveyard of
Westminster Church, in Baltimore. The place was not
marked, and, fortunately for me, my coffin was placed in
a sort of vault. I presume some alterations were being made;
at all events, my first sensation was of a draught of cold air;

I supposed I was sleeping by an open window, and I endeavored to draw the blanket around me. Gradually—I can
hardly tell how—I began obscurely to realize my position.
I was not agitated; probably my nerves were in a state of
insensibility from my long torpor. I have often, since I escaped from my tomb, felt a deeper thrill of horror at my
position than I did at the moment. My coffin had decayed
sufficiently to enable me to leave it without much difficulty.
Some stones had been removed from the sides of the vault,
and I emerged through the aperture. I was, as yet, scarcely
alive, and had no more strength than an infant. It was
night: I heard the clock of the church strike midnight as I
lifted myself into the open air. Under the wall of the church
I found, rolled up, a rough coat and a pair of overalls,
doubtless the property of a workman. I appropriated them,
for my own garments were dropping to pieces. In the
pocket of the coat was a piece of bread, which I ate, and it
gave me a little vigor. But I was greatly emaciated, and my
mind was bewildered. I believe I spent that night in the
station-house, and the following day I was removed to a
hospital, where I remained two weeks, slowly recovering
the use of my faculties. Of course I did not soon realize the
lapse of time, and the questions I asked and the remarks
I let fall doubtless led the attendants to suppose me demented. But," he added, breaking off, "I must apologize for
my loquacity. This is the first time I have spoken of this
subject. I dislike even to dwell upon it in thought. And my
further experiences are commonplace, and would not interest you."

"I have never before listened to so interesting a narrative:
it surpasses even your own published romances," I said. "But
is it not your intention, Mr. Poe, to re-enter the literary
profession?"

"I think not," he replied. "I have never found it remu-
nerative. And the art must have advanced so far since my
time that I should have no chance in the competition. Be-

sides, all the men of my generation are gone, and the sense of loneliness, and of vanished associations, would render the experiment too painful."

"As regards the question of remuneration—do you happen to recollect what was paid you for your story of 'The Murders in the Rue Morgue'?"

"I could not say, precisely, but it might be forty or fifty dollars."

"And it contains upward of twelve thousand words. Well, Mr. Poe, I saw your original manuscript of the story in the collection of a friend of mine the other day, and I am confident he would have refused a thousand dollars for it. I am willing to guarantee that you could sell anything you chose to write at the rate of a dollar a word. If fact, if I were your agent, I would agree to pay you that, and to make a handsome commission for myself besides."

"You fairly astonish me," said Poe, in his low voice. "Literature must indeed have taken a step forward since my day. Writers, then, are among the wealthiest classes of the community?"

"No, I can hardly say that," I returned. "There are so many of us, you see, that we somewhat interfere with one another's profits. Besides, we have suffered from the lack of an international copyright law, subjecting us to the rivalry of stolen English books at nominal prices—"

"Is it possible," exclaimed Poe, "that no such law yet exists? Is the situation unchanged since 1842, when Dickens was over here, co-operating with Webster and Clay? I was hardly prepared to learn this!"

"I am glad to be able to tell you that a measure was actually passed on the last day of the recent session of Congress," said I. "It is true that most of the members were absent, and that nearly all of those present were asleep: nevertheless, the vote was favorable, and the law is expected to go into effect next July. So we may look forward to better days. But, in any case, such a question would have

no application to you. Apart from the extraordinary sensation that would be caused by your reappearance, you are
still as far above the level of average writers as you were
in the forties. I doubt if any living man could rival your
prose style. I am certain none of us have a tithe of your
genius. As to your poetry, there you stand alone, and you
always will. Another 'Raven,' or 'To Helen'—"

"I should hardly care," said Poe, with a wave of his hand,
"to attempt that vein again. There can be no enduring
merit in such verses. They were constructed on a poetical
theory which I now perceive to have been fallacious. The
true music of poetry should lie, not in its sound to the ear,
but in its sense to the mind. It should be a rational pursuit,
not a passion. I should be more inclined to try my hand at a
blank-verse drama, in the style of my *Politian*. Or perhaps
a prose comedy of contemporary life would be better yet."

"You are no doubt the best judge of what you would like
to do," said I; "but it is my impression that a continuance of
your old manner would be expected by the public, and
might be more popular. Suppose, however, you begin with
a series of short stories, in the style of 'The Gold-Bug'?"

Poe shook his head meditatively. "The short story," said
he, "is not a satisfactory form of fiction. To properly gauge
the quality of a genius, we must see it in longer flights. If I
returned to the region of romance at all, it would be to
write a long novel, like *Martin Chuzzlewit* or *The Last Days
of Pompeii*. But, to tell the truth, fiction in any form has few
charms for me. I am more impressed by the realities of life
than by its fancies. I should like to write a treatise embody-
ing my ideas on the equitable division of land among its
inhabitants. Such a work, I think, would be useful, and
would constitute a reasonable basis for a reputation. What
you intimate concerning the present popularity of my short
tales and poems is, I confess, a disappointment to me. It
seems to show a regrettable frivolity in the human mind.
Perhaps, had my readers, like myself, passed forty years in

the tomb, they would be disposed to modify their point of view."

I thought this not improbable, but, as the contingency was never likely to occur, I wished that Mr. Poe had shown a greater willingness to accommodate himself to actual circumstances. I began to perceive, moreover, that although the great writer's prolonged absence from the activities of the world had wrought no noticeable change in his personal appearance, it had had a singularly disenchanting effect on his mind. All traces of his weird imagination seemed to have died out of him. He was contentedly filling the position of amanuensis to a prosperous banker, and his thoughts were running on political economy. The amazing experience of which he had been the subject, instead of stimulating transcendental speculations in his soul, was merely a disagreeable matter, about which he did not care to think. I even suspected that he felt irritated with himself for having been the hero of so unique and sensational an occurrence. His love of fame was gone; to spare himself a little temporary annoyance he was satisfied to conceal his identity and live unknown and unsought. Could it be that the qualities which gave Poe his renown were but a transient ebullition of youthful spirits, having no deep roots in his nature? Was this the real man that sat here chatting with me, and was the other, whom the world knew and honored, but an artificial *rôle* that he deliberately played, with no sincere and hearty purpose?

"The more I reflect upon it," said he, breaking in upon my speculations, "the more reluctant I feel to embark again on the uncertain sea of literature. What is really worth having in this life? Surely nothing save the sense of reasonable security against vicissitudes, the certainty of bodily support and comfort from day to day, the feeling that one is performing a useful, if humble, work in the world, the freedom from the agitations of passion, the hopes and despairs of ambition! I was never happy in my former existence; I am happy now. Why should I tempt a renewal of those old doubts and emotions? Our experience is given to us, we may suppose, as a lesson. We act foolishly, and we are taught the folly of our actions. Few of us are granted the opportunity to profit by our instruction. That opportunity has been vouchsafed to me, and I should be remiss in my duty did I venture to disregard it. No, my dear sir, I shall never resume the pen. I am conscious of no impulse to do so, and I will not act against my nature."

"Mr. Poe," I said, looking him in the face, "are you not making a virtue of necessity? Is it not because you feel the decay in you of the powers you once possessed that you profess to care no longer to use them? Are you not concealing the loss of your genius by pretending to be indifferent to the honor that genius commands?"

I had hoped that this attack would have the effect of rousing him from his apathy. If any sparks of the old fire yet lingered in him, surely they would burst into flame now! But Poe sipped his coffee, and betrayed no symptoms of disturbance.

"I am not conscious of concealing any deficiency," he said. "In my view, I have advanced in wisdom and philosophy, rather than retrograded. Nevertheless, I do not care to dispute your hypothesis. The result, in any case, is the same."

"So be it!" returned I, with a sigh, uncorking my wine. "But, before we part, permit me to pour you out a glass of this vintage."

"You will excuse me, I am sure," he replied, courteously. "I have an unconquerable aversion to all forms of liquor. Were I to drink a glass, it would simply make me ill; and that could be a gratification to neither of us. If you will allow me, I will respond to your compliment in this coffee."

We bowed, and drank. Immediately after, Poe arose, and, with a graceful inclination, went out.

Two weeks later, I chanced to see in the newspaper a notice of the death by the grippe of Edgar Allan Arnold. As I was slightly acquainted with his employer, Mr. Dressel, I presented myself at the funeral, which was from the banker's house. I looked at the quiet face in the coffin: it was Poe's.

"He was a capital hand with a pen, and a quiet, sensible fellow; rather dull, except for the practical things of life; but I am very sorry to lose him," Mr. Dressel remarked.

I suppose the truth may be that Poe was really a very old man when he died the second time, though, physically, he still retained the appearance of youth. But his mind was aged; his heart was dried up; the glory and the beliefs of youth were gone; he was like other old men, whom Providence is preparing for the final farewell to this world by removing from them all appreciation of what makes the world seem beautiful. But, then, why did Providence bring him back? What is the moral of his story?

IN WHICH AN AUTHOR AND HIS CHARACTER ARE WELL MET

Charles Vincent Emerson Starrett is today best known as one of the nation's leading book reviewers, appearing regularly in the Chicago *Tribune*. In the past he has had published over a hundred books: novels, short stories, reviews, criticism, bibliography, biography, and very recently autobiography, *Born in a Bookshop, Chapters from the Chicago Renascence.*

Perhaps his best-known book is *The Private Life of Sherlock Holmes* (1933), which was an early attempt to collate the elements of the career of that great figure. Starrett was also instrumental in the formation of the Baker Street Irregulars, that straight-faced, tongue-in-cheek fraternity dedicated to the furtherance of the legend of the world's greatest detective.

It is obviously impossible for a man to be an admirer of Sherlock Holmes without having also a profound respect for Edgar Allan Poe, who created the prototype of the "Profile by Gaslight" in Auguste Dupin. As an admirer of Poe, Starrett was also involved with one of the most unusual and widespread searches for a copy of *Tamerlane*, the little pamphlet which constituted Edgar Allan Poe's first "book." As an aspiring young writer in the 1920s, Starrett finally succeeded in "cracking" *The Saturday Evening Post* with an article titled: "Have You a 'Tamerlane' in Your Attic?" It assessed the value of this book at ten thousand dollars and asked people nationwide to search their attics and other repositories of old books to see if this little rarity reposed there. Letters poured in by the hundreds from people who thought they had the scarce title. None proved to possess the real thing. Finally, one weekend Starrett had to leave town. When he returned, there was a letter from a Mrs. Ada Dodd in Worcester, Massachusetts, who unquestionably had located the "McCoy." Starrett dashed her off a letter, but it was too late. She had been put in contact with the famed rare book dealer Charles Goodspeed in Boston, who, true to his name, wasted no time selling the book for her at a sum substantially greater than ten thousand dollars.

All this is by way of validating Vincent Starrett's impeccable credentials for writing a story in which Edgar Allan Poe is the chief character. It appeared initially in *Seaports in the Moon,* a collection of stories by Starrett involving famed historical and literary figures, published in 1928. The book has been a collector's item among devotees of fantasy ever since.

The story deals with Edgar Allan Poe's last days and presents an extremely well-written presentation of the nature of the man and his attempted seduction by the lady in black.

In Which an Author and His Character Are Well Met

By Vincent Starrett

> *Ill-fated and mysterious man!—bewildered in the brilliancy of thine own imagination, and fallen in the flames of thine own youth! Again in fancy I behold thee!*
>
>   —E. A. POE.

Three quarters of a century after the momentous events just narrated, the steam packet from Richmond set down upon the docks at Baltimore a small, dark man of shabby-genteel appearance, who glanced quickly about him, as if expecting recognition, then strode briskly into the city. Afternoon was waning, and over the sky was spreading a dark threat of storm. In the shops, the proprietors were beginning to light their lamps. Presently, a thin rain began to fall, and the traveler hastened his steps toward shelter. Despite the bleakness of the occasion, a high humor perched jauntily upon him; and unwonted humor that he wore at the rakish angle of a new hat. His stick tapped the boards with arrogant challenge; his restless eyes gleamed with a sardonic mirth. So arresting was the hauteur of his cameo-like features that a passing woman stopped to look back and admire. Sensing her admiration, he paused before the window of a small shop and ostentatiously adjusted his stock before resuming his march.

At the intersection of two thoroughfares, under the canopy of a cheap hotel, he halted and stared around him at the bustling life in the streets; at the homing throngs that passed him in either direction. For a moment his heart sank. *Face on face in the city—would never the faces end?* There was at least a poem in the situation. *Face on face in the city—and never the face of a friend!* A wave of self-pity overwhelmed him and passed slowly. After a time, he smiled. This was the city of his youth. How he had loathed and loved it! For twenty years, it had been whispered, no friend had seen this man smile; but upon this gray day he smiled again, and, smiling, jingled in his pocket the few silver pieces that remained to him. This was an occasion of holiday. The follies of youth were long behind him. Ahead, a new and glittering chapter was opening its pages. He peered into the future, and suddenly life seemed almost bewilderingly bright. What of the paltry dollars in his pocket? At a single blow, perhaps, he would recoup his fallen fortunes and live forever at his ease. Only one episode must be allowed to intervene—dinner! The boat journey had been long and chilling. Dinner—and a bottle of wine!

He looked dubiously at the garish entrance to the hostelry, and mentally calculated the sum of money in his pocket. Then, with firm step and smiling eye, he entered the place.

At the cashier's rostrum, in the dining room, sat an aging spinster, watching the diners with listless gaze. She was almost offensively plain. Her straight teeth projected from her mouth as if driven forth by the violence of her shrill tongue. She was lank, dry, and yellow. Ten years dropped from her shoulders as he bowed, and twenty as, with his air of commanding diffidence, he wished her good evening. Her eyes followed him with a wild hope as he sought a corner table and melted into the deepening shadows.

An ancient darky shambled forward and cried out in surprise. "Lord-a-marcy, Massa Poe! Am dat you?"

The somber poet, thus revealed, smiled wryly. "You are a clever rascal, Jeff," he replied. "In the entire city, you are the first to recognize and welcome me. I shall admit the indictment on one condition only: that you bring me instantly a bottle and a glass. Need I say more?"

Widely grinning, the black servitor departed upon his errand. The poet, waiting for his wine, drummed restlessly upon the table. A wax taper gleamed before him, and upon this he fixed his melancholy gaze. After a moment, while the spinster gasped at her desk, he leaned forward and, removing it from its holder, pinched out the flame. Then, quietly, he transferred the candle to his pocket and again leaned back in his chair.

"Another taper, Jeff," he said, when the bottle had been placed before him; and when it had been brought, he filled his glass and held it to the light. For an instant, he hesitated, then raised the glass to his lips and drained it at a draught.

"'Fo' God, Massa Poe," observed the astonished Negro, "yo' cert'nly swallered dat licker powerful quick!"

"It is to celebrate my swearing-off," said the poet solemnly, and he filled his glass again. "Tomorrow, I shall be done with it forever." Again he tilted the liquid to his lips, and shuddered when he set down the glass.

On the other side of the dining room, a man arose and came forward. He was a tall man, in immaculate linen garments, which gave him somewhat the appearance of a Singhalese planter. A great diamond blazed on one of his fingers. Under a glossy black moustache, his white teeth gleamed like the denture of a piano keyboard. Immediately, there was an outcry.

"Poe!" exclaimed the tall man delightedly.

"Legrand!" cried the poet, springing to his feet.

They shook hands heartily, while the diners stared and raised their brows.

"This *is* a surprise," said the man called Legrand. "I thought you were in Richmond."

"I am in Aberystwyth, as you perceive," retorted the sardonic poet. "But how fortuitous a meeting! You are the very man I have been wishing to see. Have you dined?"

"I was about to order when I saw you. You will join me, I hope?"

"I was about to extend the same invitation. Do sit down. I have a fascinating story for you. Quite in your line, you know. Buried treasure, and all that sort of thing."

"Good God!" said Legrand. "Again?"

They seated themselves at the poet's table. "Does it concern the lady behind the cage?" continued Legrand, with a smile. "She is eying us with a somewhat proprietary air."

The poet was not deeply flattered. He was aware of the fatal effect he had upon women of whatever age and station. Such things were always happening. Was it his fault that his black hair lay in curls upon his high, white forehead? That his eyes were of tragic brilliance above his well-turned nose and neat black moustache? He shrugged and bent his head over the penciled card of dinner dishes. For a moment, he looked anxiously at the right-hand column for the enlightening figures there displayed. Had he accepted Legrand's invitation, or had Legrand accepted *his*? At length, he ordered, and lay back luxuriously in his chair.

It was a pleasant place, he reflected, this large dining room with its little gleaming tapers and dark-shadowed corners. Not at all the sort of place in which he ordinarily appeased his hunger.

Legrand, when the order had been given, watched him for a time in silence. Poe felt his companion's gaze and knew the thoughts that were passing in his mind. Neatly, even nattily dressed, as he was, the poet realized that there must be about him the unconcealable hints of poverty so long associated with his name. He resented the silent sympathy.

"My dear fellow," said Legrand, at last, "I can't tell you how glad I am to see you. We hear a great deal about you, these days. You are becoming quite famous."

The melancholy poet again drained his glass before replying. "And infamous," he added, shrugging. "It is all the same, you know. Let them but shout loudly enough, and I care not what they say."

"But what a cynic!" continued the other. "I should have thought that by this time you would be quite—what is the phrase?—'o'erswol'n with pride.'"

"Not a stiver of it," asserted Poe. "Believe me, Legrand, I have too few friends worthy of the name, to wish to forget any of them. My pride is reserved for the mounting number of my foes. In youth, you know, we hope to succeed to please those whom we love; in age, to spite those whom we hate." He laughed lightly. "My ill luck in making enemies has been little short of phenomenal. Fortunately, they have all written books."

His friend laughed also. "I suspect, however, that you have just stated the reason why you enjoy such enmity," he ventured.

"Ha!" cried the poet. "So you, too, read my reviews! Well, it is true. They like me not at all, these little essayists and poetasters. And so, like sheep, they forgather and trample me."

"I trust it has not spoiled your appetite for grilled kidneys?"

"It has not," declared Poe, with decision; and he turned eagerly to the steaming plate that the old Negro set before him.

Legrand raised his brows inquiringly. "A bottle of wine to celebrate your return?" he asked. "I note that you have not sworn off."

The black waiter paused uncertainly, and the poet made an eloquent gesture. "A bottle of wine, Jeff," he ordered, "to celebrate my return. And some cheroots, too."

They attacked their kidneys with gusto, nodding brightly at each other from time to time.

"By the way, Poe," said Legrand suddenly, "did you know that the words *abstemious* and *facetious* contain all the vowels in their consecutive order?"

The poet laughed. "It's true, isn't it? What genius discovered that, I wonder?"

"I saw it stated in a newspaper the other day, with other useful and informing items. I am interested in the curiosities of the alphabet, you may remember."

"I remember it very well," said Poe seriously. "The fact is, Legrand, I have been thinking about your talents in that direction for some hours."

At this point, the Negro returned with the bottle of wine, and for a time conversation languished. Legrand, as he watched an entire tumbler of the liquor disappearing down his friend's throat, appeared as astonished as the black waiter had been.

"Hold on, Poe!" he cried humorously. "That's no way to drink wine."

The poet leaned back in his chair. He smiled gently and half-closed his eyes. For some minutes, he puffed languidly at his cheroot and watched the smoke rings float away into the mysterious shadows. Save for the glimmering tapers, the room was almost without light. The lamps burned but feebly. Outside, the rain was falling more heavily. Poe's tragic eyes were fixed upon the taper before him. At length he spoke in a dreamy undertone.

"Wax tapers, Legrand," he said in his melodious voice. "How usual, and yet how lovely! We think of them, when we think of them at all, as commonplaces. Yet they are the veritable flambeaux of faëry. A white metamorphosis from the flowers, crowned with the most intangible of all visible mysteries."

"Charming!" cried his companion. "Why, one might make a poem of it, Poe."

The poet gestured gracefully. "One shall," he murmured. "Yes, I shall do it tonight, and send it off to Graham, to-morrow."

He reached for the wine bottle and found it empty. "Another bottle, Jeff," he called, "To celebrate Mr. Poe's return."

Legrand appeared to be worried. "Well, one more, Poe," he agreed, "but that's all."

"Mystery," continued the poet, unheeding. "And yet, it is all about us. It is at the heart of everything. It is life and it is death. And what do any of us know? To dream—that has been the business of my life; and I have framed for myself a bower of dreams. In them, *you* have had your part. Come," he cried abruptly, "let us drink! It is early—but let us drink! It is late—but what matters it? Let us drink! Let us pour out an offering . . ."

His words trailed into nothingness, and again silence lay heavily between them.

"My dear fellow," said Legrand, at length, "can I help you in any way while you are in the city? I owe a great deal to you, you know. My very existence, in fact."

"Mystery," continued the dreamer, resuming the tone of his desultory conversation. "Mystery and despair! Man's career is a pendulum that swings ceaselessly between hope and fear. Life is a struggle between them. Between a desire to believe that life is important and a conviction that it is not. It is not truth that man needs, but if it were, who should give it to him? What he requires is a beautiful legend, to soothe and comfort him. It is all that he shall ever discover. Death! What is death? Not death, but that Time can offer him only age, may be man's tragedy." He laughed harshly. "Wherefore, let us drink!"

"Poe," said his friend, leaning swiftly across the table, "are you in need of money?"

The poet set down his glass and ran his fingers upward through his curling hair. The directness of the question apparently had broken his moody train of thought.

"Why, yes," he replied, after a moment. "I am always in need of money. But I have enough for the moment. It is sufficient until tomorrow. And tomorrow, there will be plenty, Legrand, as you shall hear."

"You would not mind if I offered to lend you some?"

"Ah, I should mind it greatly. Believe me, my embarrassment is only temporary."

Legrand was silent. After a time, he asked: "What are your plans for the evening?"

"To drink," said the poet. "To drink, Legrand, and when I have finished, to drink again. And then, when I have finished drinking, once more—to drink!"

"By God, you shall do nothing of the sort! Look here, Poe. I have a set of rooms. Suppose you spend the night with me, and in the morning, with fresh minds, we shall attack the problem—"

"It is your accusing conscience talking, Legrand," said the poet. "You have made me drunk, it whispers, and so you must look after me." He snapped his fingers. "Fiddlesticks! I am no more drunk than yourself. I am alive! I see clearly! Listen, Legrand! Last night, I had a dream. Do you believe in presentiments?"

His companion moved uneasily. His expression seemed to indicate dismay and a measure of suspicion.

"No matter," continued the other, growing more cheerful as he talked. "They are, I believe, often subconscious conclusions, and so may have a definite value. Well, I have a presentiment that, by this time tomorrow, I shall be rolling in riches!"

"My dear fellow!" exclaimed Legrand. "Are you sure that you feel quite well?"

"You should be the last to ask it. I am not drunk, nor have I taken leave of my senses. Last night—listen!—I dreamed that I stood within an ancient house; a house falling into ruin and decay; peopled by lonely, imprisoned echoes in the wall, and shadowy memories, tearless and waiting. I progressed from room to room, and the lonely echoes woke and whispered around me; gaunt memories sprang forth to welcome and reproach me. At length, in a bare chamber, high under dripping eaves, I found an ancient chest, and inside a treasure—jewels and gold and tarnished silver vessels, and on the top of all a parchment sheet that told the tragic story."

"Oh, you're drunk as an owl!" cried Legrand. "Come out of it, Poe. Let's go home."

"A parchment sheet of writing," continued the poet relentlessly, "whereby it was made known that all this wealth was mine, and had been awaiting me these many, many years. Can you guess, Legrand, what house that old house was?"

"Tell me, if you care to."

"It was my grandfather's house!"

For an instant, Legrand stared stupidly. Then, "The devil!" he exclaimed.

"No, my grandfather: General David Poe. He was a quartermaster general, Legrand, during the Revolution, and an intimate of Lafayette. How well I used to know the story! There was no denying the place. I had been there before; I knew it when I saw it. Now do you think me drunk? For years, I have wondered that my grandfather left nothing to his children. It was said that he had died quite poor. His widow also died in poverty. Legrand, something happened back in those early days, something curious and strange; and now, at last, the hiding place of the treasure has been revealed to me in a dream. You ask my plans for the evening. I will tell you them. I intend to collect the treasure of my ancestor."

All this he said in a fierce, low whisper, leaning forward toward his friend across the table, who now listened with sparkling eyes.

"Damn it, Poe!" exploded Legrand, "it is almost too amazing to be true."

"You will help me?"

"I am at your service."

"Then we shall leave at once. But we shall need another candle."

A new taper had been placed within the holder, and

plucking it from its place the poet pinched out the flame and deposited it with the other in his pocket. "And now," he cried, "a final glass—to our success!"

"Success!" echoed Legrand, and raised his glass.

They drank the toast solemnly and sank back into their chairs.

"Success," muttered the poet, and leaned forward to the table. He laid his head upon his hand and breathed heavily. Presently, his hand slipped down; his head drooped forward and was pillowed on his arm. His breathing became stertorous and harsh.

After a time, a hand was laid upon his shoulder, and he was gently shaken. He looked up wildly into the face of the old Negro who had waited upon him. Legrand had vanished.

"Was yo'-all quite finished, Massa Poe?" asked the Negro respectfully. "'Ca'se if you is, we is gwine to close up de dining room."

"Where is the gentleman who was with me?" demanded the poet thickly. "When did he go?"

The old Negro turned his face aside for a moment to hide a smile. Then his features became grave as he replied: "Dey wa'n't no one else with yo', Massa Poe. Dat other genelman, he wasn't here at all, sah."

"Not here!" cried Poe. He dashed his hand across his eyes. "Not here! Why, I've been talking with him for an hour!"

"Yassah," said the darky, "yo's done a powerful lot of talkin', Massa Poe; but dere wa'n't no one else with yo'. Yo' was jes' kin' of talkin' to yo'self, sah."

The poet sank back in his chair and seemed to shrivel. "Good God!" he muttered in a low voice; and suddenly he staggered to his feet. "Am I insane?"

His eyes fell upon the row of empty bottles on the table, and for some moments he stood regarding them. At last, quietly, he asked: "How long have I been sleeping?"

"About two hours, sah."

"Two hours! It must be ten o'clock." He strode to the

window and pushed aside the curtains. The rain was still falling monotonously in the streets. He returned to the table. "I'm sorry if I have been a trouble, Jeff," he said. "Bring me my bill and I'll get out." And after a moment he whispered again, "Good God!"

In the street, he began to feel better. His head was clearer, his legs firmer. He welcomed the rain that beat against his face. The darkness was a bandage about his eyes. For a few minutes, he stood and let the water cool his raging blood. Then, with a stronger step, he moved away in the darkness toward the old home of his father's.

It was midnight when he crossed the deserted garden and climbed the knoll to the ruined dwelling. The door flew open to welcome him, and in the frame stood a woman, tall and beautiful, who extended a hand to him and drew him quickly within. In the darkness, they stood looking into each other's eyes.

"I have waited long for you to come," she whispered. "Look well into my face, Edgar Poe, and tell me: do you know me?"

He shook his head, embarrassed, like a child that is questioned by an elder. "I seem to know you, lady," he replied; "there is that about your eyes that is familiar; or perhaps it is your hair. I think that once I knew you very well."

Her laughter was like the chiming of old bells.

"You have never known me," she said, "and yet for years I have been near you, your neighbor in a dozen streets and cities, your destined bride through all your years of life."

"Of course," he smiled. "How well I know you now! It was your eager voice that puzzled me, your radiant youth and loveliness. I had not thought that such a thing could be. I know you now. You are the Lady Death, my long-lost love!"

She laughed, showing her faultless teeth, confident of her

beauty and perpetual youth. Her eyes became coquettish, and she nestled against his shoulder.

"I am so glad you find me not entirely a fright," she admitted. "And now, after all these years, you will go with me?"

He hesitated and drew back. He pressed her hand in his, and it was cold as ice. He attempted to articulate, and his tongue clucked against the top of his mouth.

"You know how long and dearly I have loved you," he stammered, at length. "It is not that I am unfaithful. From the beginning, I have dreamed only of your arms about me, and your lips on mine, our mingled bodies and our long repose. And yet—"

"And yet?"

"Somehow, I have just begun to live. Tonight I came here with my heart aflame. It seemed that a vision led me."

"It was I."

But he shook his head and held her from him for a time, looking deeply into her eyes. "You are very beautiful," he sighed; "but I have never lived. It grieves me to seem ungracious; yet I must beg your pardon and go upon my way. Some other day—or night—perhaps—"

"What is it you would do?" she asked.

"Dwell for a time within the lap of luxury. Lie for a time beside the hussy Life."

"Her body is less soft than mine."

"Still, with your permission, I should like to try her shameful ease."

"Stay with me," she pleaded. "See, we have the house to ourselves. Upstairs there is a chamber with old hangings, and a bed wide as a field of lilies. There your father was born, and there your grandfather died. What could be more appropriate than that you and I—"

He pushed her resolutely away. "Not tonight," he said firmly. "Besides, I am not feeling very well. Some other time, I promise you. I have your address, you know. I always keep it by me. You will come to me when I send for you?"

She sighed and drifted from him. "I will come," she whispered, "for I cannot do otherwise."

"That is well," he answered, "and don't feel too badly about this, if you please, because, after all—"

Then he noticed that she was gone. A cold breeze whistled through the half-open door, and he knew that his clothes were dripping wet. Somehow, he had lost his hat. He pushed his fingers upward through the wet mass of his hair and tightly closed his eyes. Thus he stood for a moment, silent; then, pushing forward across the wide reception hall, he stumbled over the first step of the ascending flight and began his upward climb. . . .

In the morning, a ray of sunlight, piercing the grime of an attic window, fell upon the body of a man lying across an ancient chest. His hair was matted and unkempt. His eyes were closed. After a time, they opened and stared in bewilderment at the scene about him. Old rafters, thick with the dust of ages; cobwebs larger and more terrible than the meshes of a dream; and a chaos of old furniture and boxes, draped with the moldering, discarded garments of three generations. Like Rip van Winkle returning to the world, the derelict groaned and stretched his aching limbs. Memory swept over him like a roll of drums, and with difficulty he got upon his feet. A cracked and dusty mirror stood at an angle against the sloping roof, and he staggered forward and wiped a portion of its surface, recoiling in horror from the image that looked forth at him. He sank down again upon the chest, and buried his face in his hands, murmuring incoherently.

Thus he sat for a time, then, rising, flung back the lid of the ancient coffer. A hideous smile distorted his features. Instead of jewels and hoarded gold, he looked upon a musty tangle of old garments, out of which, like the shoulder of a man, thrust upward an epaulette of tarnished silver. It was the uniform of General David Poe. Unceremoniously, he hauled it forth and dropped it to the floor. Then, methodically, he began to draw forth piece after piece and add it to the heap.

At the bottom he came upon a velvet bag, no larger than a woman's vanity case, drawn tight at the throat by a drawstring. Inside was something hard and metallic, and something too that crackled like old paper. Without emotion, he untied the string and shook the contents of the bag out upon the boards.

The slender vial that tumbled forth pleased him greatly, and for a few moments he turned it in his hands, as a child plays with a toy. Then he examined it with greater care, and in a moment came upon the legend engraved on the surface of the setting. And then, for a long time, he sat very still and stared with dazed and frightened eyes at the impossible thing that he held within his hand.

The waters of Bimini! The precious drops de León sought —and failed to find!

Slowly, his wits came back. It was, of course, incredible; beyond belief. This was some trifle that once had graced the boudoir of his father's mother, that slender Revolutionary maiden whose eyes looked forth, so full of mischief, from beneath long, sweeping lashes, in the dainty miniature that was all that was left to tell that she had lived. Were it a vial of that veritable water from the fountain, that slim hoyden would be living still, and breaking hearts on every hand. And yet . . .

Again his mind departed for a time. Then he recalled that there had been a paper with the vial. He snatched it from the bag and carried it to the window. Brown, faded writing, and paper turning yellow. For a moment, the words danced before his eyes and ran together; then they settled into place, and he read what his grandfather had written.

This pretty phiall with the pretty name was given me by Tom Endicott, mine old adjutant, who had it of a fellow in his company, when he was a Captaine, who swore that he had won it at dice from a drunken villain of Tarrytown, near the city of New York, who vowed that he had taken it from that Major André who was hanged because he was a spy. The originall owner was one of those three drinking, card-playing louts, who while idling in the woods near the place called Tarrytown, did set upon and capture that British Major, taking from him all that he had of value upon his person. The later story as it comes to me is to this effect: that the unfortunate Major André cried out bitterly upon being bereft of his phiall, and pleaded with his captors that it be returned, they assuming it to be a love token, since the young Major was very handsome and beloved of the ladies. It is further asserted, although with less authority, that upon the scaffold the poor young man did again cry out for his phiall, to the great amazement of his executioners, who had no word of any such bottle, it having been withheld from them by this afore-mentioned villain who took it from him. I know not what the virtue of the phiall may be, save that it is of gold and set with diamonds in a pretty design, but that its effect upon those who see it is powerful and potent, is proved by the circumstance that twice after I had myself shown it in a public gathering, my dwelling was thereafter entered by thieves, who took nothing but turned things mightily about in their search. Many times also have I been offered money for the phiall, which I have at all times declined. Having no faith in magic, but an abiding trust in Him who breathed into me the breath of life, I have foreborne to search out the truth of the phiall, which is of such an attraction, however, that I have likewise foreborne to destroy it. It is, in all likelihood, merely a pretty toy intended to contain a lady's toilet water, and about which an undue excitement is created.

To this document was signed the name of the author, David Poe, and when he had reached it, the grandson of David Poe turned quickly upon his heel and paced the floor in uncontrollable agitation. After a time, with burning eyes, he read the communication for a second time; then, putting paper and vial into his pocket, hurried forth into the streets. His head was splitting and his throat was parched and contracted. He knew, however, what he needed. He needed liquor—liquor—liquor in large and satisfying draughts.

On a street corner stood a large and flashy gentleman, with a cold eye and a bland and oily tongue. He saw the hurrying figure that approached him, and with determined friendship barred the way. His great hand was extended after the cordial fashion of his kind.

"Good morning, neighbor," he boomed. "John Rafferty, ward committeeman and captain of this precinct. A great day after the rain! Have you voted yet, this morning?"

"Not yet," laughed the poet wildly, pushing past; "nor have I drunk yet, this morning, Mr. Rafferty. Don't stop me, I implore you, for I am going to get a drink."

Mr. Rafferty's shrewd eyelids flickered; his shrewd and understanding hand fell heartily upon the poet's shoulder.

"Ha-ha!" he roared. "Ha-ha-ha! That's a good one. Drink first and vote afterward, hey? You've certainly got the right system, brother."

"Ha-ha!" cried the poet. "It is very amusing, isn't it? You see why I am in a hurry. I'm sorry I can't ask you to join me."

"No offense, neighbor," said Mr. Rafferty jovially. "I was about to have a drink myself. Why not join *me*?" He seized the poet's arm and urged him forward in the direction he had been following. "You are a man after my own heart, Mr. Jo—I don't believe I caught the name, neighbor."

"I didn't mention it," replied the poet, "but it is Poe, not Joe. I am Edgar Allan Poe."

"Poe!" cried Mr. Rafferty. "Know the name very well. Very

well, indeed. Well, Mr. Poe, you're quite right. A man may not have time to vote, but he's always got time to drink. You look to me like a perfectly good Whig, too. How about it?"

"Oh, a Whig, of course," asserted Poe. "A Whig, a Baptist, and a somnambulist." He laughed sardonically, and reluctantly fell into step beside the implacable stranger. . . . After all, a drink was what he wanted. "Very good of you, I'm sure," he added more courteously. "By all means, let us have a drink. As for the voting, I'm afraid I can't join you in that. The fact is, I don't vote in this town. It's rather a drawback, I understand."

Mr. Rafferty chuckled. "You'd be surprised!" he said.

They made two turns and entered the doorway of a grisly barroom. Mr. Rafferty was greeted with acclaim. The place began to fill. . . .

"Well, one more, then," said the poet, after a few moments at the bar. "Did you ever hear, Mr. Rafferty, of the four boxes that govern the world? They are the cartridge box, the ballot box, the jury box, and the bandbox."

"Ha-ha-ha," roared Mr. Rafferty, with appreciation. "That's a good one, Mr. Poe. Well, here's to crime!"

They raised their glasses to each other. . . .

"I must really go, now," said the poet, an hour later; and four days afterward, in the hospital whither he had been taken, he awoke for a moment and said again: "I must go now, gentlemen; I must really go!"

His physicians were greatly surprised by the remark and puzzled about it for some time.

Shortly before he died, he raised his head a few inches from the pillow and asked for his coat, which was brought to him. The vial had slipped through a torn pocket into the lining, and when he felt the little mound it made, he smiled peacefully and for a time was silent.

"You need not fear to tell me the truth," he whispered, after a while. "How long have I to live?"

Two physicians, young but whiskered like pirates, consulted together, with little glances at the bed. At length one of them spoke.

"We are not prepared, Mr. Poe, to say that you are—ah—not going to—ah—recover," he said. "If you have friends, however, whom you would like to see, we should be happy to—ah—send for them."

"Friends!" murmured the poet, with a little smile. But he gave them a name, the first that came into his head, although he had not seen the man for years.

A little later, when their attention was otherwise occupied, he managed to extract the vial from its hiding place and draw it beneath the covers. With infinite toil and patience, as his strength decreased, he picked at the withholding wax about the stopper. . . . A faintness began to overwhelm him.

In desperation, he brought the vial into view and conveyed it to his mouth, gnawing at the stopper with his teeth; but a nurse rushed forward and snatched it from his grasp. With a terrible cry, he fell back upon his pillow. The physicians came forward quickly.

"What is it, doctor?" asked one of the other, his eyes upon the vial.

"Hanged if I know," answered the physician who had received it.

They turned their accusing eyes upon the poet, just too late to receive his explanation.

This short story is unquestionably one of the most ingenious tales written by any author involving the presence of Edgar Allan Poe. Intimate knowledge of the life and works of Poe are displayed in "When It Was Moonlight," which is at once a mystery story and a tale of supernatural horror. It involves Poe's analytical abilities and pretends to show the basis of at least three of his most famous tales: "The Premature Burial," "The Black Cat," and "The Cask of Amontillado." The Philadelphia period of Poe's life is dealt with in this story, and his aunt, Mrs. Maria Poe Clemm, appears as one of the characters.

The author, Manly Wade Wellman, has been a popular figure in many of the literary areas into which Poe himself had ventured. He is noted as a writer of science fiction, supernatural horror, mystery, and historical fiction. Born in Portuguese West Africa, Manly Wade Wellman came to the United States when seven. This early background served as the basis for some of the unusual stories he wrote for *Weird Tales*. His first sale of fiction was an interplanetary novelette, *When Planets Clashed*, appearing in Hugo Gernsback's *Wonder Stories Quarterly*, Spring 1931. He became a popular and well-known figure in the science fiction magazines, selling regularly until the end of World War II.

Along with many other science fiction writers, he branched into writing comic book continuities, then veered into mystery and detective stories, in which fields he won a two-thousand-dollar first prize for the most original detective story of 1945 from *Ellery Queen's Mystery Magazine*. Ten years later, he would receive the Mystery Writers of America's Edgar Award for *Dead and Gone* as the best fact crime book of 1955.

He has also turned to historical novels and teen-age books, and the total number of his works between hard covers must now be approaching fifty, of which *Who Fears the Devil* (Arkham House, 1963), a collection of folk tales of the mountain people, is especially noteworthy.

"When It Was Moonlight" initially appeared in *Unknown*, an off-trail fantasy magazine, in the issue of February 1940. This is the first time it has ever been reprinted.

When It Was Moonlight

By Manly Wade Wellman

> *Let my heart be still a moment, and this mystery explore.*
>
> *—The Raven.*

His hand, as slim as a white claw, dipped a quillful of ink and wrote in one corner of the page the date—March 3, 1842. Then:

THE PREMATURE BURIAL
By Edgar A. Poe

He hated his middle name, the name of his miserly and spiteful stepfather. For a moment he considered crossing out even the initial; then he told himself that he was only wool-gathering, putting off the drudgery of writing. And write he must, or starve—the Philadelphia *Dollar Newspaper* was clamoring for the story he had promised. Well, today he had heard a tag of gossip—his mother-in-law had it from a neighbor—that revived in his mind a subject always fascinating.

He began rapidly to write, in a fine copperplate hand:

> There are certain themes of which the interest is all-absorbing, but which are entirely too horrible for the purposes of legitimate fiction—

This would really be an essay, not a tale, and he could do it justice. Often he thought of the whole world as a vast fat cemetery, close-set with tombs in which not all the occupants were at rest—too many struggled unavailingly against their smothering shrouds, their locked and weighted coffin lids. What were his own literary labors, he mused, but a struggle against being shut down and throttled by a society as heavy and grim and senseless as clods heaped by a sexton's spade?

He paused, and went to the slate mantelshelf for a candle. His kerosene lamp had long ago been pawned, and it was dark for midafternoon, even in March. Elsewhere in the house his mother-in-law swept busily, and in the room next to his sounded the quiet breathing of his invalid wife. Poor Virginia slept, and for the moment knew no pain. Returning with his light, he dipped more ink and continued down the sheet:

> To be buried while alive is, beyond question, the most terrific of these extremes which has ever fallen to the lot of mere mortality. That it has frequently, very frequently, fallen will scarcely be denied—

Again his dark imagination savored the tale he had heard that day. It had happened here in Philadelphia, in this very quarter, less than a month ago. A widower had gone, after weeks of mourning, to his wife's tomb, with flowers. Stooping to place them on the marble slab, he had heard noise beneath. At once joyful and aghast, he fetched men and crowbars, and recovered the body, all untouched by decay. At home that night, the woman returned to consciousness.

So said the gossip, perhaps exaggerated, perhaps not. And the house was only six blocks away from Spring Garden Street, where he sat.

Poe fetched out his notebooks and began to marshal bits of narrative for his composition—a gloomy tale of resurrection in Baltimore, another from France, a genuinely creepy citation from the *Chirurgical Journal* of Leipzig; a sworn case of revival, by electrical impulses, of a dead man in London. Then he added an experience of his own, romantically embellished, a dream adventure of his boyhood in

Virginia. Just as he thought to make an end, he had a new inspiration.

Why not learn more about that reputed Philadelphia burial and the one who rose from seeming death? It would point up his piece, give it a timely local climax, ensure acceptance—he could hardly risk a rejection. Too, it would satisfy his own curiosity. Laying down the pen, Poe got up. From a peg he took his wide black hat, his old military cloak that he had worn since his ill-fated cadet days at West Point. Huddling it round his slim little body, he opened the front door and went out.

March had come in like a lion and, lionlike, roared and rampaged over Philadelphia. Dry, cold dust blew up into Poe's full gray eyes, and he hardened his mouth under the gay dark moustache. His shins felt goosefleshy; his striped trousers were unseasonably thin and his shoes badly needed mending. Which way lay his journey?

He remembered the name of the street, and something about a ruined garden. Eventually he came to the place, or what must be the place—the garden was certainly ruined, full of dry, hardy weeds that still stood in great ragged clumps after the hard winter. Poe forced open the creaky gate, went up the rough-flagged path to the stoop. He saw a bronzed nameplate—"Gauber," it said. Yes, that was the name he had heard. He swung the knocker loudly, and thought he caught a whisper of movement inside. But the door did not open.

"Nobody lives there, Mr. Poe," said someone from the street. It was a grocery boy, with a heavy basket on his arm. Poe left the doorstep. He knew the lad; indeed, he owed the grocer eleven dollars.

"Are you sure?" Poe prompted.

"Well"—and the boy shifted the weight of his burden—"if anybody lived here, they'd buy from our shop, wouldn't they? And I'd deliver, wouldn't I? But I've had this job for six months, and never set foot inside that door."

Poe thanked him and walked down the street, but did not take the turn that would lead home. Instead he sought the shop of one Pemberton, a printer and a friend, to pass the time of day and ask for a loan.

Pemberton could not lend even one dollar—times were hard—but he offered a drink of Monongahela whisky, which Poe forced himself to refuse; then a supper of crackers, cheese, and garlic sausage, which Poe thankfully shared. At home, unless his mother-in-law had begged or borrowed from the neighbors, would be only bread and molasses. It was past sundown when the writer shook hands with Pemberton, thanked him with warm courtesy for his hospitality, and ventured into the evening.

Thank heaven, it did not rain. Poe was saddened by storms. The wind had abated and the March sky was clear save for a tiny fluff of scudding cloud and a banked dark line at the horizon, while up rose a full moon the color of frozen cream. Poe squinted from under his hat brim at the shadow-pattern on the disk. Might he not write another story of a lunar voyage—like the one about Hans Pfaal, but dead serious this time? Musing thus, he walked along the dusk-filling street until he came again opposite the ruined garden, the creaky gate, and the house with the doorplate marked: "Gauber."

Hello, the grocery boy had been wrong. There was light inside the front window, water-blue light—or was there? Anyway, motion—yes, a figure stooped there, as if to peer out at him.

Poe turned in at the gate, and knocked at the door once again.

Four or five moments of silence; then he heard the old lock grating. The door moved inward, slowly and noisily. Poe fancied that he had been wrong about the blue light, for he saw only darkness inside. A voice spoke:

"Well, sir?"

The two words came huskily but softly, as though the

door-opener scarcely breathed. Poe swept off his broad black hat and made one of his graceful bows.

"If you will pardon me—" He paused, not knowing whether he addressed man or woman. "This is the Gauber residence?"

"It is," was the reply, soft, hoarse, and sexless. "Your business, sir?"

Poe spoke with official crispness; he had been a sergeant major of artillery before he was twenty-one, and knew how to inject the proper note. "I am here on public duty," he announced. "I am a journalist, tracing a strange report."

"Journalist?" repeated his interrogator. "Strange report? Come in, sir."

Poe complied, and the door closed abruptly behind him, with a rusty snick of the lock. He remembered being in jail once, and how the door of his cell had slammed just so. It was not a pleasant memory. But he saw more clearly, now he was inside—his eyes got used to the tiny trickle of moonlight.

He stood in a dark hallway, all paneled in wood, with no furniture, drapes, or pictures. With him was a woman, in full skirt and down-drawn lace cap, a woman as tall as he and with intent eyes that glowed as from within. She neither moved nor spoke, but waited for him to tell her more of his errand.

Poe did so, giving his name and, stretching a point, claiming to be a subeditor of the *Dollar Newspaper*, definitely assigned to the interview. "And now, madam, concerning this story that is rife concerning a premature burial—"

She had moved very close, but as his face turned toward her she drew back. Poe fancied that his breath had blown her away like a feather; then, remembering Pemberton's garlic sausage, he was chagrined. To confirm his new thought, the woman was offering him wine—to sweeten his breath.

"Would you take a glass of canary, Mr. Poe?" she invited,

and opened a side door. He followed her into a room papered in pale blue. Moonglow, drenching it, reflected from that paper and seemed an artificial light. That was what he had seen from outside. From an undraped table his hostess lifted a bottle, poured wine into a metal goblet, and offered it.

Poe wanted that wine, but he had recently promised his sick wife, solemnly and honestly, to abstain from even a sip of the drink that so easily upset him. Through thirsty lips he said: "I thank you kindly, but I am a temperance man."

"Oh," and she smiled. Poe saw white teeth. Then: "I am Elva Gauber—Mrs. John Gauber. The matter of which you ask I cannot explain clearly, but it is true. My husband was buried, in the Eastman Lutheran Churchyard—"

"I had heard, Mrs. Gauber, that the burial concerned a woman."

"No, my husband. He had been ill. He felt cold and quiet. A physician, a Dr. Mechem, pronounced him dead, and he was interred beneath a marble slab in his family vault." She sounded weary, but her voice was calm. "This happened shortly after the New Year. On Valentine's Day, I brought flowers. Beneath his slab he stirred and struggled. I had him brought forth. And he lives—after a fashion—today."

"Lives today?" repeated Poe. "In this house?"

"Would you care to see him? Interview him?"

Poe's heart raced, his spine chilled. It was his peculiarity that such sensations gave him pleasure. "I would like nothing better," he assured her, and she went to another door, an inner one.

Opening it, she paused on the threshold, as though summoning her resolution for a plunge into cold, swift water. Then she started down a flight of steps.

Poe followed, unconsciously drawing the door shut behind him.

The gloom of midnight, of prison—yes, of the tomb—fell at once upon those stairs. He heard Elva Gauber gasp:

"No—the moonlight—let it in—" And then she fell, heavily and limply, rolling downstairs.

Aghast, Poe quickly groped his way after her. She lay against a door at the foot of the flight, wedged against the panel. He touched her—she was cold and rigid, without motion or elasticity of life. His thin hand groped for and found the knob of the lower door, flung it open. More dim reflected moonlight, and he made shift to drag the woman into it.

Almost at once she sighed heavily, lifted her head, and rose. "How stupid of me," she apologized hoarsely.

"The fault was mine," protested Poe. "Your nerves, your health, have naturally suffered. The sudden dark—the closeness—overcame you." He fumbled in his pocket for a tinderbox. "Suffer me to strike a light."

But she held out a hand to stop him. "No, no. The moon is sufficient." She walked to a small, oblong pane set in the wall. Her hands, thin as Poe's own, with long grubby nails, hooked on the sill. Her face, bathed in the full light of the moon, strengthened and grew calm. She breathed deeply, almost voluptuously. "I am quite recovered," she said. "Do not fear for me. You need not stand so near, sir."

He had forgotten that garlic odor, and drew back contritely. She must be as sensitive to the smell as . . . as . . . what was it that was sickened and driven away by garlic? Poe could not remember, and took time to note that they were in a basement, stone-walled and with a floor of dirt. In one corner water seemed to drip, forming a dank pool of mud. Close to this, set into the wall, showed a latched trap door of planks, thick and wide, cleated crosswise, as though to cover a window. But no window would be set so low. Everything smelt earthy and close, as though fresh air had been shut out for decades.

"Your husband is here?" he inquired.

"Yes." She walked to the shutterlike trap, unlatched it, and drew it open.

The recess beyond was as black as ink, and from it came a feeble mutter. Poe followed Elva Gauber, and strained his eyes. In a little stone-flagged nook a bed had been made up. Upon it lay a man, stripped almost naked. His skin was as white as dead bone, and only his eyes, now opening, had life. He gazed at Elva Gauber, and past her at Poe.

"Go away," he mumbled.

"Sir," ventured Poe formally, "I have come to hear of how you came to life in the grave—"

"It's a lie," broke in the man on the pallet. He writhed halfway to a sitting posture, laboring upward as against a crushing weight. The wash of moonlight showed how wasted and fragile he was. His face stared and snarled bare-toothed, like a skull. "A lie, I say!" he cried, with a sudden strength that might well have been his last. "Told by this monster who is not—my wife—"

The shutter-trap slammed upon his cries. Elva Gauber faced Poe, withdrawing a pace to avoid his garlic breath.

"You have seen my husband," she said. "Was it a pretty sight, sir?"

He did not answer, and she moved across the dirt to the stair doorway. "Will you go up first?" she asked. "At the top, hold the door open, that I may have—" She said "life," or, perhaps, "light." Poe could not be sure which.

Plainly she, who had almost welcomed his intrusion at first, now sought to lead him away. Her eyes, compelling as shouted commands, were fixed upon him. He felt their power, and bowed to it.

Obediently he mounted the stairs, and stood with the upper door wide. Elva Gauber came up after him. At the top her eyes again seized his. Suddenly Poe knew more than ever before about the mesmeric impulses he loved to write about.

"I hope," she said measuredly, "that you have not found your visit fruitless. I live here alone—seeing nobody, caring for the poor thing that was once my husband, John Gauber.

My mind is not clear. Perhaps my manners are not good. Forgive me, and good night."

Poe found himself ushered from the house, and outside the wind was howling once again. The front door closed behind him, and the lock grated.

The fresh air, the whip of gale in his face, and the absence of Elva Gauber's impelling gaze suddenly brought him back, as though from sleep, to a realization of what had happened—or what had not happened.

He had come out, on this uncomfortable March evening, to investigate the report of a premature burial. He had seen a ghastly sick thing, which had called the gossip a lie. Somehow, then, he had been drawn abruptly away—stopped from full study of what might be one of the strangest adventures it was ever a writer's good fortune to know. Why was he letting things drop at this stage?

He decided not to let them drop. That would be worse than staying away altogether.

He made up his mind, formed quickly a plan. Leaving the doorstep, he turned from the gate, slipped quickly around the house. He knelt by the foundation at the side, just where a small oblong pane was set flush with the ground.

Bending his head, he found that he could see plainly inside, by reason of the flood of moonlight—a phenomenon, he realized, for generally an apartment was disclosed only by light within. The open doorway to the stairs, the swamp mess of mud in the corner, the out-flung trap door, were discernible. And something stood or huddled at the exposed niche—something that bent itself upon and above the frail white body of John Gauber.

Full skirt, white cap—it was Elva Gauber. She bent herself down, her face was touching the face or shoulder of her husband.

Poe's heart, never the healthiest of organs, began to drum and race. He pressed closer to the pane, for a better glimpse of what went on in the cellar. His shadow cut away some of the light. Elva Gauber turned to look.

Her face was as pale as the moon itself. Like the moon, it was shadowed in irregular patches. She came quickly, almost running, toward the pane where Poe crouched. He saw her, plainly and at close hand.

Dark, wet, sticky stains lay upon her mouth and cheeks. Her tongue roved out, licking at the stains—

Blood!

Poe sprang up and ran to the front of the house. He forced his thin, trembling fingers to seize the knocker, to swing it heavily again and again. When there was no answer, he pushed heavily against the door itself—it did not give. He moved to a window, rapped on it, pried at the sill, lifted his fist to smash the glass.

A silhouette moved beyond the pane, and threw it up. Something shot out at him like a pale snake striking—before he could move back, fingers had twisted in the front of his coat. Elva Gauber's eyes glared into his.

Her cap was off, her dark hair fallen in disorder. Blood still smeared and dewed her mouth and jowls.

"You have pried too far," she said, in a voice as measured and cold as the drip from icicles. "I was going to spare you, because of the odor about you that repelled me—the garlic. I showed you a little, enough to warn any wise person, and let you go. Now—"

Poe struggled to free himself. Her grip was immovable, like the clutch of a steel trap. She grimaced in triumph, yet she could not quite face him—the garlic still clung to his breath.

"Look in my eyes," she bade him. "Look—you cannot refuse, you cannot escape. You will die, with John—and the two of you, dying, shall rise again like me. I'll have two fountains of life while you remain—two companions after you die."

"Woman," said Poe, fighting against her stabbing gaze, "you are mad."

She snickered gustily. "I am sane, and so are you. We both know that I speak the truth. We both know the futility of your struggle." Her voice rose a little. "Through a chink in the tomb, as I lay dead, a ray of moonlight streamed and struck my eyes. I woke. I struggled. I was set free. Now at night, when the moon shines— *Ugh!* Don't breathe that herb in my face!"

She turned her head away. At that instant it seemed to Poe that a curtain of utter darkness fell, and with it sank down the form of Elva Gauber.

He peered in the sudden gloom. She was collapsed across the window sill, like a discarded puppet in its booth. Her hand still twisted in the bosom of his coat, and he pried himself loose from it, finger by steely, cold finger. Then he turned to flee from this place of shadowed peril to body and soul.

As he turned, he saw whence had come the dark. A cloud had come up from its place on the horizon—the fat, sooty bank he had noted there at sundown—and now it obscured the moon. Poe paused, in mid-retreat, gazing.

His thoughtful eye gauged the speed and size of the cloud. It curtained the moon, would continue to curtain it for—well, ten minutes. And for that ten minutes Elva Gauber would lie motionless, lifeless. She had told the truth about the moon giving her life. Hadn't she fallen like one slain on the stairs when they were darkened? Poe began grimly to string the evidence together.

It was Elva Gauber, not her husband, who had died and gone to the family vault. She had come back to life, or a mockery of life, by touch of the moon's rays. Such light was an unpredictable force—it made dogs howl, it flogged mad-men to violence, it brought fear, or black sorrow, or ecstasy. Old legends said that it was the birth of fairies, the transformation of werewolves, the motive power of broom-

riding witches. It was surely the source of the strength and
evil animating of what had been the corpse of Elva Gauber
—and he, Poe, must not stand there dreaming.

He summoned all the courage that was his, and scrambled
in at the window through which slumped the woman's form.
He groped across the room to the cellar door, opened it,
and went down the stairs, through the door at the bottom,
and into the stone-walled basement.

It was dark, moonless still. Poe paused only to bring forth
his tinderbox, strike a light, and kindle the end of a tightly
twisted linen rag. It gave a feeble steady light, and he found
his way to the shutter, opened it, and touched the naked,
wasted shoulder of John Gauber.

"Get up," he said. "I've come to save you."

The skullface feebly shifted its position to meet his gaze.
The man managed to speak, moaningly:

"Useless. I can't move—unless she lets me. Her eyes keep
me here—half alive. I'd have died long ago, but somehow—"

Poe thought of a wretched spider, paralyzed by the sting
of a mud wasp, lying helpless in its captive's close den until
the hour of feeding comes. He bent down, holding his blazing tinder close. He could see Gauber's neck, and it was a
mass of tiny puncture wounds, some of them still beaded
with blood drops fresh or dried. He winced, but bode firm
in his purpose.

"Let me guess the truth," he said quickly. "Your wife was
brought home from the grave, came back to a seeming of
life. She put a spell on you, or played a trick—made you a
helpless prisoner. That isn't contrary to nature, that last.
I've studied mesmerism."

"It's true," John Gauber mumbled.

"And nightly she comes to drink your blood?"

Gauber weakly nodded. "Yes. She was beginning just
now, but ran upstairs. She will be coming back."

"Good," said Poe bleakly. "Perhaps she will come back to
more than she expects. Have you ever heard of vampires?

Probably not, but I have studied them, too. I began to guess, I think, when first she was so repelled by the odor of garlic. Vampires lie motionless by day, and walk and feed at night. They are creatures of the moon—their food is blood. Come."

Poe broke off, put out his light, and lifted the man in his arms. Gauber was as light as a child. The writer carried him to the slanting shelter of the closed-in staircase, and there set him against the wall. Over him Poe spread his old cadet cloak. In the gloom, the gray of the cloak harmonized with the gray of the wall stones. The poor fellow would be well hidden.

Next Poe flung off his coat, waistcoat, and shirt. Heaping his clothing in a deeper shadow of the stairway, he stood up, stripped to the waist. His skin was almost as bloodlessly pale as Gauber's, his chest and arms almost as gaunt. He dared believe that he might pass momentarily for the unfortunate man.

The cellar sprang full of light again. The cloud must be passing from the moon. Poe listened. There was a dragging sound above, then footsteps.

Elva Gauber, the blood drinker by night, had revived.

Now for it. Poe hurried to the niche, thrust himself in, and pulled the trap door shut after him.

He grinned, sharing a horrid paradox with the blackness around him. He had heard all the fabled ways of destroying vampires—transfixing stakes, holy water, prayer, fire. But he, Edgar Allan Poe, had evolved a new way. Myriads of tales whispered frighteningly of fiends lying in wait for normal men, but who ever heard of a normal man lying in wait for a fiend? Well, he had never considered himself normal, in spirit, or brain, or taste.

He stretched out, feet together, hands crossed on his bare midriff. Thus it would be in the tomb, he found himself thinking. To his mind came a snatch of poetry by a man named Bryant, published long ago in a New England review

—Breathless darkness, and the narrow house. It was breathless and dark enough in this hole, heaven knew, and narrow
as well. He rejected, almost hysterically, the implication of
being buried. To break the ugly spell, which daunted him
where thought of Elva Gauber failed, he turned sideways to
face the wall, his naked arm lying across his cheek and
temple.

As his ear touched the musty bedding, it brought to him
once again the echo of footsteps, footsteps descending
stairs. They were rhythmic, confident. They were eager.

Elva Gauber was coming to seek again her interrupted
repast.

Now she was crossing the floor. She did not pause or turn
aside—she had not noticed her husband, lying under the
cadet cloak in the shadow of the stairs. The noise came
straight to the trap door, and he heard her fumbling for the
latch.

Light, blue as skimmed milk, poured into his nook. A
shadow fell in the midst of it, full upon him. His imagination, ever outstripping reality, whispered that the shadow
had weight, like lead—oppressive, baleful.

"John," said the voice of Elva Gauber in his ear, "I've
come back. You know why—you know what for." Her voice
sounded greedy, as though it came through loose, trembling
lips. "You're my only source of strength now. I thought to-
night, that a stranger—but he got away. He had a cursed
odor about him, anyway."

Her hand touched the skin of his neck. She was prodding
him, like a butcher fingering a doomed beast.

"Don't hold yourself away from me, John," she was commanding, in a voice of harsh mockery. "You know it won't
do any good. This is the night of the full moon, and I have
power for anything, anything!" She was trying to drag his
arm away from his face. "You won't gain by—" She broke
off, aghast. Then, in a wild dry-throated scream:

"You're not John!"

Poe whipped over on his back, and his bird-claw hands shot out and seized her—one hand clinching upon her snaky disorder of dark hair, the other digging its fingertips into the chill flesh of her arm.

The scream quivered away into a horrible breathless rattle. Poe dragged his captive violently inward, throwing all his collected strength into the effort. Her feet were jerked from the floor and she flew into the recess, hurtling above and beyond Poe's recumbent body. She struck the inner stones with a crashing force that might break bones, and would have collapsed upon Poe; but, at the same moment, he had released her and slid swiftly out upon the floor of the cellar.

With frantic haste he seized the edge of the back-flung trap door. Elva Gauber struggled up on hands and knees, among the tumbled bedclothes in the niche; then Poe had slammed the panel shut.

She threw herself against it from within, yammering and wailing like an animal in a trap. She was almost as strong as he, and for a moment he thought that she would win out of the niche. But, sweating and wheezing, he bore against the planks with his shoulder, bracing his feet against the earth. His fingers found the latch, lifted it, forced it into place.

"Dark," moaned Elva Gauber from inside. "Dark—no moon—" Her voice trailed off.

Poe went to the muddy pool in the corner, thrust in his hands. The muck was slimy but workable. He pushed a double handful of it against the trap door, sealing cracks and edges. Another handful, another. Using his palms like trowels, he coated the boards with thick mud.

"Gauber," he said breathlessly, "how are you?"

"All right—I think." The voice was strangely strong and clear. Looking over his shoulder, Poe saw that Gauber had come upright of himself, still pale but apparently steady. "What are you doing?" Gauber asked.

"Walling her up," jerked out Poe, scooping still more mud. "Walling her up forever, with her devil."

He had a momentary flash of inspiration, a symbolic germ of a story; in it a man sealed a woman into such a nook of the wall, and with her an embodiment of active evil—perhaps in the form of a black cat.

Pausing at last to breathe deeply, he smiled to himself. Even in the direst of danger, the most heartbreaking moment of toil and fear, he must ever be coining new plots for stories.

"I cannot thank you enough," Gauber was saying to him. "I feel that all will be well—if only she stays there."

Poe put his ear to the wall. "Not a whisper of motion, sir. She's shut off from moonlight—from life and power. Can you help me with my clothes? I feel terribly chilled."

His mother-in-law met him on the threshold when he returned to the house in Spring Garden Street. Under the white widow's cap, her strong-boned face was drawn with worry.

"Eddie, are you ill?" She was really asking if he had been drinking. A look reassured her. "No," she answered herself, "but you've been away from home so long. And you're dirty, Eddie—filthy. You must wash."

He let her lead him in, pour hot water into a basin. As he scrubbed himself, he formed excuses, a banal lie about a long walk for inspiration, a moment of dizzy weariness, a stumble into a mud puddle.

"I'll make you some nice hot coffee, Eddie," his mother-in-law offered.

"Please," he responded, and went back to his room with the slate mantelpiece. Again he lighted the candle, sat down, and took up his pen.

His mind was embellishing the story inspiration that had come to him at such a black moment, in the cellar of the Gauber house. He'd work on that tomorrow. The *United*

States Saturday Post would take it, he hoped. Title? He would call it simply "The Black Cat."

But to finish the present task! He dipped his pen in ink. How to begin? How to end? How, after writing and publishing such an account, to defend himself against the growing whisper of his insanity?

He decided to forget it, if he could—at least to seek healthy company, comfort, quiet—perhaps even to write some light verse, some humorous articles and stories. For the first time in his life, he had had enough of the macabre.

Quickly he wrote a final paragraph:

> There are moments when, even to the sober eye of Reason, the world of our sad Humanity may assume the semblance of a Hell—but the imagination of man is no Carathis, to explore with impunity its every cavern. Alas! The grim legion of sepulchral terrors cannot be regarded as altogether fanciful—but, like the Demons in whose company Afrasiab made his voyage down the Oxus, they must sleep, or they will devour us—they must be suffered to slumber, or we will perish.

That would do for the public, decided Edgar Allan Poe. In any case, it would do for the Philadelphia *Dollar Newspaper*.

His mother-in-law brought in the coffee.

The possibilities of what Edgar Allan Poe might have written had he lived even a few more years continues to haunt most students of literature. It is humanly natural that leading present-day writers who acknowledge the influence of Poe, such as Robert Bloch, would conjecture on the subject. As the title suggests, this story deals with the world's greatest collector of Poe, whose acquisitive instinct was boundless.

Robert Bloch might be called a second-generation influence of Edgar Allan Poe. Bloch idolized H. P. Lovecraft and Lovecraft had earlier worshiped Edgar Allan Poe. A number of the Lovecraft stories were powerfully influenced by Edgar Allan Poe. Robert Bloch was in turn at first highly imitative of H. P. Lovecraft.

The similarity of Bloch's fantasies to those of H. P. Lovecraft delighted readers and his work proved readily salable. Lovecraft's stories were appearing less frequently and those of Bloch were excellent pastiches. As the years passed, it became apparent that the tales told in the Lovecraft manner, which had proved an easy method by which a seventeen-year-old writer could attain professionalism, would also prove a trap. Scores of the stories sold, but Bloch's reputation remained on a perpetual plateau.

Gradually he developed his own powerfully imaginative approach, laying the stress on the terrors of the mind rather than terrors of the soul or superanimated disgust. His first big success in this vein was "Yours Truly, Jack the Ripper" (*Weird Tales,* July 1943), telling of the search for Jack the Ripper by one of his victims and of the unpleasant moment of encounter. This tale was anthologized many times and used as the basis for several radio dramatizations.

Bloch's problem was a sick wife and the necessity of grinding out an endless barrage of fiction at full speed just to meet the rent. He did not have the time to give his best ideas the thought and polish they required for full impact.

Twenty-five years of effort preceded the Alfred Hitchcock adaptation of his novel *Psycho,* which caused a sensation at the very time when Bloch was in Hollywood and able to take advantage of the publicity. It has since become apparent that he possesses one of the most original imaginations of this era in the presentation of psychological terror. His interest in Edgar Allan Poe is now a compliment to the long-term vitality and influence of the master rather than a literary debt.

The Man Who Collected Poe

By Robert Bloch

AUTHOR'S INTRODUCTION

Would Edgar Allan Poe be able to sell his stories if he were writing today? This is a question which has long intrigued editors, authors, readers, and critics of fantasy. It is a question I have sought to answer in the only possible way—by writing a story of Poe in the manner which Poe himself might have written it. I do not claim a tenth of his talent or a tithe of his genius . . . but I have proposed deliberately, insofar as possible, to re-create his style. Poe scholars will recognize my deliberate inclusion of sentences and sections from "The Fall of the House of Usher," and the casual reader will quite easily discover them. The result is, I believe, a "Poe story" in a rather unique and special sense . . . and one which it gave me great pleasure to write as a tribute to a figure to whom I, like every other writer of fantasy, must own indebtedness.

—Robert Bloch

During the whole of a dull, dark, and soundless day in the autumn of the year, when the clouds hung oppressively low in the heavens, I had been passing alone, by automobile, through a singularly dreary tract of country, and at length found myself, as the shades of the evening drew on, within view of my destination.

I looked upon the scene before me—upon the mere house, and the simple landscape features of the domain—upon the bleak walls—upon the vacant eye-like windows—upon a few rank sedges—and upon a few white trunks of decayed trees —with a feeling of utter confusion commingled with dismay. For it seemed to me as though I had visited this scene once before, or read of it, perhaps, in some frequently rescanned tale. And yet assuredly it could not be, for only three days had passed since I had made the acquaintance of Launcelot Canning and received an invitation to visit him at his Maryland residence.

The circumstances under which I met Canning were simple; I happened to attend a bibliophilic meeting in Washington and was introduced to him by a mutual friend. Casual conversation gave place to absorbed and interested discussion when he discovered my preoccupation with works of fantasy. Upon learning that I was traveling upon a vacation with no set itinerary, Canning urged me to become his guest for a day and to examine, at my leisure, his unusual display of memorabilia.

"I feel, from our conversation, that we have much in common," he told me. "For you see, sir, in my love of fantasy I bow to no man. It is a taste I have perhaps inherited from my father and from his father before him, together with their considerable acquisitions in the genre. No doubt you would be gratified with what I am prepared to show you, for in all due modesty, I beg to style myself the world's leading collector of the works of Edgar Allen Poe."

I confess that his invitation as such did not enthrall me, for I hold no brief for the literary hero-worshiper or the scholarly collector as a type. I own to a more than passing interest in the tales of Poe, but my interest does not extend to the point of ferreting out the exact date upon which Mr. Poe first decided to raise a moustache, nor would I be unduly intrigued by the opportunity to examine several hairs preserved from that hirsute appendage.

So it was rather the person and personality of Launcelot Canning himself which caused me to accept his proffered hospitality. For the man who proposed to become my host might have himself stepped from the pages of a Poe tale. His speech, as I have endeavored to indicate, was characterized by a courtly rodomontade so often exemplified in Poe's heroes—and beyond certainty, his appearance bore out the resemblance.

Launcelot Canning had the cadaverousness of complexion, the large, liquid, luminous eye, the thin, curved lips, the delicately modeled nose, finely molded chin, and dark, web-like hair of a typical Poe protagonist.

It was this phenomenon which prompted my acceptance and led me to journey to his Maryland estate, which, as I now perceived, in itself manifested a Poe-etic quality of its own, intrinsic in the images of the gray sedge, the ghastly tree-stems, and the vacant and eye-like windows of the mansion of gloom. All that was lacking was a tarn and a moat—and as I prepared to enter the dwelling I half-expected to encounter therein the carved ceilings, the somber tapestries, the ebon floors and the phantasmagoric armorial trophies so vividly described by the author of *Tales of the Grotesque and Arabesque.*

Nor upon entering Launcelot Canning's home was I too greatly disappointed in my expectations. True to both the atmospheric quality of the decrepit mansion and to my own fanciful presentiments, the door was opened in response to my knock by a valet who conducted me, in silence, through dark and intricate passages to the study of his master.

The room in which I found myself was very large and lofty. The windows were long, narrow, and pointed, and at so vast a distance from the black oaken floor as to be altogether inaccessible from within. Feeble gleams of encrimsoned light made their way through the trellised panes, and served to render sufficiently distinct the more prominent objects around; the eye, however, struggled in vain to reach the remoter angles of the chamber or the recesses of the vaulted and fretted ceiling. Dark draperies hung upon the walls. The general furniture was profuse, comfortless, antique, and tattered. Many books and musical instruments lay scattered about, but failed to give any vitality to the scene.

Instead they rendered more distinct that peculiar quality of quasi-recollection; it was as though I found myself once again, after a protracted absence, in a familiar setting. I had read, I had imagined, I had dreamed, or I had actually beheld this setting before.

Upon my entrance, Launcelot Canning arose from a sofa on which he had been lying at full length, and greeted me with a vivacious warmth which had much in it, I at first thought, of an overdone cordiality.

Yet his tone, as he spoke of the object of my visit, of his earnest desire to see me, and of the solace he expected me to afford him in a mutual discussion of our interests, soon alleviated my initial misapprehension.

Launcelot Canning welcomed me with the rapt enthusiasm of the born collector—and I came to realize that he was indeed just that. For the Poe collection he shortly proposed to unveil before me was actually his birthright.

Initially, he disclosed, the nucleus of the present accumulation had begun with his grandfather, Christopher Canning, a respected merchant of Baltimore. Almost eighty years ago he had been one of the leading patrons of the arts in his community and as such was partially instrumental in arranging for the removal of Poe's body to the southeastern corner of the Presbyterian Cemetery at Fayette and Green streets, where a suitable monument might be erected. This event occurred in the year 1875, and it was a few years prior to that time that Canning laid the foundation of the Poe collection.

"Thanks to his zeal," his grandson informed me, "I am today the fortunate possessor of a copy of virtually every existing specimen of Poe's published works. If you will step over here"—and he led me to a remote corner of the vaulted study, past the dark draperies, to a bookshelf which rose remotely to the shadowy ceiling—"I shall be pleased to corroborate that claim. Here is a copy of *Al Aaraaf, Tamerlane and other Poems* in the 1829 edition, and here is the still earlier *Tamerlane and other Poems* of 1827. The Boston edition, which, as you doubtless know, is valued today at fifteen thousand dollars. I can assure you that Grandfather Canning parted with no such sum in order to gain possession of this rarity."

He displayed the volumes with an air of commingled pride and cupidity which is ofttimes characteristic of the collector and is by no means to be confused with either literary snobbery or ordinary greed. Realizing this, I remained patient as he exhibited further treasures—copies of the *Philadelphia Saturday Courier* containing early tales, bound volumes of *The Messenger* during the period of Poe's editorship, *Graham's Magazine*, editions of the *New York Sun* and the *New York Mirror* boasting, respectively, of "The Balloon Hoax" and "The Raven," and files of *The Gentleman's Magazine*. Ascending a short library ladder, he handed down to me the Lea and Blanchard edition of *Tales of the Grotesque and Arabesque*, the *Conchologist's First Book*, the Putnam *Eureka*, and, finally, the little paper booklet, published in 1843 and sold for twelve and a half cents, entitled *The Prose Romances of Edgar A. Poe*; an insignificant trifle containing two tales which is valued by present-day collectors at fifty thousand dollars.

Canning informed me of this last fact, and, indeed, kept up a running commentary upon each item he presented. There was no doubt but that he was a Poe scholar as well as a Poe collector, and his words informed tattered specimens of the *Broadway Journal* and *Godey's Lady's Book* with a singular fascination not necessarily inherent in the flimsy sheets or their contents.

"I owe a great debt to Grandfather Canning's obsession," he observed, descending the ladder and joining me before the bookshelves. "It is not altogether a breach of confidence to admit that his interest in Poe did reach the point of an obsession, and perhaps eventually of an absolute mania. The knowledge, alas, is public property, I fear.

"In the early seventies he built this house, and I am quite sure that you have been observant enough to note that it in itself is almost a replica of a typical Poe-esque mansion. This was his study, and it was here that he was wont to pore over the books, the letters, and the numerous mementos of Poe's life.

"What prompted a retired merchant to devote himself so fanatically to the pursuit of a hobby, I cannot say. Let it suffice that he virtually withdrew from the world and from all other normal interests. He conducted a voluminous and lengthy correspondence with aging men and women who had known Poe in their lifetime—made pilgrimages to Fordham, sent his agents to West Point, to England and Scotland, to virtually every locale in which Poe had set foot during his lifetime. He acquired letters and souvenirs as gifts, he bought them, and—I fear—stole them, if no other means of acquisition proved feasible."

Launcelot Canning smiled and nodded. "Does all this sound strange to you? I confess that once I, too, found it almost incredible, a fragment of romance. Now, after years spent here, I have lost my own objectivity."

"Yes, it is strange," I replied. "But are you quite sure that there was not some obscure personal reason for your grandfather's interest? Had he met Poe as a boy, or been closely associated with one of his friends? Was there, perhaps, a distant, undisclosed relationship?"

At the mention of the last word, Canning started visibly, and a tremor of agitation overspread his countenance.

"Ah!" he exclaimed. "There you voice my own inmost conviction. A relationship—assuredly there must have been one —I am morally, instinctively certain that Grandfather Canning felt or knew himself to be linked to Edgar Poe by ties

of blood. Nothing else could account for his strong initial
interest, his continuing defense of Poe in the literary con-
troversies of the day, and his final melancholy lapse into
a world of delusion and illusion.

"Yet he never voiced a statement or put an allegation
upon paper—and I have searched the collection of letters in
vain for the slightest clue.

"It is curious that you so promptly divine a suspicion held
not only by myself but by my father. He was only a child at
the time of my Grandfather Canning's death, but the at-
tendant circumstances left a profound impression upon his
sensitive nature. Although he was immediately removed
from this house to the home of his mother's people in Baltimore, he lost no time in returning upon assuming his in-
heritance in early manhood.

"Fortunately being in possession of a considerable income,
he was able to devote his entire lifetime to further research.
The name of Arthur Canning is still well known in the world
of literary criticism, but for some reason he preferred to
pursue his scholarly examination of Poe's career in privacy.
I believe this preference was dictated by an inner sensibility;
that he was endeavoring to unearth some information which
would prove his father's, his, and for that matter, my own,
kinship to Edgar Poe."

"You say your father was also a collector?" I prompted.

"A statement I am prepared to substantiate," replied my
host, as he led me to yet another corner of the shadow-
shrouded study. "But first, if you would accept a glass of
wine?"

He filled, not glasses, but veritable beakers from a large
carafe, and we toasted one another in silent appreciation.
It is perhaps unnecessary for me to observe that the wine
was a fine old amontillado.

"Now, then," said Launcelot Canning. "My father's special
province in Poe research consisted of the accumulation and
study of letters."

Opening a series of large trays or drawers beneath the bookshelves, he drew out file after file of glassined folios, and for the space of the next half-hour I examined Edgar Poe's correspondence—letters to Henry Herring, to Dr. Snodgrass, Sarah Shelton, James P. Moss, Elizabeth Poe— missives to Mrs. Rockwood, Helen Whitman, Anne Lynch, John Pendleton Kennedy—notes to Mrs. Richmond, to John Allan, to Annie, to his brother, Henry—a profusion of documents, a veritable epistolary cornucopia.

During the course of my perusal my host took occasion to refill our beakers with wine, and the heady draught began to take effect—for we had not eaten, and I own I gave no thought to food, so absorbed was I in the yellowed pages illumining Poe's past.

Here was wit, erudition, literary criticism; here were the muddled, maudlin outpourings of a mind gone in drink and despair; here was the draft of a projected story, the fragments of a poem; here was a pitiful cry for deliverance and a paean to living beauty; here was a dignified response to a dunning letter and an editorial pronunciamento to an admirer; here was love, hate, pride, anger, celestial serenity, abject penitence, authority, wonder, resolution, indecision, joy, and soul-sickening melancholia.

Here was the gifted elocutionist, the stammering drunkard, the adoring husband, the frantic lover, the proud editor, the indigent pauper, the grandiose dreamer, the shabby realist, the scientific inquirer, the gullible metaphysician, the dependent stepson, the free and untrammeled spirit, the hack, the poet, the enigma that was Edgar Allan Poe.

Again the beakers were filled and emptied.

I drank deeply with my lips, and with my eyes more deeply still.

For the first time the true enthusiasm of Launcelot Canning was communicated to my own sensibilities—I divined the eternal fascination found in a consideration of Poe the writer and Poe the man; he who wrote Tragedy, lived

Tragedy, was Tragedy; he who penned Mystery, lived and died in Mystery, and who today looms on the literary scene as Mystery incarnate.

And Mystery Poe remained, despite Arthur Canning's careful study of the letters. "My father learned nothing," my host confided, "even though he assembled, as you see here, a collection to delight the heart of a Mabbott or a Quinn. So his search ranged further. By this time I was old enough to share both his interest and his inquiries. Come," and he led me to an ornate chest which rested beneath the windows against the west wall of the study.

Kneeling, he unlocked the repository, and then drew forth, in rapid and marvelous succession, a series of objects each of which boasted of intimate connection with Poe's life.

There were souvenirs of his youth and his schooling abroad—a book he had used during his sojourn at West Point—mementos of his days as a theatrical critic in the form of playbills, a pen used during his editorial period, a fan once owned by his girl-wife, Virginia, a brooch of Mrs. Clemm's; a profusion of objects including such diverse articles as a cravat-stock and—curiously enough—Poe's battered and tarnished flute.

Again we drank, and I own the wine was potent. Canning's countenance remained cadaverously wan—but, moreover, there was a species of mad hilarity in his eye—an evident restrained hysteria in his whole demeanor. At length, from the scattered heap of curiosa, I happened to draw forth and examine a little box of no remarkable character, whereupon I was constrained to inquire its history and what part it had played in the life of Poe.

"In the *life* of Poe?" A visible tremor convulsed the features of my host, then rapidly passed in transformation to a grimace, a rictus of amusement. "This little box—and you will note how, by some fateful design or contrived coincidence it bears a resemblance to the box he himself con-

ceived of and described in his tale "Berenice"—this little
box is concerned with his death, rather than his life. It is,
in fact, the selfsame box my grandfather Christopher Canning clutched to his bosom when they found him down
there."

Again the tremor, again the grimace. "But stay, I have
not yet told you of the details. Perhaps you would be interested in seeing the spot where Christopher Canning was
stricken; I have already told you of his madness, but I did no
more than hint at the character of his delusions. You have
been patient with me, and more than patient. Your understanding shall be rewarded, for I perceive you can be fully
entrusted with the facts."

What further revelations Canning was prepared to make
I could not say, but his manner was such as to inspire a
vague disquiet and trepidation in my breast.

Upon perceiving my unease he laughed shortly and laid
a hand upon my shoulder. "Come, this should interest you
as an *aficionado* of fantasy," he said. "But first, another drink
to speed our journey."

He poured, we drank, and then he led the way from that
vaulted chamber, down the silent halls, down the staircase,
and into the lowest recesses of the building until we reached
what resembled a donjon-keep, its floor and the interior of
a long archway carefully sheathed in copper. We paused
before a door of massive iron. Again I felt in the aspect of
this scene an element evocative of recognition or recollection.

Canning's intoxication was such that he misinterpreted, or
chose to misinterpret, my reaction.

"You need not be afraid," he assured me. "Nothing has
happened down here since that day, almost seventy years
ago, when his servants discovered him stretched out before
this door, the little box clutched to his bosom; collapsed, and
in a state of delirium from which he never emerged. For
six months he lingered, a hopeless maniac—raving as wildly

from the very moment of his discovery as at the moment he died—babbling his visions of the giant horse, the fissured house collapsing into the tarn, the black cat, the pit, the pendulum, the raven on the pallid bust, the beating heart, the pearly teeth, and the nearly liquid mass of loathsome— of detestable putridity from which a voice emanated.

"Nor was that all he babbled," Canning confided, and here his voice sank to a whisper that reverberated through the copper-sheathed hall and against the iron door. "He hinted other things far worse than fantasy; of a ghastly reality surpassing all of the phantasms of Poe.

"For the first time my father and the servants learned the purpose of the room he had built beyond this iron door, and learned too what Christopher Canning had done to establish his title as the world's foremost collector of Poe.

"For he babbled again of Poe's death, thirty years earlier, in 1849—of the burial in the Presbyterian cemetery—and of the removal of the coffin in 1874 to the corner where the monument was raised. As I told you, and as was known then, my grandfather had played a public part in instigating that removal. But now we learned of the private part—learned that there was a monument and a grave, but no coffin in the earth beneath Poe's alleged resting place. The coffin now rested in the secret room at the end of this passage. That is why the room, the house itself, had been built.

"I tell you, he had stolen the body of Edgar Allan Poe— and as he shrieked aloud in his final madness, did not this indeed make him the greatest collector of Poe?

"His ultimate intent was never divined, but my father made one significant discovery—the little box clutched to Christopher Canning's bosom contained a portion of the crumbled bones, the veritable dust that was all that remained of Poe's corpse."

My host shuddered and turned away. He led me back along that hall of horror, up the stairs, into the study.

Silently, he filled our beakers and I drank as hastily, as deeply, as desperately as he.

"What could my father do? To own the truth was to create a public scandal. He chose instead to keep silence; to devote his own life to study in retirement.

"Naturally the shock affected him profoundly; to my knowledge he never entered the room beyond the iron door, and, indeed, I did not know of the room or its contents until the hour of his death—and it was not until some years later that I myself found the key among his effects.

"But find the key I did, and the story was immediately and completely corroborated. Today I am the greatest collector of Poe—for he lies in the keep below, my eternal trophy!"

This time I poured the wine. As I did so, I noted for the first time the imminence of a storm; the impetuous fury of its gusts shaking the casements, and the echoes of its thunder rolling and rumbling down the time-corroded corridors of the old house.

The wild, overstrained vivacity with which my host hearkened, or apparently hearkened, to these sounds did nothing to reassure me—for his recent revelation led me to suspect his sanity.

That the body of Edgar Allan Poe had been stolen—that this mansion had been built to house it—that it was indeed enshrined in a crypt below—that grandsire, son, and grandson had dwelt here alone, apart, enslaved to a sepulchral secret—was beyond sane belief.

And yet, surrounded now by the night and the storm, in a setting torn from Poe's own frenzied fancies, I could not be sure. Here the past was still alive, the very spirit of Poe's tales breathed forth its corruption upon the scene.

As thunder boomed, Launcelot Canning took up Poe's flute, and, whether in defiance of the storm without or as a mocking accompaniment, he played; blowing upon it with drunken persistence, with eerie atonality, with nerve-

shattering shrillness. To the shrieking of that infernal in-
strument the thunder added a braying counterpoint.

Uneasy, uncertain, and unnerved, I retreated into the
shadows of the bookshelves at the farther end of the room,
and idly scanned the titles of a row of ancient tomes. Here
was the *Chiromancy* of Robert Flud, the *Directorium In-
quisitorum*, a rare and curious book in quarto Gothic that
was the manual of a forgotten church; and betwixt and between the volumes of pseudo-scientific inquiry, theological
speculation, and sundry incunabula, I found titles that arrested and appalled me. *De Vermis Mysteriis* and the *Liber
Eibon*, treatises on demonology, on witchcraft, on sorcery
moldered in crumbling bindings. The books were old, but
the books were not dusty. They had been read—

"Read them?" It was as though Canning divined my inmost thoughts. He had put aside his flute and now approached me, tittering as though in continued drunken
defiance of the storm. Odd echoes and boomings now
sounded through the long halls of the house, and curious
grating sounds threatened to drown out his words and his
laughter.

"Read them?" said Canning. "I study them. Yes, I have
gone beyond grandfather and father, too. It was I who pro-
cured the books that held the key, and it was I who found
the key. A key more difficult to discover, and more important, than the key to the vaults below. I often wonder if Poe
himself had access to these selfsame tomes, knew the selfsame secrets. The secrets of the grave and what lies beyond,
and what can be summoned forth if one but holds the key."

He stumbled away and returned with wine. "Drink," he
said. "Drink to the night and the storm."

I brushed the proffered glass aside. "Enough," I said. "I
must be on my way."

Was it fancy or did I find fear frozen on his features?
Canning clutched my arm and cried, "No, stay with me! This
is no night on which to be alone; I swear I cannot abide the

thought of being alone, I can bear to be alone no more!"

His incoherent babble mingled with the thunder and the echoes; I drew back and confronted him. "Control yourself," I counseled. "Confess that this is a hoax, an elaborate imposture arranged to please your fancy."

"Hoax? Imposture? Stay, and I shall prove to you beyond all doubt"—and so saying, Launcelot Canning stooped and opened a small drawer set in the wall beneath and beside the bookshelves. "This should repay you for your interest in my story, and in Poe," he murmured. "Know that you are the first other person than myself to glimpse these treasures."

He handed me a sheaf of manuscripts on plain white paper; documents written in ink curiously similar to that I had noted while perusing Poe's letters. Pages were clipped together in groups, and for a moment I scanned titles alone.

"'The Worm of Midnight,' by Edgar Poe," I read, aloud. "'The Crypt,'" I breathed. And here, "'The Further Adventures of Arthur Gordon Pym'"—and in my agitation I came close to dropping the precious pages. "Are these what they appear to be—the unpublished tales of Poe?"

My host bowed.

"Unpublished, undiscovered, unknown, save to me—and to you."

"But this cannot be," I protested. "Surely there would have been a mention of them somewhere, in Poe's own letters or those of his contemporaries. There would have been a clue, an indication, somewhere, someplace, somehow."

Thunder mingled with my words, and thunder echoed in Canning's shouted reply.

"You dare to presume an imposture? Then compare!" He stooped again and brought out a glassined folio of letters. "Here—is this not the veritable script of Edgar Poe? Look at the calligraphy of the letter, then at the manuscripts. Can you say they are not penned by the selfsame hand?"

I looked at the handwriting, wondered at the possibilities of a monomaniac's forgery. Could Launcelot Canning, a victim of mental disorder, thus painstakingly simulate Poe's hand?

"Read, then!" Canning screamed through the thunder. "Read, and dare to say that these tales were written by any other than Edgar Poe, whose genius defies the corruption of Time and the Conqueror Worm!"

I read but a line or two, holding the topmost manuscript close to eyes that strained beneath wavering candlelight; but even in the flickering illumination I noted that which told me the only, the incontestable truth. For the paper, the curiously *unyellowed* paper, bore a visible watermark; the name of a firm of well-known modern stationers, and the date—1949.

Putting the sheaf aside, I endeavored to compose myself as I moved away from Launcelot Canning. For now I knew the truth; knew that one hundred years after Poe's death a semblance of his spirit still lived in the distorted and disordered soul of Canning. Incarnation, reincarnation, call it what you will; Canning was, in his own irrational mind, Edgar Allan Poe.

Stifled and dull echoes of thunder from a remote portion of the mansion now commingled with the soundless seething of my own inner turmoil, as I turned and rashly addressed my host.

"Confess!" I cried. "Is it not true that you have written these tales, fancying yourself the embodiment of Poe? Is it not true that you suffer from a singular delusion born of solitude and everlasting brooding upon the past; that you have reached a stage characterized by the conviction that Poe still lives on in your own person?"

A strong shudder came over him and a sickly smile quivered about his lips as he replied. "Fool! I say to you that I have spoken the truth. Can you doubt the evidence of your senses? This house is real, the Poe collection exists, and the stories exist—they exist, I swear, as truly as the body lying in the crypt below!"

I took up the little box from the table and removed the lid. "Not so," I answered. "You said your grandfather was found with this box clutched to his breast, before the door of the vault, and that it contained Poe's dust. Yet you cannot escape the fact that the box is empty." I faced him furiously. "Admit it, the story is a fabrication, a romance. Poe's body does not lie beneath this house, nor are these his unpublished works, written during his lifetime and concealed."

"True enough." Canning's smile was ghastly beyond belief. "The dust is gone because I took it and used it—because in the works of wizardry I found the formulae, the arcana whereby I could raise the flesh, re-create the body from the essential salts of the grave. Poe does not *lie* beneath this house—he *lives!* And the tales are *his posthumous works!*"

Accented by thunder, his words crashed against my consciousness.

"That was the end-all and the be-all of my planning, of my studies, of my work, of my life! To raise, by sorcery, the veritable spirit of Edgar Poe from the grave—reclothed and animate in flesh—set him to dwell and dream and do his work again in the private chambers I built in the vaults below—and this I have done! To steal a corpse is but a ghoulish prank; mine is the achievement of true genius!"

The distinct, hollow, metallic, and clangorous yet apparently muffled reverberation accompanying his words caused him to turn in his seat and face the door of the study, so that I could not see the workings of his countenance—nor could he read my own reaction to his ravings.

His words came but faintly to my ears through the thunder that now shook the house in a relentless grip; the wind rattling the casements and flickering the candle-flame from the great silver candelabra sent a soaring sighing in an anguished accompaniment to his speech.

"I would show him to you, but I dare not; for he hates me as he hates life. I have locked him in the vault, alone, for the resurrected have no need of food or drink. And he sits there, pen moving over paper, endlessly moving, endlessly pouring out the evil essence of all he guessed and hinted at in life and which he learned in death.

"Do you not see the tragic pity of my plight? I sought to raise his spirit from the dead, to give the world anew of his genius—and yet these tales, these works, are filled and fraught with a terror not to be endured. They cannot be shown to the world, he cannot be shown to the world; in bringing back the dead I have brought back the fruits of death!"

Echoes sounded anew as I moved toward the door—moved, I confess, to flee this accursed house and its accursed owner.

Canning clutched my hand, my arm, my shoulder. "You cannot go!" he shouted above the storm. "I spoke of his escaping, but did you not guess? Did you not hear it through the thunder—the grating of the door?"

I pushed him aside and he blundered backward, upsetting the candelabra, so that flames licked now across the carpeting.

"Wait!" he cried. "Have you not heard his footstep on the stair? *Madman, I tell you that he now stands without the door!*"

A rush of wind, a roar of flame, a shroud of smoke rose all about us. Throwing open the huge, antique panels to which Canning pointed, I staggered into the hall.

I speak of wind, of flame, of smoke—enough to obscure all vision. I speak of Canning's screams, and of thunder loud enough to drown all sound. I speak of terror born of loathing and of desperation enough to shatter all my sanity.

Despite these things, I can never erase from my consciousness that which I beheld as I fled past the doorway and down the hall.

There without the doors there *did* stand a lofty and en-shrouded figure; a figure all too familiar, with pallid features, high, domed forehead, moustache set above a mouth. My glimpse lasted but an instant, an instant during which the man—the corpse—the apparition—the hallucination, call it what you will—moved forward into the chamber and clasped Canning to his breast in an unbreakable embrace. Together, the two figures tottered toward the flames, which now rose to blot out vision forevermore.

From that chamber, and from that mansion, I fled aghast. The storm was still abroad in all its wrath, and now fire came to claim the house of Canning for its own.

Suddenly there shot along the path before me a wild light, and I turned to see whence a gleam so unusual could have issued—but it was only the flames, rising in supernatural splendor to consume the mansion, and the secrets, of the man who collected Poe.

Michael Avallone is a fast-rising young mystery writer whose list of credits has grown so unwieldy that even a comprehensive sketch must inevitably neglect most of his "children." Best known for his successful series of Ed Noon mysteries, Michael Avallone has truly tried to pattern his writing career after Poe by writing weird tales and science fiction as well.

Like many writers, Michael Avallone is a frustrated editor and he assuages this hunger by cooking up anthologies of the supernatural and Gothic whenever the opportunity offers. A paperback collection which appears to show the discriminating touch of Boris Karloff in small type will be found to have actually been selected by Michael Avallone. A collection of Gothic short stories appropriately titled *Gothic Sampler* requires no C. Auguste Dupin to determine who hides behind the façade of Edwina Noone

Less well known is Michael Avallone's flyer as editor of two digest magazines, titled *Space Science Fiction* and *Tales of the Frightened*. Both were published in 1957 and both lasted but two issues. It was in the August 1957 number of *Tales of the Frightened* that "The Man Who Thought He Was Poe" first appeared. The story fitted no editorial policies. It received the "kiss of death" treatment from all editors submitted to: "This is a wonderful story and should find a place somewhere; however, it is not really a mystery story . . ."

"The Man Who Thought He Was Poe" epitomizes the romance and mystery that lingers about the life of that unfortunate genius. It would scarcely seem strange if some might want to submerge their own reality to become part of a legend.

The Man Who Thought He Was Poe

By Michael Avallone

"*. . . and the Raven, never flitting, still is sitting, still is sitting on the pallid bust of—*" He closed the book swiftly as the shuffling figure of his wife loomed in the open doorway, the pat-pat of her slippered feet warning him. He frowned at her over his reading glasses, big horn-rimmed monstrosities of another age. Another life.

Hastily adjusting the papers on his littered desk to cover the small, rare edition of the *Tales,* he coughed testily. Damn the woman! She was forever snooping, prowling, prying. Why couldn't she leave him alone?

"Confound you, Agatha! What is it now? It's after two and you should be asleep."

She looked down at him where he was, closed in with old books, out-of-date furniture, reading by the light thrown fitfully from a kerosene lamp of ancient vintage. She sighed wearily with vast regret, a large, rawboned woman too conscious of her bad choice of mate, her own non-conformation to the role of wife to the pedantic Roderick Legrande. Yet, she loved him because he was weak. There are such women.

"Roderick, come to bed. You've read long enough, haven't you? Put it off until morning."

"Leave me alone! I can't stand to be interrupted like this at odd hours when I'm reading." His words hammered at her with the repetition and fury of other nights. Other interruptions.

She leaned over him, sorrowfully, coaxing him as she might a small child. "Rod, hasn't this business gone far enough?"

His eyes narrowed suspiciously. It was the first time she had ever hinted at a difference, the opening gun of any marital hostility or divergence of opinion.

"What do you mean by that?" he croaked hoarsely.

His anger fanned her mounting impatience. "What do I mean by that?" she repeated fiercely, unable to hold it in now that he was pretending that everything was as it had always been.

"What don't I mean? You sold all our modern furnishings,

made me get rid of everything I'd ever wanted in a home. And then what did you do? You fitted the house with period furniture, sold the radio, and installed a phonograph that to this day I'll never know where you got! And look at yourself. Writing by lamplight with a goosequill and dressed like something out of Charles Dickens. Good Lord! Rod, can't you see what's happened to you? This is 1957—not 1857!"

She ran down, exhausted and spent, the full tide of her anger ebbing as she saw his sickly face, bent shoulders, and wasted body.

He glared up at her, a fantastic figure indeed. The exaggerated length of the quill in his bony fingers made him suddenly conscious of how it dated him as she had said. Like something out of the last century. Antique, outmoded, feeble.

The warm feel of the exquisitely bound volume concealed beneath his hand steadied him again. He sensed his bond with the past, the older, better things, and pounded the desk with theatrical self-righteousness.

"Damn you everlastingly, you infernal meddler!" He was shouting now, wildly gesticulating. "What is so wrong with my longing for the past or outfitting myself in the garment and style of a better age? What is so wonderful in all this progress that can be measured in the discordant sounds of subway trains and maudlin jazz music? Progress, indeed! Electric lights are proven artificial forms of illumination that damage valuable eyesight, and as for your seeming forgetfulness of your duties and solicitude as wife, I am prepared for your apology and entreatment of my forgiveness." He paused triumphantly at the end of his stream of imposing, flowery discourse and folded his arms.

The color drained from her face. She attempted to say something, to prick his false bubble with the proper amount of scorn, but no words came. Muffling a sob, she turned swiftly and swept from the room, slamming the door with vibrant fury and hurt.

Grimacing, he set his teeth as the sound of her feet running up the steps of the landing to the bedroom came down to him. He cursed and flung down his feathered pen. That was modern times for you! People rushing to get someplace, setting up hideous dins, unmindful of the well-being of others. Progress was also the lowly wife telling you off and striving to rule.

The issue of his glorying in the past was lost on him. He wasn't aware of his own shortcomings, his own bigotry in things. He had gone too far back to correlate the present.

Selecting a meerschaum pipe from the elegantly carved rack on his desk, he filled it with studied pomp from the large humidor squatting beside it. Damn her anyway! Blast her for owning such a plain, coarse figure, for being unfortunately endowed with such a trite, unromantic name as Agatha. Agatha Beggs, when he had married her six years ago. Why couldn't she have been called Lenore, or Eulalie, or Ulalume—or even Helen? Poe was right, bless his fevered brow! Those were names a lover could conjure with!

His fretful mental mood caused him to fill the tiny chamber with smoke. Why hadn't she seen fit to do as he had in the long ago? Change her name, of course. He himself had been George Legrande once, born of ignorant French immigrant parents. But once he had come in contact with the magic of Poe in the school library that had all been changed. Oh, he could tell the difference between amontillado and sherry all right! It was that simple. It merely wanted the devoted reading of "The Gold Bug" and "The Fall of the House of Usher."

George Legrande was prosaic, unimposing, dull. The dual heroes of the respective Poe classics were not. William Legrande and Roderick Usher. The former, a brilliant adventurer of mathematical stature; the latter, a moody, impetuous scion of ancient, brooding aristocracy. He was already

George Legrande by right of birth. He became Roderick Legrande by right of choice in a Providence courthouse as soon as he came of legal age. This was before he had met Agatha and yielded to the temptations of flesh from which even the most restricted man cannot escape.

The declaration of independence in name-changing was only the first salvo in his willful yearning for the time-dusted nostalgias of the days of Edgar Allan. He had been afraid to go beyond it until long after his marriage. He had worn the proper clothes, had spoken with the terse urgency of the day, and had given in to but a few of his odd caprices. He had only dared to collect old books, cameos, period pieces, and musty bric-a-brac so that his friends and wife thought him merely a zealous antiquarian. Even Agatha had been proud of him then. Why wasn't she proud now?

He frowned with the memory of her impatience and suspicion as the home had been slowly, subtly overrun with the relics he had garnered from all the many corners of the city. Soon the new, up-to-date, in-the-time furniture went rapidly and the whole house at the edge of Ashlynne Square presented a family portrait of nineteenth-century life.

Roderick's own job as bookkeeper for the Ashlynne Gas and Electric Company didn't interfere in any way with his trip back through time. He was pretty much to himself with his ledgers and files; to the rest of the help he was just a "character," a still-young fellow who had a few eccentricities. It seemed there was one in every organization.

Not long after that, he was never seen without a muffler of some sort, or mittens, and wore vests that were always outstanding for their cut and the gold watch with the linked chain forever dangling from their pockets.

The lamp flickered and cast a dying gaze over the room. He smiled in contentment at the gathering gloom as it settled over his rocking chair and made blurred magic of the cabinet and the roll-top desk in the far corner. Tightening his scarf about his throat, he lurched to the fireplace and stoked the steadily crackling logs with a heavy andiron. Flame licked up at him from an opening made by the probe of the rod and he reveled in a feeling of rest, security, and comfort. Why couldn't Agatha feel as he did about the old place? Wasn't it far more comfortable like this? Better than some four-room apartment where you always had to badger the janitor for steam, for hot water?

He sighed ponderously. Better indeed.

He went back to his reading of Poe's "Raven" with the alacrity of the small boy who has to put off playing with his Erector set until the guests have left. Beaming, he found his spot again.

"... *and the Raven, never flitting, still is sitting, still is sitting on the pallid bust of Pallas just above my chamber door ...*"—here he flung a quick glance above the entrance of his own door. His slavery to the Poe tradition was complete. There above the arch of the threshold, stoically squatting on the famous bust of the most beautiful of all famous women, was a black, stern, stuffed raven. The imitation was complete in every detail. The blank eyes of Pallas Athene set in the rounded, classic face; the Raven, bird of omen, black as coal, beak poised in an attitude of "grave decorum," beady eyes glistening with message, seeming ever ready to croak the fabulous cry of old, "*Nevermore!*"

He raced through the remainder of the poem with the speed of long familiarity and countless re-readings. At its doleful climax, he closed the book with gross reverence and went back to his pipe.

Poe was so right, he mused. Life is but a haunted dream, a dim candle, a wraith-like travail through lands of poignant memory, deep despair. Why do people blandly continue to think of empty things, unimportant theories and modern excitement?

If only Agatha—

"RODERICK!"

She was calling him from the head of the stairs with no real emergency in her tone save the loud, trumpeting plainness that he detested so heartily. He bit the end of his pipe in annoyance. What the devil did she want now?

"Yes, what is it?" he barked from the doorway. Atop the landing, her wide figure moved in the semidarkness, one arm joining the balustrade in blending shadow.

"If you ever find time to leave that dream world of yours," her words rippled down on a wave of sarcasm, "will you bring some fresh meat up from the cellar?"

"Meat? At this ungodly hour?"

"Yes—I'll need the chops for dinner tomorrow and with one thing and another I may forget it at the last minute. You don't mind, do you?" There was the barest lilt of mockery in her voice.

He clattered out from the study grumpily and headed for the alcove directly under the stairs. "That infernal refrigerator! Why couldn't an ordinary icebox have sufficed?" He winced at the thought of its cost, its mammoth size, its modernity.

She leaned over the railing so that he could hear her rejoinder.

"There isn't room in the kitchen, remember? Thanks to you and your love for old houses. We barely get by with two chairs and a table."

"Go to bed, Agatha! I'll get it for you."

All the way down the rickety cellar steps, the thought nettled him. The refrigerator. It had been her only triumph over his mode of life. It was the one thing he had not been able to control when furnishing the house and she had defied him on the whole issue. They had to have fresh meat. He couldn't dispute the point. Keeping it in the cellar was a necessity due to its streamlined grandeur of size. That was what really bothered him. He still felt that she had purchased such a big model, such an ultramodern one, as a flaunt to his code, his feelings, his ancient ideas.

The feeble light of the lone bulb that dangled perilously from a length of corded wire cast a wavery glow over the thing. Everything else here in the cellar was old. The refrigerator was still new, its white porcelain shoulders offsetting the incredible age of the antiques that formed its company.

Round, bulging, aged-in-the-wood barrels; a spinning wheel teetering precariously on a broken, warped base as if the next closing of the upstairs door would cause it to fall. In one corner, flanking a mountainous pile of yellowed newspapers, the faded glory of a century-old painting peered out past the cobwebs and layers of dust encroaching on its scene.

He paused to survey them once again with all the fervor that had prompted his ownership. They were his links, his tracks back to the past.

It was a cellar out of the pages of ancient historians. The low, spiderwebbed rafters; the heavy, closely bunched blocks of rounded stone that walled the four sides formed a torture chamber that only wanted the proper equipment to justify the name.

Forgetting his original purpose, he glided to another recess where a scratched and scarred piano gleamed out at him from the shrouded depths with its contrasting white teeth of keyboard. He ran his fingers over the unused ivories and reveled in the out-of-tune notes that sounded hollowly in the low-ceilinged chamber. This was his age, his era. "If Milady would be so kind. This is our waltz." A slim, dainty, powdered dream. Small, elegant feet. Not big and awkward like Agatha.

Agatha. He remembered the meat and the refrigerator, a spasm contorting his face. How he would love to be rid of both! Then he could delight in his fancies uninterrupted. There would be no prying eyes, no criticism. And someday, somewhere, he could begin anew, commence the whole romance of courtship with someone more to his tastes, his fitting mate . . . but, no, it wasn't possible . . . or was it?

A chill spread through him slowly, almost cautiously, as

if he had it under control. Was it possible that he had been
unconsciously thinking of it all the time so that the staggering
suggestion did not shock him as it should have? Was that
it? His thin face powered itself into his bony hands in sudden fear. Good God!

Slowly with dragging, thoughtful steps, he moved toward
the refrigerator and whipped the broad door wide.

"Agatha, I've been thinking—"

"What about, Roderick?"

"The refrigerator. I must confess in spite of my previous
thoughts on the subject that it is performing its functions
rather well. So much so that I have reversed my former attitude and shall now do all in my power to retain it in perfect working order."

"Well, it's about time, I must say! I thought you understood that by having such a thing I am able to stock up
on meat products without going to the butcher's so often. I
have so many other things to do around the house. The time
spent on shopping for food can be used to better advantage."

"That's true, Agatha. Besides, there is the fresh meat—"

"Of course, Roderick. I'm glad you changed your mind
about it."

"I'm afraid it's none too soon."

"Whatever do you mean?"

"The cooling system seemed faulty to me last night. Some
sort of leak. Nothing I can't repair myself. So after supper,
I'll be working down the cellar—"

"Wouldn't you rather I called the handyman from the
company? There's a guarantee—"

"Oh, no. By no means. I'll fix it myself. I'm not without
ability along that line, you know. So if you hear any strange
noises from the basement after supper, pay no mind. It
will only be me."

"As you say, Roderick."

She had been too pleased by his affability to argue the

point. He had been too anxious to allay her suspicions to be short-tempered with her.

His plan was very simple. Poe himself had pointed the way with the bizarre cunning of the master. The method was in the tale "The Black Cat." It was cold, it was clear, it was proper. The only difference lay in the motive. The harassed protagonist of "The Black Cat," driven to extremes of alcoholism, had killed his wife in a fit of passion while they were both in the cellar of their home. The body had been disposed of by the process of sealing it in a section of decomposed wall. But he would go Edgar Allan one better. The floor of his cellar was earthen. Thick, damp soil. He would dig deep and dig hard and no one would know of his crime. He chuckled grimly to himself. There would be no black cat buried with her to reveal his secret by its terrible squalling. And he would not boast of the foundations of his house, of the firm, rock-like anchorage that it bedded on. He had no one to boast to.

He would arrange it so that it would seem that Agatha, tired of his misanthropic life, had run away in the dead of night. He was not unaware of the strange light people held him in.

"Did you fix it? You certainly took long enough."

"Yes, I did. But it was the first time I have ever experimented with a thing like that and I wanted to repair it properly." *It had taken longer digging the hole than he had thought it would. There was a good deal of rock formation under the old house.*

"I never thought one could get his hands so dirty working on a refrigerator, Roderick. You look as if you'd been ditch-digging." *What was behind that remark? Did she suspect or had she just winged blithely past the truth?*

"Fact is, Agatha, I have moved the machine around a bit. It is nearer the steps than it was before. That way you can get at it more easily." *For another day or so anyway. After that it won't matter.*

"Roderick—why not clean the whole cellar up? Throw all that old stuff out? It frightens me, this fixation of yours for old things." *It won't frighten you much longer, Agatha.*

"Don't you like to remember the past, Agatha?" *Do it now, my dear. You haven't much time.*

"Not the way you do. Ugh! Old, dirty, crumbling things. Decayed furniture. Always reading that Poe person. Can't you see what it's done to you? To—us?"

Agatha dear, you have just signed your death warrant. Destroyed the last vestige of human pity within me.

Friday night came with that maddening slowness that typifies anything one waits for. Up until that point, Legrande had felt no qualms, displayed no outward signs of his inner tension, his eagerness for the little game of death to begin. He had been sober and calm when dinnertime came, but once the meal began, he toyed with his food and punctuated his eating with sly glances at his watch beneath his napkin. Agatha was oddly silent herself, only speaking to ask him to pass the salt and briefly commenting on the vagaries of the weather.

He knew he was nervous, could feel it in the sticky clasp of his napkin to his fingers, the closed-in feel of his starched collar. "Bread, please," he mumbled and was amazed when he caught himself repeating the idiotic phrase so that she could hear and comply. Her full, peasant's face stared at him dumbly for an instant.

The meal wore on with aggravating slowness, stillness. His reflection paled back at him from the oval, concave mirror hanging beyond her chair. He saw the thinning black of his hair, the sharp lines prematurely etched in his cadaverous cheeks, and forgot the moment's concern in self-fascination. He was really so much like Poe, he thought. The same bitter, disappointed mouth, the high forehead, the eyes with lights in them . . .

"Roderick, are you feeling well?"

He came back from the world of the mirror. "Quite well." He stole a second from his watch. Why hadn't it begun yet? It was almost time. He couldn't have misjudged his calculations. He'd never be able to carry her down into the cellar. It would have to be done down there. But first, she would have to be *in* the cellar. Unsuspecting, of her own volition, for a perfectly good reason—

"Did you like the lamb, Roderick?" she was asking. "I feel as if it was especially good tonight."

"It was, my dear," he agreed without meaning. Damnation! Wouldn't it ever happen?

BOOO-MMMM!

A muffled roar noised up from what seemed directly below the table, and Agatha dropped her fork with a squeal of fright. The dishes rattled and Roderick shivered. The sound was brief, ending as swiftly as it had come.

She stared at him in questioning wonder. "Gracious, what was that?"

"It sounded like it came from the cellar—" Masking the stab of elation within his breast, he pushed back from his chair and bounded out of the room into the hall corridor, confident she would follow out of curiosity alone, possibly wifely concern. He was glad all over, glad that the thing had begun, would soon be over.

He paused for the barest instant at the top of the cellar steps, waiting for the scrape of her chair, the rapid click of her heels. They came in that sequence and he pounded down the wooden steps, the blood mounting in his veins. It would not be long now.

He was down the steps and into the heart of the cellar before the weight of her heavy heel thudded on the first step. He had to hurry now. The scattered remnants of blown wiring and tin can that he had set electrically the evening before were strewn chaotically in the narrow bin where he had placed them. In a breathless moment, spurred by each descending thump of her shoes, he had spread several stacks of the yellowed newspapers over the minor ruin. It had been a simple enough trick. All that was needed was some powder and an elemental knowledge of electricity.

"Roderick, what was it? What made that terrible noise?" she was demanding in tempo to her falling feet. Gradually, her body seemed to lower itself into view with timidity as if waiting for his reassurances that everything was all right.

"I can't be certain, dear. But come ahead and we'll see. Possibly the refrigerator is leaking and—"

"Oh, no. That can't be!" She hove into sight, her face bright and red in the proximity of the dangling bulb. "It sounded like an explosion of some kind."

"That may be." He had stationed himself at the door of the porcelain giant as if investigating his opinion. "But there doesn't appear to be anything of the sort. Do you suppose something fell and caused the noise?"

She drew in closer, fanning her skirts as she did so, lulled on by the private congeniality of his tone. For once they both were interested in the same thing, something they had not been guilty of in years.

"Well, this is your sanctum sanctorum, Roderick. You would know more about that than I. Does it look as if something dropped accidentally? It would have to be something heavy, of course, like—say the piano." She moved over to it, not remarking that it was farther out from its recess than was normal, not questioning the abnormal expanse of yawning blackness beyond it. But how could she? She had seldom been in the cellar and then only to go to the refrigerator. She certainly wouldn't dally down here for any length of time. It would be out of keeping with her professed feelings for old things.

His eyes never left her back as his hand, nervously twitching, reached slowly for the handle of the spade that poked up from its narrow stall.

"No, it doesn't seem to be anything I can see—how about you?" she murmured, and the turning loudness of her voice warned him. At the last second, his hand whipped back from its desired goal. She was facing him again.

He wondered if he was controlling his face as much as he wanted to. A roaring flush was in his cheeks at her near discovery of his plan. Pounding, pounding—

"I'm confounded if I can see what made that sound, Agatha." He coughed with a sudden spasm. "It couldn't be that we imagined it?"

Her large eyes showed her scorn. "Don't be an ass! There most certainly was a noise of some kind and I mean to find out what it was." She swept by him with her big body toward the refrigerator, her back once again turned helplessly to his murderous design. Lightning-swift, with the boldness of desperation, he swung the spade clear from its narrow bin and held it noiselessly behind him. It was now or never. He could not hold her down here much longer.

Cautiously, he tiptoed behind her as she half-crouched before her time-saver, oblivious of the terror at her very heels.

The light played on the little scene; the saffron glow of the bulb adding the touch of the unreal to everything. *No, it would not be long now.*

"I'm pleased to see you moved it as you said you would. It is much easier this way, isn't it?" *Was she saying that?* He could hardly restrain a mad giggle as he raised the spade in a high parabola of premeditated murder above his head.

"Still, I don't understand what could have made such a noise. Perhaps the mechanism has run down. . . ." *Why did she have to keep on babbling that drivel? Just another second, Agatha. Hold your position. Don't move. That's it, that's it. Now, now . . .* His muscles tensed for the killing blow and the digging implement started down as if he were driving a spike into a railroad tie—

"AGATHA!"

The cry knifed through his lungs with his overpowering bewilderment, the complete change of the tableau. Arms as fierce and as strong as those of the Seducers and Temptresses of old were crushing him, punishing him with their steel, bending his scrawny form back without mercy or remorse. The wooden shaft of the spade spiraled from his senseless fingers. She had whirled as if windswept at the zero hour of her life and encompassed him with the embrace of Death.

"—you crawling, slimy monster!" The words hissed out at him, close to his face on the wings of hot, furious breath. "I knew it all along! You and your petty deceits! Your stupid inconsistencies! Did you think me the complete foolish, trusting wife? Did you imagine for one second that you had me deceived?"

He gagged with the pressure of her blocky hands, the overhead bulb dancing before his clouding vision like some gigantic, new species of fly. "Aga—" he choked. The blood in his skull ran riot and the pounding sensation of faintness lurched on as in a dream. Dimly, he heard an enormous click as of some mechanical thing in operation. . . .

"You would do away with me, was that it? You pedantic, morbid monstrosity! Old things, dead things, antiques! Musty diaries and decadent histories of people not worth knowing! You can have it all now, Roderick! I give it to you of my own free will! I want the present and progress." A draft of cold air funneled up his legs in dread newness— oh, good God!

"I've been down here before, Roderick, as you shall presently discover. Now!"

He was so sickly. He was so pale. She was so strong. She

balled him up like some hateful package and threw him away.

The door of the refrigerator clanged shut behind him. The light was on. There was no meat and there were no shelves. Only room for a man. Room enough for his body.

In the awful nakedness of the interior, he hurled himself desperately against the cold walls. His hands drummed madly—her voice mocked from somewhere on the other side of the door, beyond the edge of darkness.

"You see, Roderick, I read Poe too. Remember 'The Cask of Amontillado,' dear? The catacombs, the mason's sign, and Montresor burying poor Fortunato behind that wall of bricks—"

"FOR THE LOVE OF GOD, AGATHA!"

"Manuscript Found in a Drawer" is one of a trilogy of short stories inspired by Poe and written by Charles Norman. One has appeared in *Vogue,* a second involving the counterfeiting of a copy of *Tamerlane* remains unpublished, and this one is published for the first time as part of this collection.

The tale is not only an attempt to write a murder mystery in the manner of Edgar Allan Poe but also involves Poe himself, implying that except for the events described in this story, that master's life might have been changed and lengthened.

Charles Norman, who is a director of the Mystery Writers of America, has gained a reputation as a writer of mystery stories; his work has appeared in *Ellery Queen's Mystery Magazine* and *The Saint,* among others. However, in the more ethereal atmosphere of scholarship, he is better known for his superbly researched biographies. One of the best of these is *The Genteel Murderer,* a life of Thomas Griffiths Wainewright, the famed British art connoisseur, noted for his literary criticism under the pen name of Janus Weathercock, who ended his life in Tasmania where he was sentenced to penal servitude for forgery.

Manuscript Found in a Drawer

By Charles Norman

As usual, after dinner in Thornton's house, we talked about his hobby, a mild word for what amounted to an obsession. Also, I knew him too well not to guess that he had found another treasure, and I waited for him to display it. Thornton was a collector. First editions were all very well, he would say—when you couldn't get hold of the original manuscripts. He was that kind of collector. Now, from the table beside him—we were having coffee in his library—he took a blue leather slipcase and extracted several pieces of paper.

"Read this," he said; "it won't take long."

I found myself holding five sheets of notepaper with an unfamiliar watermark, all of them closely written over in an old-fashioned copperplate hand as clear as print. There was a lamp behind my chair; I leaned back and began to read, noticing, as I did so, that Thornton was watching me intently.

"My name is Roger Desforth, of Richmond, Virginia [the little manuscript, for such it was, began]. It is my hope that this account of my last day on earth will fall into the hands of the American minister, or other countryman of mine. As I am a bachelor, and without near kin, it is my wish that the proceeds from my goods and other possessions—including those on this side of the Atlantic, if they prove salvageable—should go to Edgar Allan Poe, Esquire, residing at present in my native city, as a slight token of my esteem. I have already instructed my banker, in a separate communication, that the money I have left on deposit with him likewise should go to Mr. Poe. I am happy in the thought that I may be of some use to him in the further- ance of his career. Even at this moment I can recall how his large, luminous eyes flashed as he talked to me about his approaching marriage and the prospects which he had both as a writer and editor, for he had in mind a periodical of his own. He was planning a trip north, to put his affairs in order, with a stopover, if I recall correctly, in Baltimore.

"I had once or twice submitted a few trifles to him—in his capacity as editor—which he professed to admire; but in spite of such encouragement it was soon clear to *me*, at least, that my true bent did not lie in the direction of author- ship. His interest in my effusions—which were, I know, greatly influenced by his own wonderful style—sprang from their bizarre settings. So it is for his perusal that I

set down my last story, conscious it is of a kind he himself
excelled in. Little did I dream that I would ever find myself
an *actor* in one of them; but such is the case. As I do not
know how much time is vouchsafed me—for *time is running out*—I will perforce be brief.

"I have been all my life a restless wanderer, forever in
quest of the antiquities which were my passion as well
as my livelihood and, I dare say, I was a good enough observer and reporter. But that was all. I ceased to write for
publication, and our acquaintance came to an end. I went
abroad, then returned to Richmond; and it was there that I
saw him again, in the autumn of this year. He was now engaged, to a widow whom he had known in his youth as I
learned from him, and who happened to be related to some
distant cousins of mine. How he found time from his rounds
of social calls, in her company, to give me the benefit of
his advice concerning my next Continental tour, I cannot
say. I learned, however, for the first time, that he had spent
some years in Europe himself, in many out-of-the-way places
as well as its famous capitals; and, indeed, I might have
known, even before he told me this, that his foreign tales
were assuredly the work of an observer on the spot.

"Thus, it is due to him that I am here; although, of
course, I hold *him* entirely blameless for the *dénouement*.
For it was from him that I heard about this city of untouched treasures, to which he directed my steps. I was all
ears; and, so great was my excitement, generated by his
inimitable descriptions, that I hurried here at once. I quickly
found an apartment, much of it bare, which I deemed fortunate; for after a first survey I foresaw that I would need all
the room possible for acquisitions. What I—and he—could
not foresee was how my sojourn here would end.

"I had spent the afternoon, as usual, in the shops of
dealers, and had come, as night was falling, to the foot of
that narrow and crooked street upon whose summit the
medieval cathedral, long unused and partly in ruins, over-

looked the quarter. I had seen much to covet. One purchase I had made—*a Spanish dagger* whose scabbard was ornamented with jewels and whose blade flashed brighter than any stone. In my mind I saw it resting, amid its own glitters, on a cabinet which is a little carved masterpiece—smooth, glowing, and monumentally solid—which stands beside me as I write and in which I plan to deposit this record.

"Despite this anticipated pleasure, the proper display of my purchase, which is the true reward of all acquisitions, I was still reluctant to return to my lodgings; and thus it was that without deliberation, I began the steep ascent, pausing from time to time to regard the massive pile above me—the nimble, obscene gargoyles leering with round evil eyes of stone, the rectangular shadows on the slopes of roof, the broken buttresses beneath. I arrived at the entrance. A momentary feeling of caution—*or was it presentiment?*—made me hesitate. It passed. But it was with an ever increasing sense of my aloneness that I pushed back a sepultural door, and found myself, when my eyes had become accustomed to the gloom, within a vast hollow oppressive with emptiness.

⍺ "I looked up. The rose-red glow faded from the splinters of stained glass; darkness, sudden and deep, was massed outside; and, just as suddenly, I was confounded by utter darkness within. I felt, on the instant, an imperative need to be out of the place. Groping my way back to the door, I grasped the latch—and found myself unable to open it! Terror seized me. But this, too, passed. I grew calm. I had spent many a night, in my wanderings, in stranger lodgings than this one—if, indeed, the ruined cathedral was to prove my lodging for the night; besides, I told myself, I had upon me a curio of inestimable value—*the Spanish dagger.*

"At that moment I perceived, at the far end of the nave, a light that wavered, advancing toward me. It was a torch. My first feeling was one of immense relief and gratitude; but my second, and that which I permitted to guide me, was one of caution. After all, I thought, I am alone, a foreigner, in a deserted building, in a deserted quarter of a half-forgotten city crumbling into ruin. I crouched low.

"Slowly, in the wavering torchlight, a procession loomed. In a swirl of shadows I saw the robes that denoted a secret order. And now, in the center of that robed band, I made out a solitary figure whose eyes, peering wildly to left and right, held terror and anguish—the expression of one who had *betrayed*—who was being *punished!* The procession passed me. The patter of sandals on stone ceased.

"Surely, I thought, I must be dreaming; or is it some fantastic revel that I have read about and now am recollecting? But the pounding of my heart, my painful breathing, the rigor which had seized my limbs, all told me it was real.

"A bell began to toll, and startled bats swooped with crackling wings. I looked at the band. In the light of the torch I saw where the wall gaped. It was a vertical cavity— an upright coffin of stone! I had one last glimpse of a terrified face; and then, swiftly, efficiently, *the wall was sealed!* The band formed itself once more, and started back whence it had come, preceded by the torchbearer.

"An uncontrollable urge to flee from this place of doom and death—to flee at once—*at all costs*—seized me. As the last robed figure shuffled past, I rose, and stepped cautiously, followed on tiptoe. Where the altar had been was an opening, and in that opening a flight of stairs. All descended in single file, and *I followed*. I had gone down eight or nine steps when I heard a dull thud overhead and felt a gust of air go by. *Someone was behind me*—someone whose hand had closed the trap door! I drew the dagger from its sheath and waited. *But no one came.* I then groped my way along a damp and narrow passage, fervently praying that it would lead to an exit under the stars. The naked dagger stayed in my hand.

"In this manner I went along for perhaps five minutes, when I became aware of a freshness in the atmosphere. It was the freshness of night, of the open air! Suddenly I was no longer in the subterranean passageway, but in a dark street of steep stone stairs in the quarter near my lodgings. There was no sign of the robed band. The torch had been snuffed out like a candle. I fled home, pursued by terror.

"It is now almost midnight, and I am alone—that is to say, *I had supposed myself alone*—in my apartment. I am writing by the light of a lamp in my favorite room, which is filled with the treasures I have gathered. There are five other rooms, most of them mere repositories for crated pieces. Although it is October, and the night is chilly, I feel oppressed to suffocation.

"A few moments after my arrival I placed the dagger in its jeweled scabbard on my prized cabinet. Feeling the need of a cigar, I made my way to the study in which I keep my smoking paraphernalia, scooped up a handful of thin Havanas, and returned to this room.

"I am not given to hallucinations. My death will substantiate the assertion I am going to make. When I returned, *the dagger was gone!* The jeweled scabbard lies where I placed it—but it is empty of its blade!

"I have just looked about me, but have seen nothing— only the smoke from my cigar drifting past the lamp to the curtained window.

"The curtain is stirring.

"Midnight, October 7, 1849."

Such was the ending of the extraordinary document which had found its way into Thornton's collection. I looked up and handed it over, unable to say a word. It was Thornton who broke the silence.

"Poor Poe!" he exclaimed. "Do you realize the significance of the date?" He was holding out the last sheet of Desforth's manuscript. I must have looked blank, for he went on: "Why, October 7, 1849—that was the day Poe died."

Of course I knew the date; but I let Thornton rattle on.

"In Baltimore," he emphasized. "After being found drunk and insensible—and broke—in the street. He had made only a few hundred dollars from all his writing, and died penniless at the age of forty."

"What if he had not gone to Baltimore?" I could not help asking.

"Ah!" Thornton exclaimed, struck with the thought. "He would have married Mrs. Shelton, and written a great deal more, and died rich. Desforth had plenty of money to leave. It went, partly, to those distant cousins of his, and partly to Mrs. Shelton."

"What about Desforth?" I inquired eagerly. "And how did you get hold of his manuscript?"

Thornton shrugged.

"A dealer in Richmond wrote me about it," he said. "You see, Mrs. Shelton and the others died before the things from Europe came. So, all this time—about a hundred years— Roger Desforth's possessions reposed in a warehouse. They were finally auctioned off—all but that piece, in which the manuscript was found."

He was pointing to a magnificent cabinet which—I realized with a start—I had not seen there before. As I gazed at it in fascination not unmixed with a feeling of premonitory horror, I heard him say: "That reminds me—there is still another memento." He opened a drawer in the cabinet and held up for my inspection a little dagger in a jeweled scabbard.

"After all," he remarked, "Desforth had paid for it; so it, too, was shipped across—after the police took it from his back."

Of all the modern writers of the strange and the terrible, none seem more akin in their writing and in certain aspects of their lives to Edgar Allan Poe than does the late Howard Phillips Lovecraft. Poe was Lovecraft's first love, and certain of his early tales shamelessly evidence imitation, none more obviously than "The Outsider," a title now almost symbolic of the life of its author.

To Poe was paid the Lovecraftian compliment: "Penetrating to every festering horror in the gaily painted mockery called existence, and in the solemn masquerade called human thought and feeling, that vision had power to project itself in blackly magical crystallisations and transmutations: till there bloomed in the sterile America of the thirties and the forties such a moon-nourished garden of gorgeous poison fungi as not even the nether slopes of Saturn might boast."

"The Dark Brotherhood" is actually written by August W. Derleth from a fragment of a story idea which H. P. Lovecraft obtained from a dream and noted before it whisked away from memory. Edgar Allan Poe's role in this story quite evidently derives from Derleth's poem "Providence: Two Gentlemen Meet at Midnight," in which the shade of Poe is conjured from an old Providence graveyard where once Poe walked. The poem is included elsewhere in this volume.

"The Dark Brotherhood" is the title story of a book edited and published by August W. Derleth under the imprint of Arkham House, composed of Lovecraft marginalia, commentary, and bibliography. Probably no man alive has done more to rescue and preserve in hard covers the best tales in the supernatural tradition written today than has August W. Derleth. In 1969, August Derleth will have spent thirty years operating Arkham House as a hobby. Except for him, many fine stories and even a few outstanding authors would have been doomed to pulp oblivion.

The Dark Brotherhood

By H. P. Lovecraft and August W. Derleth

> *It is probable that the facts in regard to the mysterious destruction by fire of an abandoned house on a knoll along the shore of the Seekonk in a little-habited district between the Washington and Red Bridges will never be entirely known. The police have been beset by the usual number of cranks, purporting to offer information about the matter, none more insistent than Arthur Phillips, the descendant of an old East Side family, long resident on Angell Street, a somewhat confused but earnest young man who prepared an account of certain events he alleges led to the fire. Though the police have interviewed all persons concerned and mentioned in Mr. Phillips' account, no corroboration—save for a statement from a librarian at the Athenaeum, attesting only to the fact that Mr. Phillips did once meet Miss Rose Dexter there—could be found to support Mr. Phillips' allegations. The manuscript follows.*

I.

The nocturnal streets of any city along the Eastern Seaboard afford the nightwalker many a glimpse of the strange and terrible, the macabre and *outré*, for darkness draws from the crevices and crannies, the attic rooms and cellar hideways of the city those human beings who, for obscure reasons lost in the past, choose to keep the day secure in their gray niches—the misshapen, the lonely, the sick, the very old, the haunted, and those lost souls who are forever seeking their identities under cover of the night, which is beneficent for them as the cold light of day can never be. These are the hurt by life, the maimed, men and women who have never recovered from the traumas of childhood or who have willingly sought after experiences not meant for man to know, and every place where the human society has been concentrated for any considerable length of time abounds with them, though they are seen only in the dark hours, emerging like nocturnal moths to move about in their narrow environs for a few brief hours before they must escape daylight once more.

Having been a solitary child, and much left to my own devices because of the persistent ill-health which was my lot, I developed early a propensity for roaming abroad by night, at first only in the Angell Street neighborhood where I lived during much of my childhood, and then, little by little, in a widened circle in my native Providence. By day, my health permitting, I haunted the Seekonk River from the city into the open country, or, when my energy was at its height, played with a few carefully chosen companions at a "clubhouse" we had painstakingly constructed in wooded areas not far out of the city. I was also much given to reading, and spent long hours in my grandfather's extensive library, reading without discrimination and thus assimilating a vast amount of knowledge, from the Greek philosophies to the history of the English monarchy, from the secrets of ancient alchemists to the experiments of Niels Bohr, from the lore of Egyptian papyri to the regional studies of Thomas Hardy, since my grandfather was possessed of very catholic tastes in books and, spurning specialization, bought and kept only what in his mind was good, by which he meant that which involved him.

But the nocturnal city invariably drew me from all else; walking abroad was my preference above all other pursuits, and I went out and about at night all through the later years of my childhood and throughout my adolescent years, in the course of which I tended—because sporadic illness kept me from regular attendance at school—to grow ever more self-sufficient and solitary. I could not now say what it was I sought with such determination in the nighted city, what it was in the ill-lit streets that drew me, why I sought old Benefit Street and the shadowed environs of Poe Street, almost unknown in the vastness of Providence, what it was I hoped to see in the furtively glimpsed faces of other night-wanderers slipping and slinking along the dark lanes and byways of the city, unless perhaps it was to escape from the harsher realities of daylight coupled with an insatiable curiosity about the secrets of city life which only the night could disclose.

When at last my graduation from high school was an accomplished fact, it might have been assumed that I would turn to other pursuits; but it was not so, for my health was too precarious to warrant matriculation at Brown University, where I would like to have gone to continue my studies, and this deprivation served only to enhance my solitary occupations—I doubled my reading hours and increased the time I spent abroad by night, by the simple expedient of sleeping during the daylight hours. And yet I contrived to lead an otherwise normal existence; I did not abandon my widowed mother or my aunts, with whom we lived, though the companions of my youth had grown away from me, and I managed to discover Rose Dexter, a dark-eyed descendant of the first English families to come into old Providence, one singularly favored in the proportions of her figure and in the beauty of her features, whom I persuaded to share my nocturnal pursuits.

With her I continued to explore nocturnal Providence, and with new zest, eager to show Rose all I had already discovered in my wanderings about the city. We met originally at the old Athenaeum, and we continued to meet there of evenings, and from its portals ventured forth into the night. What began lightheartedly for her soon grew into dedicated habit; she proved as eager as I to inquire into hidden byways and long-disused lanes, and she was soon as much at home in the night-held city as I. She was little inclined to irrelevant chatter, and thus proved admirably complementary to my person.

We had been exploring Providence in this fashion for several months when, one night on Benefit Street, a gentleman wearing a knee-length cape over wrinkled and ill-kept clothing accosted us. He had been standing on the walk not far ahead of us when first we turned into the street, and I had observed him when we went past him; he had struck me as oddly disquieting, for I thought his moustached, dark-eyed face with the unruly hair of his hatless head strangely familiar; and, at our passing, he had set out in pursuit until, at last, catching up to us, he touched me on the shoulder and spoke.

"Sir," he said, "could you tell me how to reach the cemetery where once Poe walked?"

I gave him directions, and then, spurred by a sudden impulse, suggested that we accompany him to the goal he sought; almost before I understood fully what had happened, we three were walking along together. I saw almost at once with what a calculating air the fellow scrutinized my companion, and yet any resentment I might have felt was dispelled by the ready recognition that the stranger's interest was inoffensive, for it was rather more coolly critical than passionately involved. I took the opportunity, also, to examine him as carefully as I could in the occasional patches of streetlight through which we passed, and was increasingly disturbed at the gnawing certainty that I knew him or had known him.

He was dressed almost uniformly in somber black, save for his white shirt and the flowing Windsor tie he affected. His clothing was unpressed, as if it had been worn for a long time without having been attended to, but it was not unclean, as far as I could see. His brow was high, almost dome-like; under it his dark eyes looked out hauntingly, and his face narrowed to his small, blunt chin. His hair, too, was longer than most men of my generation wore it, and yet he seemed to be of that same generation, not more than five years past my own age. His clothing, however, was definitely not of my generation; indeed, it seemed, for all that it had the appearance of being new, to have been cut to a pattern of several generations before my own.

"Are you a stranger to Providence?" I asked him presently.

"I am visiting," he said shortly.

"You are interested in Poe?"

He nodded.

"How much do you know of him?" I asked then.

"Little," he replied. "Perhaps you could tell me more?"

I needed no second invitation, but immediately gave him a biographical sketch of the father of the detective story and a master of the macabre tale, whose work I had long admired, elaborating only on his romance with Mrs. Sarah Helen Whitman, since it involved Providence and the visit with Mrs. Whitman to the cemetery whither we were bound. I saw that he listened with almost rapt attention, and seemed to be setting down in memory everything I said, but I could not decide from his expressionless face whether what I told him gave him pleasure or displeasure, and I could not determine what the source of his interest was.

For her part, Rose was conscious of his interest in her, but she was not embarrassed by it, perhaps sensing that his interest was other than amorous. It was not until he asked her name that I realized we had not had his. He gave it now as "Mr. Allan," at which Rose smiled almost imperceptibly; I caught it fleetingly as we passed under a street lamp.

Having learned our names, our companion seemed interested in nothing more, and it was in silence that we reached the cemetery at last. I had thought Mr. Allan would enter it, but such was not his intention; he had evidently meant only to discover its location, so that he could return to it by day, which was manifestly a sensible conclusion, for—though I knew it well and had walked there on occasion by night—it offered little for a stranger to view in the dark hours.

We bade him good night at the gate and went on.

"I've seen that fellow somewhere before," I said to Rose once we had passed beyond his hearing. "But I can't think where it was. Perhaps in the library."

"It must have been in the library," answered Rose with a throaty chuckle that was typical of her. "In a portrait on the wall."

"Oh, come!" I cried.

"Surely you recognized the resemblance, Arthur!" she cried. "Even to his name. He looks like Edgar Allan Poe."

And, of course, he did. As soon as Rose had mentioned it, I recognized the strong resemblance, even to his clothing, and at once set Mr. Allan down as a harmless idolater of Poe's, so obsessed with the man that he must fashion himself in his likeness, even to his outdated clothing—another of the curious specimens of humanity thronging the night streets of the city.

"Well, that is one of the oddest fellows we've met in all the while we've walked out," I said.

Her hand tightened on my arm. "Arthur, didn't you *feel* something—something *wrong* about him?"

"Oh, I suppose there is something 'wrong' in that sense about all of us who are haunters of the dark," I said. "Perhaps, in a way, we prefer to make our own reality."

But even as I answered her, I was aware of her meaning, and there was no need of the explanation she tried so earnestly to make in the spate of words that followed—there was something wrong in the sense that there was about Mr. Allan a profound note of error. It lay, now that I faced and accepted it, in a number of trivial things, but particularly in the lack of expressiveness in his features; his speech, limited though it had been, was without modulation, almost mechanical; he had not smiled, nor had he been given to

any variation in facial expression whatsoever; he had spoken
with a precision that suggested an icy detachment and aloof-
ness foreign to most men. Even the manifest interest he
showed in Rose was far more clinical than anything else. At
the same time that my curiosity was quickened, a note of
apprehension began to make itself manifest, as a result of
which I turned our conversation into other channels and
presently walked Rose to her home.

II

I suppose it was inevitable that I should meet Mr. Allan
again, and but two nights later, this time not far from my
own door. Perhaps it was absurd to think so, but I could not
escape the impression that he was waiting for me, that he
was as anxious to encounter me again as I was to meet him.

I greeted him jovially, as a fellow haunter of the night,
and took quick notice of the fact that, though his voice
simulated my own joviality, there was not a flicker of emotion on his face; it remained completely placid—"wooden,"
in the words of the romantic writers. Not the hint of a smile
touched his lips, not a glint shone in his dark eyes. And now
that I had had it called to my attention, I saw that the
resemblance to Poe was remarkable, so much so, that had
Mr. Allan put forth any reasonable claim to being a descendant of Poe's, I could have been persuaded to belief.

It was, I thought, a curious coincidence, but hardly more,
and Mr. Allan on this occasion made no mention of Poe
or anything relating to him in Providence. He seemed, it
was soon evident, more intent on listening to me; he was as
singularly uncommunicative as he had been at our first meeting, and in an odd way his manner was precisely the same—
as if we had not actually met before. But perhaps it was that
he simply sought some common ground, for once I mentioned that I contributed a weekly column on astronomy to
the Providence *Journal*. At this he began to take part in our

conversation; what had been for several blocks virtually a monologue on my part became a dialogue.

It was immediately apparent to me that Mr. Allan was not a novice in astronomical matters. Anxious as he seemed to be for my views, he entertained some distinctly different views of his own, some of them highly debatable. He lost no time in setting forth his opinion that not only was interplanetary travel possible, but that countless stars—not alone some of the planets in our own solar system—were inhabited.

"By human beings?" I asked incredulously.

"Need it be?" he replied. "Life is unique—not man. Even here on this planet life takes many forms."

I asked him then whether he had read the works of Charles Fort.

He had not. He knew nothing of him, and, at his request, I outlined some of Fort's theories, together with the facts Fort had adduced in support of those theories. I saw that from time to time, as we walked along, my companion's head moved in a curt nod, though his unemotional face betrayed no expression; it was as if he agreed. And on one occasion, he broke into words.

"Yes, it is so. What he says is so."

I had at the moment been speaking of the sighting of un-identified flying objects near Japan during the latter half of the nineteenth century.

"How can you say so?" I cried.

He launched at once into a lengthy statement, the gist of which was that every advanced scientist in the domain of astronomy was convinced that earth was not unique in having life, and that it followed therefore that, just as it could be concluded that some heavenly bodies had lower life forms than our own, so others might well support higher forms, and, accepting that premise, it was perfectly logical that such higher forms had mastered interplanetary travel and might, after decades of observation, be thoroughly familiar with earth and its inhabitants as well as with its sister planets.

"To what purpose?" I asked. "To make war on us? To invade us?"

"A more highly developed form of life would hardly need to use such primitive methods," he pointed out. "They watch us precisely as we watch the moon and listen for radio signals from the planets—we here are still in the earliest stages of interplanetary communication and, beyond that, space travel, whereas other races on remote stars have long since achieved both."

"How can you speak with such authority?" I asked then.

"Because I am convinced of it. Surely you must have come face to face with similar conclusions."

I admitted that I had.

"And you remain open-minded?"

I admitted this as well.

"Open-minded enough to examine certain proof if it were offered to you?"

"Certainly," I replied, though my skepticism could hardly have gone unnoticed.

"That is good," he said. "Because if you will permit my brothers and me to call on you at your home on Angell Street, we may be able to convince you that there is life in space—not in the shape of men, but life, and life possessing a far greater intelligence than that of your most intelligent men."

I was amused at the breadth of his claim and belief, but I did not betray it by any sign. His confidence made me reflect again upon the infinite variety of characters to be found among the nightwalkers of Providence; clearly Mr. Allan was a man who was obsessed by his extraordinary beliefs, and, like most of such men, eager to proselytize, to make converts.

"Whenever you like," I said by way of invitation.

"Except that I would prefer it to be late rather than early, to give my mother time to get to bed. Anything in the way of an experiment might disturb her."

"Shall we say next Monday night?"

"Agreed."

My companion thereafter said no more on this subject. Indeed, he said scarcely anything on any subject, and it was left for me to do the talking. I was evidently not very entertaining, for in less than three blocks we came to an alley and there Mr. Allan abruptly bade me good night, after which he turned into the alley and was soon swallowed in its darkness.

Could his house abut upon it? I wondered. If not, he must inevitably come out the other end. Impulsively I hurried around one end of that block and stationed myself deep in the shadows of the parallel street, where I could remain well hidden from the alley entrance and yet keep it in view.

Mr. Allan came leisurely out of the alley before I had quite recovered my breath. I expected him to pursue his way through the alley, but he did not; he turned down the street, and, accelerating his pace a little, he proceeded on his way. Impelled by curiosity now, I followed, keeping myself as well hidden as possible. But Mr. Allan never once looked around; he set his face straight ahead of him and never, as far as I could determine, even glanced to left or right; he was clearly bound for a destination that could only be his home, for the hour was past midnight.

I had little difficulty following my erstwhile companion, for I knew these streets well, I had known them since my childhood. Mr. Allan was bound in the direction of the Seekonk, and he held to his course without deviation until he reached a somewhat run-down section of Providence, where he made his way up a little knoll to a long-deserted house at its crest. He let himself into it and I saw him no more. I waited a while longer, expecting a light to go up in the house, but none did, and I could only conclude that he had gone directly to bed.

Fortunately, I had kept myself in the shadows, for Mr. Allan had evidently not gone to bed. Apparently he had gone through the house and around the block, for suddenly I saw him approach the house from the direction we had come, and once more he walked on, past my place of concealment, and made his way into the house, again without turning on a light.

This time, certainly, he had remained there. I waited for five minutes or a trifle more, then turned and made my way back toward my own home on Angell Street, satisfied that I had done no more in following Mr. Allan than he had evidently done on the night of our initial meeting in following me, for I had long since concluded that our meeting tonight had not been by chance, but by design.

Many blocks from the Allan house, however, I was startled to see, approaching me from the direction of Benefit Street, my erstwhile companion! Even as I wondered how he had managed to leave the house again and make his way well around me in order to enable him to come toward me, trying in vain to map the route he could have taken to accomplish this, he came up and passed me by without so much as a flicker of recognition.

Yet it was he, undeniably—the same Poe-esque appearance distinguished him from any other nightwalker. Stilling his name on my tongue, I turned and looked after him. He never turned his head, but walked steadily on, clearly bound for the scene I had not long since quitted. I watched him out of sight, still trying—in vain—to map the route he might have taken among the lanes and byways and streets so familiar to me in order to meet me so once more, face to face.

We had met on Angell Street, walked to Benefit and north, then turned riverward once more. Only by dint of hard running could he have cut around me and come back. And what purpose would he have had to follow such a course?

It left me utterly baffled, particularly since he had given me not the slightest sign of recognition, his entire mien suggesting that we were perfect strangers!

But if I was mystified at the occurrences of the night, I was even more puzzled at my meeting with Rose at the Athenaeum the following night. She had clearly been waiting for me, and hastened to my side as soon as she caught sight of me.

"Have you seen Mr. Allan?" she asked.

"Only last night," I answered, and would have gone on to recount the circumstances had she not spoken again.

"So did I! He walked me out from the library and home."

I stifled my response and heard her out. Mr. Allan had been waiting for her to come out of the library. He had greeted her and asked whether he might walk with her, after having ascertained that I was not with her. They had walked for an hour with but little conversation, and this only of the most superficial—relative to the antiquities of the city, the architecture of certain houses, and similar matters, just such as one interested in the older aspects of Providence would find of interest—and then he had walked her home. She had, in short, been with Mr. Allan in one part of the city at the same time that I had been with him in another; and clearly neither of us had the slightest doubt of the identity of our companions.

"I saw him after midnight," I said, which was part of the truth but not all the truth.

This extraordinary coincidence must have some logical explanation, though I was not disposed to discuss it with Rose, lest I unduly alarm her. Mr. Allan had spoken of his "brothers"; it was therefore entirely likely that Mr. Allan was one of a pair of identical twins. But what explanation could there be for what was an obvious and designed deception? One of our companions was *not*, could not have been the same Mr. Allan with whom we had previously

walked. But which? I was satisfied that my companion was
identical with Mr. Allan met but two nights before.

In as casual a manner as I could assume in the circumstances, I asked such questions of Rose as were designed to
satisfy me in regard to the identity of her companion, in the
anticipation that somewhere in our dialogue she would reveal some doubt of the identity of hers. She betrayed
no such doubt; she was innocently convinced that her companion was the same man who had walked with us two
nights ago, for he had obviously made references to the
earlier nocturnal walk, and Rose was completely convinced
that he was the same man. She had no reason for doubt,
however, for I held my tongue; there was some perplexing
mystery here, for the brothers had some obscure reason for
interesting themselves in us—certainly other than that they
shared our interest in the nightwalkers of the city and the
hidden aspects of urban life that appeared only with the dusk
and vanished once more into their seclusion with the dawn.

My companion, however, had made an assignation with
me, whereas Rose said nothing to indicate that her companion had planned a further meeting with her. And why
had he waited to meet her in the first place? But this line of
inquiry was lost before the insistent cognizance that neither
of the meetings I had had after leaving my companion at his
residence last night could have been Rose's companion, for
Rose lived rather too far from the place of my final meeting
last night to have permitted her companion to meet me at
the point we met. A disquieting sense of uneasiness began
to rise in me. Perhaps there were three Allans—all identical
—triplets? Or four? But no, surely the second Mr. Allan encountered on the previous night had been identical with the
first, even if the third encounter could not have been the
same man.

No matter how much thought I applied to it, the riddle
remained insoluble. I was, therefore, in a challenging frame

of mind for my Monday night appointment with Mr. Allan, now but two days away.

III

Even so, I was ill-prepared for the visit of Mr. Allan and his brothers on the following Monday night. They came at a quarter past ten o'clock; my mother had just gone upstairs to bed. I had expected, at most, three of them; there were seven—and they were as alike as peas in a pod, so much so that I could not pick from among them the Mr. Allan with whom I had twice walked the nocturnal streets of Providence, though I assumed it was he who was the spokesman for the group.

They filed into the living room, and Mr. Allan immediately set about arranging chairs in a semicircle with the help of his brothers, murmuring something about the "nature of the experiment," though, to tell the truth, I was still much too amazed and disquieted at the appearance of seven identical men, all of whom bore so strong a resemblance to Edgar Allan Poe as to startle the beholder, to assimilate what was being said. Moreover, I saw now by the light of my Welsbach gas lamp that all seven of them were of a pallid, waxen complexion, not of such a nature as to give me any doubt of their being flesh and bone like myself, but rather such as to suggest that one and all were afflicted with some kind of disease—anemia, perhaps, or some kindred illness which would leave their faces colorless; and their eyes, which were very dark, seemed to stare fixedly and yet without seeing, though they suffered no lack of perception and seemed to perceive by means of some extra sense not visible to me. The sensation that rose in me was not predominantly one of fear, but one of overwhelming curiosity tinged with a spreading sense of something utterly alien not only to my experience but to my existence.

Thus far, little had passed between us, but now that the

semicircle had been completed, and my visitors had seated themselves, their spokesman beckoned me forward and indicated a chair placed within the arc of the semicircle facing the seated men.

"Will you sit here, Mr. Phillips?" he asked.

I did as he asked, and found myself the object of all eyes, but not essentially so much their object as their focal point, for the seven men seemed to be looking not so much at me as through me.

"Our intention, Mr. Phillips," their spokesman—whom I took to be the gentleman I had encountered on Benefit Street—explained, "is to produce for you certain impressions of extra-terrestrial life. All that is necessary for you to do is to relax and to be receptive."

"I am ready," I said.

I had expected that they would ask for the light to be lowered, which seems to be integral to all such séance-like sessions, but they did not do so. They waited upon silence, save for the ticking of the hall clock and the distant hum of the city, and then they began what I can only describe as singing—a low, not unpleasant, almost lulling humming, increasing in volume, and broken with sounds I assumed were words though I could not make out any of them. The song they sang and the way they sang it was indescribably foreign; the key was minor, and the tonal intervals did not resemble any terrestrial musical system with which I was familiar, though it seemed to me more oriental than occidental.

I had little time to consider the music, however, for I was rapidly overcome with a feeling of profound malaise, the faces of the seven men grew dim and coalesced to merge into one swimming face, and an intolerable consciousness of unrolled aeons of time swept over me. I concluded that some form of hypnosis was responsible for my condition, but I did not have any qualms about it; it did not matter, for the experience I was undergoing was utterly novel and not unpleasant, though there was inherent in it a discordant note, as of some lurking evil looming far behind the relaxing sensations that crowded upon me and swept me before them. Gradually, the lamp, the walls, and the men before me faded and vanished and, though I was still aware of being in my quarters on Angell Street, I was also cognizant that somehow I had been transported to new surroundings, and an element of alarm at the strangeness of these surroundings, together with one of repulsion and alienation, began to make themselves manifest. It was as if I feared losing consciousness in an alien place without the means of returning to earth—for it was an extra-terrestrial scene that I witnessed, one of great and magnificent grandeur in its proportions, and yet one completely incomprehensible to me.

Vast vistas of space whirled before me in an alien dimension, and central in them was an aggregation of gigantic cubes, scattered along a gulf of violet and agitated radiation—and other figures moving among them—enormous, iridescent, rugose cones, rising from a base almost ten feet wide to a height of over ten feet, and composed of ridgy, scaly, semielastic matter, and sporting from their apexes four flexible, cylindrical members, each at least a foot thick, and of a similar substance, though more flesh-like, as that of the cones, which were presumably bodies for the crowning members, which, as I watched, had an ability to contract or expand, sometimes to lengthen to a distance equal to the height of the cone to which they adhered. Two of these members were terminated with enormous claws, while a third wore a crest of four red, trumpet-like appendages, and the fourth ended in a great yellow globe two feet in diameter, in the center of which were three enormous eyes, darkly opalescent, which, because of their position in the elastic member, could be turned in any direction whatsoever. It was such a scene as exercised the greatest fascination upon me and yet at the same time spread in me a repellence inspired by its total alienation and the aura of fearful disclosures which alone could give it meaning and a lurking terror. Moreover, as I saw the moving figures, which seemed to be *tending* the great cubes, with greater clarity and more distinctness, I saw that their strange heads were crowned by four slender gray stalks carrying flower-like appendages, as well as, from their nether sides, eight sinuous, elastic tentacles, moss green in color, which seemed to be constantly agitated by serpentine motion, expanding and contracting, lengthening and shortening and whipping around as if with life independent of that which animated, more sluggishly, the cones themselves. The whole scene was bathed in a wan, red glow, as from some dying sun which, failing its planet, now took second place to the violet radiation from the gulf.

The scene had an indescribable effect on me; it was as if I had been permitted a look into another world, one incredibly vaster than our own, distinguished from our own by antipodally different values and life forms, and remote from ours in time and space, and as I gazed at this far world, I became aware—as were this intelligence being funneled into me by some psychic means—that I looked upon a dying race which must escape its planet or perish. Spontaneously then, I seemed to recognize the burgeoning of a menacing evil, and with an urgent, violent effort, I threw off the bondage of the chant that held me in its spell, gave vent to the uprushing of fear I felt in a cry of protest, and rose to my feet, while the chair on which I sat fell backward with a crash.

Instantly the scene before my mind's eye vanished and the room returned to focus. Across from me sat my visitors, the seven gentlemen in the likeness of Poe, impassive and silent, for the sounds they had made, the humming and the odd word-like tonal noises, had ceased.

I calmed down, my pulse began to slow.

"What you saw, Mr. Phillips, was a scene on another star,

remote from here," said Mr. Allan. "Far out in space—indeed, in another universe. Did it convince you?"

"I've seen enough," I cried.

I could not tell whether my visitors were amused or scornful; they remained without expression, including their spokesman, who only inclined his head slightly and said, "We will take our leave then, with your permission."

And silently, one by one, they all filed out into Angell Street.

I was most disagreeably shaken. I had no proof of having seen anything on another world, but I could testify that I had experienced an extraordinary hallucination, undoubtedly through hypnotic influence.

But what had been its reason for being? I pondered that as I set about to put the living room to rights, but I could not adduce any profound reason for the demonstration I had witnessed. I was unable to deny that my visitors had shown themselves to be possessed of extraordinary faculties—but to what end? And I had to admit to myself that I was as much shaken by the appearance of no less than seven identical men as I was by the hallucinatory experience I had just passed through. Quintuplets were possible, yes—but had anyone ever heard of septuplets? Nor were multiple births of identical children usual. Yet here were seven men, all of very much the same age, identical in appearance, for whose existence there was not a scintilla of explanation.

Nor was there any graspable meaning in the scene that I had witnessed during the demonstration. Somehow I had understoood that the great cubes were sentient beings for whom the violet radiation was life-giving; I had realized that the cone creatures served them in some fashion or other, but nothing had been disclosed to show how. The whole vision was meaningless; it was just such a scene as might have been created by a highly organized imagination and telepathically conveyed to a willing subject, such as myself. That it proved the existence of extra-terrestrial life was ri-

diculous; it proved no more than that I had been the victim
of an induced hallucination.

But, once more, I came full circle. As hallucination, it
was completely without reason for being.

Yet I could not escape an insistent disquiet that troubled
me long that night before I was able to sleep.

IV

Strangely enough, my uneasiness mounted during the
course of the following morning. Accustomed as I was to the
human curiosities, to the often incredible characters and
unusual sights to be encountered on the nocturnal walks I
took about Providence, the circumstances surrounding the
Poe-esque Mr. Allan and his brothers were so *outré* that
I could not get them out of mind.

Acting on impulse, I took time off from my work that
afternoon and made my way to the house on the knoll along
the Seekonk, determined to confront my nocturnal companion. But the house, when I came to it, wore an air of singular
desertion; badly worn curtains were drawn down to the sills
of the windows, in some places blinds were up; and the
whole milieu was the epitome of abandonment.

Nevertheless, I knocked at the door and waited.

There was no answer. I knocked again.

No sound fell to my ear from inside the house.

Powerfully impelled by curiosity now, I tried the door.
It opened to my touch. I hesitated still, and looked all around
me. No one was in sight, at least two of the houses in the
neighborhood were unoccupied, and if I was under surveil-
lance it was not apparent to me.

I opened the door and stepped into the house, standing
for a few moments with my back to the door to accustom my
eyes to the twilight that filled the rooms. Then I moved cautiously through the small vestibule into the adjacent room,
a parlor sparely occupied by horsehair furniture at least

two decades old. There was no sign here of occupation by any human being, though there was evidence that someone had not long since walked here, making a path through dust visible on the uncarpeted flooring. I crossed the room and entered a small dining room, and crossed this, too, to find myself in a kitchen, which, like the other rooms, bore little sign of having been used, for there was no food of any kind in evidence, and the table appeared not to have been used for years. Yet here, too, were footprints in substantial numbers, testifying to the habitation of the house. And the staircase revealed steady use as well.

But it was the far side of the house that afforded the most disturbing disclosures. This side of the building consisted of but one large room, though it was instantly evident that it had been three rooms at one time, but the connecting walls had been removed without the finished repair of the junctions at the outer wall. I saw this in a fleeting glance, for what was in the center of the room caught and held my fascinated attention. The room was bathed in violet light, a soft glowing that emanated from what appeared to be a long, glass-encased slab, which, with a second, unlit similar slab, stood surrounded by machinery the like of which I had never seen before save in dreams.

I moved cautiously into the room, alert for anyone who might prevent my intrusion. No one and nothing moved. I drew closer to the violet-lit glass case and saw that something lay within, though I did not at first encompass this because I saw what it laid upon—nothing less than a life-sized reproduction of a likeness of Edgar Allan Poe, which, like everything else, was illuminated by the same pulsing violet light, the source of which I could not determine, save that it was enclosed by the glass-like substance which made up the case. But when at last I looked upon that which lay upon the likeness of Poe, I almost cried out in fearful surprise, for it was, in miniature, a precise reproduction of

one of the rugose cones I had seen only last night in the
hallucination induced in my home on Angell Street! And
the sinuous movement of the tentacles on its head—or what
I took to be its head—was indisputable evidence that it
was alive!

I backed hastily away with only enough of a glance at
the other case to assure myself that it was bare and unoccupied, though connected by many metal tubes to the illumined case parallel to it; then I fled, as noiselessly as possible,
for I was convinced that the nocturnal brotherhood slept
upstairs and in my confusion at this inexplicable revelation
that placed my hallucination of the previous night into another perspective, I wished to meet no one. I escaped from
the house undetected, though I thought I caught a brief
glimpse of a Poe-esque face at one of the upper windows. I
ran down the road and back along the streets that bridged
the distance from the Seekonk to the Providence River, and
ran so for many blocks before I slowed to a walk, for I was
beginning to attract attention in my wild flight.

As I walked along, I strove to bring order to my chaotic
thoughts. I could not adduce an explanation for what I had
seen, but I knew intuitively that I had stumbled upon some
menacing evil too dark and forbidding and perhaps too vast
as well for my comprehension. I hunted for meaning and
found none; mine had never been a scientifically oriented
mind, apart from chemistry and astronomy, so that I was
not equipped to understand the use of the great machines I
had seen in that house ringing that violet-lit slab where that
rugose body lay in warm, life-giving radiation—indeed, I
was not even able to assimilate the machinery itself, for
there was only a remote resemblance to anything I had ever
before seen, and that the dynamos in a powerhouse. They
had all been connected in some way to the two slabs, and
the glass cases—if the substance were glass—the one occupied, the other dark and empty, for all the tubing that tied
them each to each.

But I had seen enough to be convinced that the dark-clad brotherhood who walked the streets of Providence by night in the guise of Edgar Allan Poe had a purpose other than mine in doing so; theirs was no simple curiosity about the nocturnal characters, about fellow walkers of the night. Perhaps darkness was their natural element, even as daylight was that of the majority of their fellow men; but that their motivation was sinister, I could not now doubt. Yet at the same time I was at a loss as to what course next to follow.

I turned my steps at last toward the library, in the vague hope of grasping at something that might lead me to some clue by means of which I could approach an understanding of what I had seen.

But there was nothing. Search as I might, I found no key, no hint, though I read widely through every conceivable reference—even to those on Poe in Providence on the shelves, and I left the library late in the day as baffled as when I had entered.

Perhaps it was inevitable that I would see Mr. Allan again that night. I had no way of knowing whether my visit to his home had been observed, despite the observer I thought I had glimpsed in an upper window in my flight, and I encountered him therefore in some trepidation. But this was evidently ill-founded, for when I greeted him on Benefit Street there was nothing in his manner or in his words to suggest any change in his attitude, such as I might have expected had he been aware of my intrusion. Yet I knew full well his capacity for being without expression—humor, disgust, even anger or irritation were alien to his features, which never changed from that introspective mask which was essentially that of Poe.

"I trust you have recovered from our experiment, Mr. Phillips," he said after exchanging the customary amenities.

"Fully," I answered, though it was not the truth. I added something about a sudden spell of dizziness to explain my bringing the experiment to its precipitate end.

"It is but one of the worlds outside you saw, Mr. Phillips," Mr. Allan went on. "There are many. As many as a hundred thousand. Life is not the unique property of Earth. Nor is life in the shape of human beings. Life takes many forms on other planets and far stars, forms that would seem bizarre to humans, as human life is bizarre to other life forms."

For once, Mr. Allan was singularly communicative, and I had little to say. Clearly, whether or not I laid what I had seen to hallucination—even in the face of my discovery in my companion's house—he himself believed implicitly in what he said. He spoke of many worlds, as if he were familiar with them. On occasion he spoke almost with reverence of certain forms of life, particularly those with the astonishing adaptability of assuming the life forms of other planets in their ceaseless quest for the conditions necessary to their existence.

"The star I looked upon," I broke in, "was dying."

"Yes," he said simply.

"You have seen it?"

"I have seen it, Mr. Phillips."

I listened to him with relief. Since it was manifestly impossible to permit any man sight of the intimate life of outer space, what I had experienced was nothing more than the communicated hallucination of Mr. Allan and his brothers. Telepathic communication certainly, aided by a form of hypnosis I had not previously experienced. Yet I could not rid myself of the disquieting sense of evil that surrounded my nocturnal companion, nor of the uneasy feeling that the explanation which I had so eagerly accepted was unhappily glib.

As soon as I decently could, thereafter, I made excuses to Mr. Allan and took my leave of him. I hastened directly to the Athenaeum in the hope of finding Rose Dexter there, but if she had been there, she had already gone. I went then to a public telephone in the building and telephoned her home.

Rose answered, and I confess to an instantaneous feeling of gratification.

"Have you seen Mr. Allan tonight?" I asked.

"Yes," she replied. "But only for a few moments. I was on my way to the library."

"So did I."

"He asked me to his home some evening to watch an experiment," she went on.

"Don't go," I said at once.

There was a long moment of silence at the other end of the wire. Then, "Why not?" Unfortunately, I failed to acknowledge the edge of truculence in her voice.

"It would be better not to go," I said, with all the firmness I could muster.

"Don't you think, Mr. Phillips, I am the best judge of that?"

I hastened to assure her that I had no wish to dictate her actions, but meant only to suggest that it might be dangerous to go.

"Why?"

"I can't tell you over the telephone," I answered, fully aware of how lame it sounded, and knowing even as I said it that perhaps I could not put into words at all the horrible suspicions which had begun to take shape in my mind, for they were so fantastic, so *outré*, that no one could be expected to believe in them.

"I'll think it over," she said crisply.

"I'll try to explain when I see you," I promised.

She bade me good night and rang off with an intransigence that boded ill, and left me profoundly disturbed.

V

I come now to the final, apocalyptic events concerning Mr. Allan and the mystery surrounding the house on the forgotten knoll. I hesitate to set them down even now, for

I recognize that the charge against me will only be broadened
to include grave questions about my sanity. Yet I have no
other course. Indeed, the entire future of humanity, the
whole course of what we call civilization, may be affected
by what I do or do not write of this matter. For the cul-
minating events followed rapidly and naturally upon my
conversation with Rose Dexter, that unsatisfactory exchange
over the telephone.

After a restless, uneasy day at work, I concluded that I
must make a tenable explanation to Rose. On the following
evening, therefore, I went early to the library, where I was
accustomed to meeting her, and took a place where I could
watch the main entrance. There I waited for well over an
hour before it occurred to me that she might not come to the
library that night.

Once more I sought the telephone, intending to ask
whether I might come over and explain my request of the
previous night.

But it was her sister-in-law, not Rose, who answered my
ring.

Rose had gone out. "A gentleman called for her."

"Did you know him?" I asked.

"No, Mr. Phillips."

"Did you hear his name?"

She had not heard it. She had, in fact, caught only a
glimpse of him as Rose hurried out to meet him, but, in answer to my insistent probing, she admitted that Rose's caller
had had a moustache.

Mr. Allan! I had no further need to inquire.

For a few moments after I had hung up, I did not know
what to do. Perhaps Rose and Mr. Allan were only walking
the length of Benefit Street. But perhaps they had gone to
that mysterious house. The very thought of it filled me
with such apprehension that I lost my head.

I rushed from the library and hurried home. It was ten

o'clock when I reached the house on Angell Street. Fortunately, my mother had retired; so I was able to procure my father's pistol without disturbing her. So armed, I hastened once more into night-held Providence and ran, block upon block, toward the shore of the Seekonk and the knoll upon which stood Mr. Allan's strange house, unaware in my incautious haste of the spectacle I made for other nightwalkers and uncaring, for perhaps Rose's life was at stake—and beyond that, vaguely defined, loomed a far greater and hideous evil.

When I reached the house into which Mr. Allan had disappeared I was taken aback by its solitude and unlit windows. Since I was winded, I hesitated to advance upon it, and waited for a minute or so to catch my breath and quiet my pulse. Then, keeping to the shadows, I moved silently up to the house, looking for any sliver of light.

I crept from the front of the house around to the back. Not the slightest ray of light could be seen. But a low humming sound vibrated just inside the range of my hearing, like the hum of a power line responding to the weather. I crossed to the far side of the house—and there I saw the hint of light— not yellow light, as from a lamp inside, but a pale lavender radiance that seemed to glow faintly, ever so faintly, from the wall itself.

I drew back, recalling only too sharply what I had seen in that house.

But my role now could not be a passive one. I had to know whether Rose was in that darkened house—perhaps in that very room with the unknown machinery and the glass case with the monster in the violet radiance.

I slipped back to the front of the house and mounted the steps to the front door.

Once again, the door was not locked. It yielded to the pressure of my hands. Pausing only long enough to take my loaded weapon in hand, I pushed open the door and en-

tered the vestibule. I stood for a moment to accustom my
eyes to that darkness; standing there, I was even more
aware of the humming sound I had heard—and of more—the
same kind of chant which had put me into that hypnotic
state in the course of which I had witnessed that disturbing vision purporting to be that of life in another world.

I apprehended its meaning instantly, I thought. Rose must
be with Mr. Allan and his brothers, undergoing a similar
experience.

Would that it had been no more!

For when I pushed my way into that large room on the
far side of the house, I saw that which will be forever in-
delibly imprinted on my mind. Lit by the radiance from the
glass case, the room disclosed Mr. Allan and his identical
brothers all prone upon the floor around the twin cases,
making their chanting song. Beyond them, against the far
wall, lay the discarded life-size likeness of Poe I had seen
beneath that weird creature in the glass case bathed in
violet radiance. But it was not Mr. Allan and his brothers
that so profoundly shocked and repelled me—it was what
I saw in the glass cases!

For in the one that lit the room with its violently pul-
sating and agitated violet radiation lay Rose Dexter, fully
clothed, and certainly under hypnosis—and on top of her
lay, greatly elongated and with its tentacles flailing madly,
the rugose cone-like figure I had last seen shrunken on the
likeness of Poe. And in the connected case adjacent to it—
I can hardly bear to set it down even now—lay, identical in
every detail, *a perfect duplicate of Rose!*

What happened next is confused in my memory. I know
that I lost control, that I fired blindly at the glass cases, intending to shatter them. Certainly I struck one or both of
them, for with the impact the radiance vanished, the room
was plunged into utter darkness, cries of fear and alarm rose
from Mr. Allan and his brothers, and, amid a succession of

explosive sounds from the machinery, I rushed forward and picked up Rose Dexter.

Somehow I gained the street with Rose.

Looking back, I saw that flames were appearing at the windows of that accursed house, and then, without warning, the north wall of the house collapsed, and something—an object I could not identify—burst from the now burning house and vanished aloft. I fled still carrying Rose.

Regaining her senses, Rose was hysterical, but I succeeded in calming her, and at last she fell silent and would say nothing. And in silence I took her safely home, knowing how frightening her experience must have been, and resolved to say nothing until she had fully recovered.

In the week that followed, I came to see clearly what was taking place in that house on the knoll. But the charge of arson—lodged against me in lieu of a far more serious one because of the pistol I abandoned in the burning house— has blinded the police to anything but the most mundane matters. I have tried to tell them, insisting that they see Rose Dexter when she is well enough to talk—and willing to do so. I cannot make them understand what I now understand only too well. Yet the facts are there, inescapably.

They say the charred flesh found in that house is not human, most of it. But could they have expected anything else? Seven men in the likeness of Edgar Allan Poe! Surely they must understand that whatever it was in that house came from another world, a dying world, and sought to invade and ultimately take over Earth by reproducing themselves in the shape of men! Surely they must know that it must have been only by coincidence that the model they first chose was a likeness of Poe, chosen because they had no knowledge that Poe did not represent the average among men? Surely they must know, as I came to know, that the rugose, tentacled cone in the violet radiance was the source of their material selves, that the machinery and the tubing—which they say was too much damaged by the fire to identify, as if they could have identified its functions even undamaged!—manufactured from the material simulating flesh supplied by the cone in the violet light creatures in the shape of men from the likeness of Poe!

"Mr. Allan" himself afforded me the key, though I did not know it at the time, when I asked him why mankind was the object of interplanetary scrutiny—"To make war on us? To invade us?"—and he replied: *"A more highly developed form of life would hardly need to use such primitive methods."* Could anything more plainly set forth the explanation for the strange occupation of the house along the Seekonk? Of course, it is evident now that what "Mr. Allan" and his identical brothers afforded me in my own home was a glimpse of life in the planet of the cubes and rugose cones, which was their own.

And surely, finally, most damning of all—it must be evident to any unbiased observer why they wanted Rose. They meant to reproduce their kind in the guise of men and women, so that they could mingle with us, undetected, unsuspected, and slowly, over decades—perhaps centuries—while their world died, take over and prepare our Earth for those who would come after.

God alone knows how many of them may be here, among us, even now!

Later. I have been unable to see Rose until now, tonight, and I am hesitant to call for her. For something unutterably terrible has happened to me. I have fallen prey to horrible doubts. While it did not occur to me during that frightful experience in the shambles following my shots in that violet-lit room, I have now begun to wonder, and my concern has grown hour by hour until I find it now almost unbearable. How can I be sure that, in those frenzied minutes, I rescued the *real* Rose Dexter? If I did, surely she will reassure me tonight. If I did not—God knows what I may un-wittingly have loosed upon Providence and the world!

From *The Providence Journal*—July 17

LOCAL GIRL SLAYS ATTACKER

Rose Dexter, the daughter of Mr. and Mrs. Elisha Dexter of 127 Benevolent Street, last night fought off and killed a young man she charged with attacking her. Miss Dexter was apprehended in a hysterical condition as she fled down Benefit Street in the vicinity of the Cathedral of St. John, near the cemetery attached to which the attack took place.

Her attacker was identified as an acquaintance, Arthur Phillips. . . .

This story was especially written for this book and is published here for the first time. It deals with the period of Poe's life when he had achieved a long-cherished ambition—the ownership of his own journal —only to find that money was at least as important as editorial brilliance and literary genius in sustaining a periodical. Because Edmond Hamilton has made his primary reputation as a science fiction writer, this tale is of that genre. However, Edmond Hamilton acknowledges much closer ties to Edgar Allan Poe.

At a time when his imaginative excursions of the Interstellar Patrol excited the imaginations of the teen-agers among readers of *Weird Tales*, he took the idea of Edgar Allan Poe's "The Premature Burial," and completely inverting the theme, made of it a memorable story. That tale, "The Man Who Returned" (*Weird Tales*, February 1934), like Poe's, tells of a man who regains consciousness in a coffin. Able to force his way out, he makes his way home, only to find that whether dead or believed dead, an individual, once erased from the rolls of the living, does not easily resume his place in their world.

It is a simple statement of fact that when he worked and polished his work, Edgar Allan Poe ranked as one of the most superb stylists of all time, producing a memorable effect without the use of a superfluous word. However, it is the mark of his genius that even his flawed and hastily contrived pieces are so superbly correct as to *method* that they have served as the inspiration of scores of writers who have followed.

Castaway

By Edmond Hamilton

It seemed to him that Broadway had never looked so depressing as in this early winter twilight, with the gas lamps yet unlit and the remnants of the old poplars stirring sluggishly in a cold wind. Hoofs and wheels slapped over the cracked paving, and a tentative flake of snow drifted down.

He thought that any place would be better than this, Richmond, Charleston, even Philadelphia. But they had really been no better, he had wearied of them all. He always wearied of places, even of most people. Perhaps it was just today's disappointment, after all the other disappointments, that made him feel this way.

He reached and entered the shabby little two-room office, and the faded little man writing at a desk looked up quickly, with a dim hope.

"No. Nothing."

The hope—there had not been much—left the face of the other. He muttered, "We can't keep going much longer." Then he said, "There's a young lady to see you. She's waiting in your office."

"I am in no mood to write in young ladies' autograph albums."

"But—but she is quite a wealthy-looking young lady. . . ."

Poe smiled his white, twisted, sarcastic smile. "I see. And wealthy young ladies have wealthy papas, who might be induced to invest in a dying literary magazine."

But when he went into the inner office, he was all the courteous Virginian as he bowed to the seated girl.

"I am most honored, Miss . . ."

She did not raise her eyes as she murmured, "Ellen Donsel."

She was expensively dressed, from her fur-lined cloak to her blue rohan bonnet. Her face was plump, pink, and stupid-looking. Then she looked up at him, and Poe felt surprise. The eyes in that round face were blazing, vibrant with life and intelligence.

"I suppose," he said, "that you wish me to read my poems at some gathering, a thing which I have not the time to do. Or perhaps it's a copy of 'The Raven' in my own handwriting—"

"No," she said. "I have a message for you."

Poe looked polite inquiry. "Yes?"

"A message from . . . Aarn."

The word seemed to hang in the air, echoing like a distant bell, and for a moment neither spoke and he could hear the clip-clop of traffic out in the street.

"Aarn," he repeated, finally. "Now, that is a fine, sonorous name. Whose is it?"

"It's not a person," said Miss Donsel. "It's a place."

"Ah," said Poe. "And where may this place be?"

Her gaze stabbed him. "Don't you remember?"

He began to feel a little uneasy. Because he had written stories of the fantastic, cranks and mentally unbalanced people tended to seek him out. This girl looked normal, even commonplace. Yet the intensity of her eyes . . .

"I'm sorry," he said. "I have not heard the name before."

"Have you heard the name Lalu?" she said. "It's my name. Or the name Yann? It's *your* name. And we came from Aarn, though you came long before I did."

Poe smiled guardedly. "This fancy of yours is a rare one, madam. Tell me . . . what is it like, this place we came from?"

"It lies in the great bay of the purple mountains." Her eyes never left his. "And the river Zair flows down through the mountains, and the towers of Aarn loom above it in the sunset . . ."

He suddenly interrupted her with a bursting laugh. Then he declaimed, ". . . glittering in the red sunlight with a hundred oriels, minarets, and pinnacles; and seeming the phantom handiwork, conjointly, of the sylphs, of the fairies, of the genii, and of the gnomes."

He laughed again, shaking his head. "That is the conclusion of my tale of 'The Domain of Arnheim.' Of course . . . Aarn . . . Arnheim. And you got the name Lalu from my Ulalume, and Yann from my Yaanek . . . why, madam, I must congratulate you on your cleverness."

"No," she said. And again, "No. It was quite the other way around, Mr. Poe. You got *your* names from those I have just spoken."

He regarded the girl with interest. He had not had an experience quite like this one before, and was intrigued.

"So I came from Aarn, did I? Then why don't I remember it?"

"You do, a little," she murmured. "You remembered the place—almost. You remembered the names—almost. You put them into your stories and poems."

His interest heightened. This girl might look like a fool—except for those intense eyes—but she obviously had an unusual imagination.

"Where, then, is Aarn? On the other side of the world? In the garden of the Hesperides?"

"Quite near here, Mr. Poe. In space, that is. But not in time. It is a long way in the future."

"Then you . . . and I, you say . . . came from the future to the present. My dear young lady, it is you who should be writing tales of fantasy, not I!"

Her level gaze did not change. "You did write it. In the tale of the Ragged Mountain. About the man who went back through time for a little while."

"Why," said Poe, "so I did, now I think of it. I had forgotten that clumsy effort. But that was just a freakish fancy."

"Was it? Was it only chance that made you write of traveling in time, a thing no one had ever seriously written of before? Or was it a suppressed memory?"

"I wish it were so," he said. "I assure you that I am not in love with this nineteenth century. But, unfortunately, I can remember my whole life quite clearly, and I have no memories of Aarn."

"That is Mr. Poe speaking," the girl said. "He remembers only his own life. But you are not only Mr. Poe, you are also Yann."

He smiled. "Two people in one body? Tell me, Miss Donsel, have you read my 'William Wilson'? It tells of a man with two personalities, an alter ego—"

"I've read it," she said. "And I know that you wrote it because you *have* two personalities, though one of them cannot remember."

She leaned forward, and he thought that her eyes were more compelling than those of the mesmerists in whom he had been so interested. Her voice was almost a whisper.

"I want to make you remember. I will make you remember. It's why I came after you. . . ."

"Speaking of that, how does one travel temporally?" he interrupted, trying to keep to lightness. "In a flying machine of some sort?"

Her face remained dead serious. "The body cannot move in time. No physical, material object can. But the mind is not material, it is a web of electric force locked into the physical brain. If the mind can be unlocked from the brain, it—being pure force—can be hurled back along the dimension of time and lock itself into the brain of a man of a former age."

"But to what purpose?"

"To the purpose of dominating that brain and body and investigating the historical past through the eyes of a man living in that past. It is not easy to do and there is *danger* in it—the danger of selecting a host whose mind is so powerful that it dominates its visitant. And that is what happened to Yann, Mr. Poe—he is in your brain but dominated, numbed, affecting only your subconscious and giving it half-memories that you think are dreams and fancies."

She added, "You must have a powerful mind indeed, Mr. Poe, so to dominate Yann."

"I've been called many things but not a dullard," he said, and then, with an ironical wave of his hand around the shabby office, "You see the heights to which my intellect has brought me."

"It has happened before," she murmured. "One of us was

trapped in the brain of a Roman poet named Lucretius. . . ."

"Titus Lucretius Carus? Why, madam, I've read his *De
Rerum Natura,* and its strange theories of an atomic
science."

"Not theories," she insisted. "Half-memories. They so tor-
mented him that he killed himself. And there were others,
in other levels of time."

Poe said, admiringly, "A bizarre idea, that. It would certainly make a tale. . . ."

She interrupted. "I am speaking to you, Mr. Poe, but I
am *trying* to speak to Yann. To awaken him from his
numbed captivity in your brain, to make him remember
Aarn."

She went on, rapidly, almost fiercely, and all the time
her eyes held his. And he listened in fascination as the names
and places and things of his tales came into her speech,
sometimes altered, sometimes unchanged, all woven into a
fabric by this girl's impassioned imagination.

"There was—or I should say, here and now, that there
will be, an Age of Violence beyond anything the world
has known. And the climax of it will be a setting loose of
fiery forces that will wreak unprecedented destruction."

Poe thought of his own tale in which mankind had
perished in a worldwide explosion of flame, and the girl
seemed to catch the thought from the half-smile on his
face.

"Oh, not all of humanity were—or will be—destroyed. But
many, many, and when the Age of Violence passed, there
were thousands where there had been millions. So our
world, of centuries from now, the world in which Aarn
lives, is not the crowded, bustling place that this one is.

"Yann, *remember!* Remember our beautiful, clean, un-
crowded world! Remember the day that we drifted down
the Zair in your boat, all the way from the mountains. Down
the yellow waters with the great water lilies about us, and

the forest dark and somber beyond them, all the way until above Aarn we came to the Valley of Many-Colored Grass, and walked there amid the silver trees and looked down on the fliers skimming in the sunlight above the towers of Aarn.

"Don't you remember? That was when you first told me that you had been to the Temporal Laboratory at Tsalal, and had volunteered for the going-back. You would go back to a time not long before the Age of Violence, and would see the world as it was before the great wars shattered it, would see through the eyes of another man all the things that had been lost to history in the devastation.

"Do you remember my tears? How I begged you not to go, how I reminded you of those who had never come back, how I clung to you? But your historical researches had so obsessed you that you would not listen. And so you went. And it was as I had feared, and you did not come back.

"Yann, this is Lalu speaking! Do you know what a torture it can be to wait? Until finally I could bear it no longer and won permission from the Temporal Laboratory to come back to this time and search for you. And the weeks I've been here, in another person's body, seeking in vain, until at last I found the clue, found the names that we knew in Aarn in tales that had become famous, and knew that only the writer of them could be your host. *Yann!*"

Poe had listened, half-dreaming, as the names from his own fancied worlds had floated on the air. But that final shrill cry of agonized appeal brought him to his feet.

"My dear Miss Donsell! I do greatly admire your imaginings, but you must control yourself—"

Her eyes flamed. "Control myself? What have I been doing all these weeks, in this ugly and terrible world, confined in the body of this meaty girl?"

A cold shock stabbed through him at those words. No woman, not even in jest, would think of herself or speak of herself in that way. But then it must mean . . .

The room, the angry face, everything, seemed to waver, as though under water. He felt a strangeness rise in him, the world seemed to fall away from him, and for a moment his old dreams seemed to rise into reality around him, changed but real.

"Yann?"

Was the girl smiling? Of course, the minx was succeeding in hoodwinking the famous Mr. Poe with moonbeams and nonsense, and would happily tell all her little friends about it! The pride and arrogance that were deep in his nature made him stiffen, and the strangeness ebbed.

"I regret," he said, "that I cannot devote more time now to your ingenious *jeu d'esprit,* Miss Donsel. I can only thank you for the assiduousness with which you have studied my little tales."

He opened the door, and bowed to her. She stood up, and her face was not smiling now, but stricken.

"No use," she whispered, finally. "No use at all."

She looked at him, and said in a low voice, "Goodbye, Yann," and closed her eyes.

Poe stepped toward her. "My dear young lady, please . . ."

Her eyes opened again. He stopped short. All the intense life and intelligence had gone out of those eyes, and she stared at him with a stupid, goggling gaze.

"What?" she said. "Who . . ."

"My dear Miss Donsel . . ." he began again.

She uttered a squawking scream. She backed away from him, and put her hands up to her face, and stared at him as though he were the devil.

"What happened?" she cried. "I . . . everything went away . . . I went asleep in the middle of the day . . . How did I . . . ? What am I doing . . . here?"

So that was it, he thought. Of course! Having played the part of the imaginary Lalu, she must now mime it out that her visitant had left her.

He said, smiling acidly, "I congratulate you, not only on your imagination but on your acting abilities."

She paid no heed to him at all. She ran past him and tore open the door. It was late, and his assistant had gone home, and by the time Poe followed her into the other office, Miss Donsel had run out into the street.

He hurried after her. The gas street lamps were on, but in the passing traffic he could not at first see her. Then he heard her shrill call, and saw her climbing into a public cab that had pulled up. He started after her, and saw her face, eyes round with terror, looking back at him the moment before she disappeared into the cab. The driver spoke to his horses and the cab went on.

Poe, always short of temper, felt an angry impatience. He had let himself be made a fool of, even to listen to that chit and her clever beguilings. Probably by now she was mirthfully triumphant.

And yet . . .

He walked back to the office. Thin flakes of snow were drifting down in the sickly yellow of the lamps, and the dust in the street was beginning to turn to greasy mud. The raw wind brought the sound of brawling voices from further along the street.

"This ugly and terrible world . . ." Well, it had often seemed so to him, and tonight it grimaced more repellently than ever. He supposed it was because of all the airy fancies of the sunset towers of Aarn that the girl had picked from his own book and stuffed into his ears.

He went back into his office and sat down at the desk. As his anger cooled a little, he wondered again if there was not a tale in all that artful nonsense? But it so echoed all his other stories that they would say he was repeating himself. Yet still, the idea was intriguing—the man lost out of his time . . .

"I have reached these lands but newly, from an ultimate

*dim Thule, from a wild, weird clime that lieth sublime, out
of Space, out of Time* . . .

"Did I write those lines? Or . . . did Yann?"

For a moment Poe's face yearned, haggard and haunted.
If it were true, if beyond tomorrow was a finer world, Thule,
Aarn, Tsalal? If the phantom, lovely shape he could never
quite see, Ulalume, Lenore, Morella, Ligeia, was a memory . . .

He wanted to believe, but he could not, he must not. He
was a man of reason and a thing like this if believed could
shatter reason, could kill a man.

It would not kill him.

It would *not*.

With a hand that trembled only slightly, he opened the
desk and reached in for the bottle.

FICTION BY POE (?)

"The Lighthouse" is the title given a story of which Edgar Allan Poe wrote scarcely more than six hundred words before his death. It is naturally intriguing to speculate on what he might have had in mind if he had lived long enough or had actually not stopped at the point where the manuscript breaks. A true devotee of Edgar Allan Poe, Robert Bloch, in 1952 decided he would take a whirl at completing the story.

The finished work, under the title of "The Lighthouse" appeared in the January–February 1953 issue of *Fantastic* as a collaboration by Edgar Allan Poe and Robert Bloch. At the time, though it made a striking cover scoop for the magazine, the impact was not great despite the fact that the fragment was known primarily to specialized Poe researchers, because Bloch was still a struggling pulpster, regarded as trading off the reputation of a great literary figure.

Time has altered the picture slightly. Robert Bloch, since the publication of that story, has become a world-renowned author. He has gone on to do the scripts for many striking moving picture successes. Few deny that he is one of the most adept manipulators of literary terror alive today. In this context, his assuming the job of completing a Poe story is removed from the presumptuous to the logical, and what he did with it becomes of primary interest to all.

So as to play fair with the reader, Edgar Allan Poe's last word is "chalk" under the January 3rd entry. Robert Bloch begins with January 4th.

The Lighthouse

By Edgar Allan Poe and Robert Bloch

Jan. 1—1796.

This day—my first on the lighthouse—I make this entry in my diary, as agreed on with DeGrät. As regularly as I *can* keep the journal, I will—but there is no telling what may happen to a man all alone as I am—I may get sick or worse. . . .

So far well! The cutter had a narrow escape—but why dwell on that, since I am *here*, all safe? My spirits are beginning to revive already, at the mere thought of being—for once in my life at least—thoroughly *alone; for*, of course, Neptune, large as he is, is not to be taken into consideration as "society." Would to heaven I had ever found in "society" one half as much *faith* as in this poor dog; in such case I and "society" might never have parted—even for a year. . . .

What most surprises me is the difficulty DeGrät had in getting me the appointment—and I a noble of the realm! It could not be that the Consistory had any doubt of my ability to manage the light. *One* man has attended it before now—and got on quite as well as the three that are usually put in. The duty is a mere nothing; and the printed instructions are as plain as possible. It would never have done to let Orndoff accompany me. I should never have made any way with my book as long as he was within reach of me, with his intolerable gossip—not to mention that everlasting meerschaum. Besides, I wish to be *alone*. . . .

It is strange that I never observed, until this moment, how dreary a sound that word has—"alone"! I could half fancy there was some peculiarity in the echo of these cylindrical walls—but oh, no!—that is all nonsense. I do believe I am going to get nervous about my insulation. *That* will never do. I have not forgotten DeGrät's prophecy. Now for a scramble to the lantern and a good look around to "see what I can see." . . . To see what I can see indeed!—not very much. The swell is subsiding a little, I think—but the cutter will have a rough passage home, nevertheless. She will hardly get within sight of the Norland before noon tomorrow—and yet it can hardly be more than 190 or 200 miles.

Jan. 2.

I have passed this day in a species of ecstasy that I find it impossible to describe. My passion for solitude could scarcely have been more thoroughly gratified. I do not say *satisfied;* for I believe I should never be satiated with such delight as I have experienced today. . . .

The wind lulled after daybreak, and by the afternoon the sea had gone down materially. . . . Nothing to be seen with the telescope even, but ocean and sky, with an occasional gull.

Jan. 3.

A dead calm all day. Toward evening, the sea looked very much like glass. A few seaweeds came in sight; but besides them absolutely *nothing* all day—not even the slightest speck of cloud. . . . Occupied myself in exploring the lighthouse. . . . It is a very lofty one—as I find to my cost when I have to ascend its interminable stairs—not quite 160 feet, I should say, from the low-water mark to the top of the lantern. From the bottom *inside* the shaft, however, the distance to the summit is 180 feet at least: thus the floor is twenty feet below the surface of the sea, even at low tide. . . .

It seems to me that the hollow interior at the bottom should have been filled in with solid masonry. Undoubtedly the whole would have been thus rendered more *safe:* but what am I thinking about? A structure such as this is safe enough under any circumstances. I should feel myself secure in it during the fiercest hurricane that ever raged—and yet I have heard seamen say that, occasionally, with a wind at southwest, the sea has been known to run higher here than anywhere, with the single exception of the western opening of the Straits of Magellan.

No mere sea, though, could accomplish anything with

this solid iron-riveted wall—which, at fifty feet from high-water mark, is four feet thick, if one inch. The basis on which the structure rests seems to me to be chalk. . . .

Jan. 4.

I am now prepared to resume work on my book, having spent this day in familiarizing myself with a regular routine.

My actual duties will be, I perceive, absurdly simple—the light requires little tending beyond a periodic replenishment of the oil for the six-wick burner. As to my own needs, they are easily satisfied, and the exertion of an occasional trip down the stairs is all I must anticipate.

At the base of the stairs is the entrance room; beneath that is twenty feet of empty shaft. Above the entrance room, at the next turn of the circular iron staircase, is my storeroom, which contains the casks of fresh water and the food supplies, plus linens and other daily needs. Above that—again another spiral of those interminable stairs!—is the oil room, completely filled with the tanks from which I must feed the wicks. Fortunately, I perceive that I can limit my descent to the storeroom to once a week if I choose, for it is possible for me to carry sufficient provisions in one load to supply both myself and Neptune for such a period. As to the oil supply, I need only to bring up two drums every three days and thus ensure a constant illumination. If I choose, I can place a dozen or more spare drums on the platform near the light and thus provide for several weeks to come.

So it is that in my daily existence I can limit my movements to the upper half of the lighthouse; that is to say, the three spirals opening on the topmost three levels. The lowest is my "living room"—and it is here, of course, that Neptune is confined the greater part of the day; here, too, that I plan to write at a desk near the wall slit that affords a view of the sea without. The second-highest level is my bedroom and kitchen combined. Here the weekly rations of food and water are contained in cupboards for that purpose; here, too, is the ingenious stove fed by the selfsame oil that lights the beacon above. The topmost level is the service room giving access to the light itself and to the platform surrounding it. Since the light is fixed, and its reflectors set, there is no need for me ever to ascend to the platform save when replenishing the oil supply or making a repair or adjustment as per the written instructions—a circumstance which may well never arise during my stay here.

Already I have carried enough oil, water, and provender to the upper levels to last me for an entire month—I need stir from my two rooms only to replenish the wicks.

For the rest, I am free! utterly free—my time is my own, and in this lofty realm I rule as king. Although Neptune is my only living subject, I can well imagine that I am sovereign o'er all I see—ocean below and stars above. I am master of the sun that rises in rubicund radiance from the sea at dawn, emperor of wind and monarch of the gale, sultan of the waves that sport or roar in roiling torrents about the base of my palace pinnacle. I command the moon in the heavens, and the very ebb and flow of the tide does homage to my reign.

But enough of fancies—DeGrät warned me to refrain from morbid or from grandiose speculation—now I shall take up in all earnestness the task that lies before me. Yet this night, as I sit before the window in the starlight, the tides sweeping against these lofty walls can only echo my exultation; I am free—and, at last, alone!

Jan. 11.

A week has passed since my last entry in this diary, and as I read it over, I can scarce comprehend that it was I who penned those words.

Something has happened—the nature of which lies unfathomed. I have worked, eaten, slept, replenished the wicks twice. My outward existence has been placid. I can ascribe the alteration in my feelings to nought but some inner alchemy; enough to say that a disturbing change has taken place.

Alone! I, who breathed the word as if it were some mystic incantation bestowing peace, have come—I realize it now—to loathe the very sound of the syllables. And the ghastliness of meaning I know full well.

It is a dismaying, it is a dreadful thing, to be alone. Truly alone, as I am, with only Neptune to exist beside me and by his breathing presence remind me that I am not the sole inhabitant of a blind and senseless universe. The sun and stars that wheel overhead in their endless cycle seem to rush across the horizon unheeding—and, of late, unheeded, for I cannot fix my mind upon them with normal constancy. The sea that swirls or ripples below me is nought but a purposeless chaos of utter emptiness.

I thought myself to be a man of singular self-sufficiency, beyond the petty needs of a boring and banal society. How wrong I was!—for I find myself longing for the sight of another face, the sound of another voice, the touch of other hands whether they offer caresses or blows. Anything, anything for reassurance that my dreams are indeed false and that I am *not,* actually, alone.

And yet I *am.* I am, and I will be. The world is two hundred miles away; I will not know it again for an entire year. And it in turn—but no more! I cannot put down my thoughts while in the grip of this morbid mood.

Jan. 13.

Two more days—two more centuries!—have passed. Can it be less than two weeks since I was immured in this prison tower? I mount the turret of my dungeon and gaze at the horizon; I am not hemmed in by bars of steel but by columns and pillars and webs of wild and raging water. The sea has changed; gray skies have wrought a wizardry so that I stand surrounded by a tumult that threatens to become a tempest.

I turn away, for I can bear no more, and descend to my room. I seek to write—the book is bravely begun, but of late I can bring myself to do nothing constructive or creative—and in a moment I fling aside my pen and rise to pace, to endlessly pace the narrow, circular confines of my tower of torment.

Wild words, these? And yet I am not alone in my affliction—Neptune, Neptune the loyal, the calm, the placid feels it too.

Perhaps it is but the approach of the storm that agitates him so—for Nature bears closer kinship with the beast. He stays constantly at my side, whining now, and the muffled roaring of the waves without our prison causes him to tremble. There is a chill in the air that our stove cannot dissipate, but it is not cold that oppresses him. . . .

I have just mounted to the platform and gazed out at the spectacle of gathering storm. The waves are fantastically high; they sweep against the lighthouse in titanic tumult. These solid walls of stone shudder rhythmically with each onslaught. The churning sea is gray no longer—the water is black, black as basalt and as heavy. The sky's hue has deepened so that at the moment no horizon is visible. I am surrounded by a billowing blackness thundering against me. . . .

Back below now, as lightning flickers. The storm will break soon, and Neptune howls piteously. I stroke his quivering flanks, but the poor animal shrinks away. It seems that he fears even my presence; can it be that my own features betray an equal agitation? I do not know—I only feel that I am helpless, trapped here and awaiting the mercy of the storm. I cannot write much longer.

And yet I will set down a further statement. I must, if only to prove to myself that reason again prevails. In writing of my venture up to the platform—my viewing of the sea and sky—I omitted to mention the meaning of a single moment. There came upon me, as I gazed down at the black and boiling madness of the waters below, a wild and willful craving to become one with it. But why should I disguise the naked truth?—I felt an insane impulse to hurl myself into the sea!

It has passed now; passed, I pray, forever. I did not yield to this perverse prompting and I am back here in my quarters, writing calmly once again. Yet the fact remains—the hideous urge to destroy myself came suddenly, and with the force of one of those monstrous waves.

And what—I force myself to realize—was the meaning of my demented desire? It was that I sought escape, escape from loneliness. It was as if by mingling with the sea and the storm I would no longer be *alone.*

But I defy the elements. I defy the powers of the earth and of the heavens. Alone I am, alone I *must* be—and come what may, I shall survive! My laughter rises above all your thunder!

So—ye spirits of the storm—blow, howl, rage, hurl your watery weight against my fortress—I am greater than you in all your powers. But wait! Neptune . . . something has happened to the creature—I must attend him.

Jan. 16.

The storm is abated. I am back at my desk now, alone— truly alone. I have locked poor Neptune in the storeroom below; the unfortunate beast seems driven out of his wits by the forces of the storm. When last I wrote he was worked into a frenzy, whining and pawing and wheeling in circles. He was incapable of responding to my commands and I had no choice but to drag him down the stairs by the scruff of his neck and incarcerate him in the storeroom where he could not come to harm. I own that concern for *my* safety was involved—the possibility of being imprisoned in this lighthouse with a mad dog must be avoided.

His howls, throughout the storm, were pitiable indeed, but now he is silent. When last I ventured to gaze into the room I perceived him sleeping, and I trust that rest and calm will restore him to my full companionship as before.

Companionship!

How shall I describe the horrors of the storm I faced *alone?*

In this diary entry I have prefaced a date—*January 16*—but that is merely a guess. The storm has swept away all track of time. Did it last a day, two days, three—as I now surmise—a week, or a century? I do *not* know.

I know only an endless raging of waters that threatened, time and again, to engulf the very pinnacle of the lighthouse. I know only an eternity of ebony, an aeon of billowing black composed of sea and sky commingled. I only know that there were times when my own voice outroared the storm—but how can I convey the cause of *that?* There was a time, perhaps a full day, perhaps much longer, when I could not bear to rise from my couch but lay with my face buried in the pillows, weeping like a child. But mine were not the pure tears of childhood innocence—call them, rather, the tears of Lucifer upon the realization of his eternal fall from grace. It seemed to me that I was truly the victim of an endless damnation; condemned forever to remain a prisoner in a world of thunderous chaos.

There is no need to write of the fancies and fantasies which assailed me through those unhallowed hours. At times I felt that the lighthouse was giving way and that I would be swept into the sea. At times I knew myself to be a victim of a colossal plot—I cursed DeGrät for sending me, knowingly, to my doom. At times (and these were the worst moments of all) I felt the full force of loneliness, crashing down upon me in waves higher than those wrought by water.

But all has passed, and the sea—and myself—are calm again. A peculiar calmness, this; as I gaze out upon the water there are certain phenomena I was not aware of until this very moment.

Before setting down my observations, let me reassure myself that I am, indeed, *quite* calm; no trace of my former tremors or agitation yet remains. The transient madness induced by the storm has departed and my brain is free of phantasms—indeed, my perceptive faculties seem to be sharpened to an unusual acuity.

It is almost as though I find myself in possession of an additional sense, an ability to analyze and penetrate beyond former limitations superimposed by Nature.

The water on which I gaze is placid once more. The sky is only lightly leaden in hue. But wait—low on the horizon creeps a sudden flame! It is the sun, the Arctic sun in sullen splendor, emerging momentarily from the pall to incarnadine the ocean. Sun and sky, sea and air about me, turn to blood.

Can it be I who but a moment ago wrote of returned, regained sanity? I, who have just shrieked aloud, "Alone!"—and half-rising from my chair, heard the muffled booming echo reverberate through the lonely lighthouse, its sepulchral accent intoning *"Alone!"* in answer? It may be that I am, despite all resolution, going mad; if so, I pray the end comes soon.

Jan. 18.

There will be no end! I have conceived a notion, a theory which my heightened faculties soon will test. I shall embark upon an experiment. . . .

Jan. 26.

A week has passed here in my solitary prison. Solitary?—

perhaps, but not for long. The experiment is proceeding. I must set down what has occurred.

The sound of the echo set me to thinking. One sends out one's voice and it comes back. One sends out one's thoughts and—can it be that there is a response? Sound, as we know, travels in waves and patterns. The emanations of the brain, perhaps, travel similarly. And they are not confined by physical laws of time, space, or *duration*.

Can one's thoughts produce a reply that *materializes*, just as one's voice produces an echo? An echo is a product of a certain vacuum. A thought . . .

Concentration is the key. I have been concentrating. My supplies are replenished, and Neptune—visited during my venture below—seems rational enough, although he shrinks away when I approach him. I have left him below and spent the past week here. Concentration, I repeat, is the key to my experiment.

Concentration, by its very nature, is a difficult task: I addressed myself to it with no little trepidation. Strive but to remain seated quietly with a mind "empty" of all thought, and one finds in the space of a very few minutes that the errant body is engaged in all manner of distracting movement—foot tapping, finger twisting, facial grimacing.

This I managed to overcome after a matter of many hours —my first three days were virtually exhausted in an effort to rid myself of nervous agitation and assume the inner and outer tranquillity of the Indian fakir. Then came the task of "filling" the empty consciousness—filling it completely with *one* intense and concentrated effort of will.

What echo would I bring forth from nothingness? What companionship would I seek here in my loneliness? What was the sign or symbol I desired? What symbolized to me the whole absent world of life and light?

DeGrät would laugh me to scorn if he but knew the concept that I chose. Yet I, the cynical, the jaded, the decadent, searched my soul, plumbed my longing, and found that which I most desired—a simple sign, a token of all the earth removed: a fresh and growing flower, a *rose!*

Yes, a simple rose is what I have sought—a rose, torn from its living stem, perfumed with the sweet incarnation of life itself. Seated here before the window I have dreamed, I have mused, I have then concentrated with every fiber of my being upon a *rose.*

My mind was filled with redness—not the redness of the sun upon the sea, or the redness of blood, but the rich and radiant redness of the rose. My soul was suffused with the scent of a rose: as I brought my faculties to bear exclusively upon the image, these walls fell away, the walls of my very flesh fell away, and I seemed to merge in the texture, the odor, the color, the actual *essence* of a rose.

Shall I write of this, the seventh day, when seated at the window as the sun emerged from the sea, I felt the commanding of my consciousness? Shall I write of rising, descending the stairs, opening the iron door at the base of the lighthouse and peering out at the billows that swirled at my very feet? Shall I write of stooping, of grasping, of holding?

Shall I write that I have indeed descended those iron stairs and returned here with my wave-borne trophy—*that this very day, from waters two hundred miles distant from any shore, I have reached down and plucked a fresh rose?*

Jan. 28.

It has not withered! I keep it before me constantly in a vase on this table, and it is a priceless ruby plucked from dreams. It is real—as real as the howls of poor Neptune, who senses that something odd is afoot. His frantic barking does not disturb me; nothing disturbs me, for I am master of a power greater than earth or space or time. And I shall use this power, now, to bring me the final boon. Here in my tower I have become quite the philosopher: I have learned my lesson well and realize that I do not desire wealth, or fame, or the trinkets of society. My need is simply this—Companionship. And now, with the power that is mine to control, I shall have it!

Soon, quite soon, I shall no longer be alone!

Jan. 30.

The storm has returned, but I pay it no heed; nor do I mark the howlings of Neptune, although the beast is now literally dashing himself against the door of the storeroom. One might fancy that his efforts are responsible for the shuddering of the very lighthouse itself, but no; it is the fury of the northern gale. I pay it no heed, as I say, but I fully realize that this storm surpasses in extent and intensity anything I could imagine as witness to its predecessor.

Yet it is unimportant; even though the light above me flickers and threatens to be extinguished by the sheer velocity of wind that seeps through these stout walls; even though the ocean sweeps against the foundations with a force that makes solid stone seem flimsy as straw; even though the sky is a single black roaring mouth that yawns low upon the horizon to engulf me.

These things I sense but dimly, as I address myself to the appointed task. I pause now only for food and a brief respite—and scribble down these words to mark the progress of resolution toward an inevitable goal.

For the past several days I have bent my faculties to my will, concentrating utterly and to the uttermost upon the summoning of a Companion.

This Companion will be—I confess it!—a woman; a woman far surpassing the limitations of common mortality. For she is, and must be fashioned, of dreams and longing, of desire and delight beyond the bounds of flesh.

She is the woman of whom I have always dreamed, the One I have sought in vain through what I once presumed, in my ignorance, was the world of reality. It seems to me now that I have always known her, that my soul has contained her presence forever. I can visualize her perfectly— I know her hair, each strand more precious than a miser's gold; the riches of her ivory and alabaster brow, the perfection of her face and form are etched forever in my consciousness. DeGrät would scoff that she is but the figment of a dream—but DeGrät did not see the rose.

The rose—I hesitate to speak of it—has gone. It was the rose which I set before me when first I composed myself to this new effort of will. I gazed at it intently until vision faded, senses stilled, and I lost myself in the attempt of conjuring up my vision of a Companion.

Hours later, the sound of rising waters from without aroused me. I gazed about, my eyes sought the reassurance of the rose and rested only upon a *foulness*. Where the rose had risen proudly in its vase, red crest rampant upon a living stem, I now perceived only a noxious, utterly detestable strand of ichorous decay. No rose this, but only seaweed; rotted, noisome, and putrescent. I flung it away, but for long moments I could not banish a wild presentiment—was it true that I had deceived myself? Was it a weed, and only a weed I plucked from the ocean's breast? Did the force of my thought momentarily invest it with the attributes of a rose? Would anything I called up from the depths—the depths of sea or the depths of consciousness—be *truly* real?

The blessed image of the Companion came to soothe these fevered speculations, and I knew myself saved. There *was* a rose; perhaps my thought had created it and nourished it —only when my entire concentration turned to other things did it depart, or resume another shape. And with my Companion, there will be no need for focusing my faculties elsewhere. She, and she alone, will be the recipient of everything my mind, my heart, my soul possesses. If will, if sentiment, if love are needed to preserve her, these things she shall have in entirety. So there is nothing to fear. Nothing to fear. . . .

Once again now I shall lay my pen aside and return to the great task—the task of "creation," if you will—and I shall not fail. The fear (I admit it!) of loneliness is enough to drive me forward to unimaginable brinks. She, and she alone, can save me, shall save me, *must* save me! I can see her now—the golden glitter of her—and my consciousness calls to her to rise, to appear before me in radiant reality. Somewhere upon these storm-tossed seas she *exists*, I know it—and wherever she may be, my call will come to her and she will respond.

Jan. 31.

The command came at midnight. Roused from the depths of the most profound innermost communion by a thunderclap, I rose as though in the grip of somnambulistic compulsion and moved down the spiral stairs.

The lantern I bore trembled in my hand; its light wavered in the wind, and the very iron treads beneath my feet shook with the furious force of the storm. The booming of the waves as they struck the lighthouse walls seemed to place me within the center of a maelstrom of ear-shattering sound, yet over the demoniacal din I could detect the frenzied howls of poor Neptune as I passed the door behind which he was confined. The door shook with the combined force of the wind and of his still desperate efforts to free himself—but I hastened on my way, descending to the iron door at the base of the lighthouse.

To open it required the use of both hands, and I set the lantern down at one side. To open it, moreover, required the summoning of a resolution I scarcely possessed—for beyond that door was the force and fury of the wildest storm that ever shrieked across these seething seas. A sudden wave might dash me from the doorway, or, conversely, enter and inundate the lighthouse itself.

But consciousness prevailed; consciousness drove me forward.

I *knew*, I thrilled to the certainty that *she* was without the iron portal—I unbolted the door with the urgency of one who rushes into the arms of his beloved.

The door swung open—blew open—roared open—and the storm burst upon me; a ravening monster of black-mouthed waves capped with white fangs. The sea and sky surged forward as if to attack, and I stood enveloped in chaos. A flash of lightning revealed the immensity of utter nightmare.

I saw it not, for the same flash illumined the form, the lineaments of *she* whom I sought.

Lightning and lantern were unneeeded—her golden glory outshone all as she stood there, pale and trembling, a goddess arisen from the depths of the sea!

Hallucination, vision, apparition? My trembling fingers sought, and found, their answer. Her flesh was real—cold as the icy waters from whence she came, but palpable and permanent. I thought of the storm, of doomed ships and drowning men, of a girl cast upon the waters and struggling toward the succor of the lighthouse beacon. I thought of a thousand explanations, a thousand miracles, a thousand riddles or reasons beyond rationality. Yet only one thing mattered—my Companion was here, and I had but to step forward and take her in my arms.

No word was spoken, nor could one be heard in all that inferno. No word was needed, for she smiled. Pale lips parted as I held out my arms, and she moved closer. Pale lips parted—and I saw the pointed teeth, set in rows like those of a shark. Her eyes, fishlike and staring, swam closer. As I recoiled, her arms came up to cling, and they were cold as the waters beneath, cold as the storm, cold as death.

In one monstrous moment I *knew*, knew with uttermost

certainty, that the power of my will had indeed summoned, the call of my consciousness *had* been answered. But the answer came not from the living, for nothing lived in this storm. I had sent my will out over the waters, but the will penetrates all dimensions, and my answer had come from *below* the waters. *She* was from below, where the drowned dead lie dreaming, and I had awakened her and clothed her with a horrid life. A life that thirsted, and must drink. . . .

I think I shrieked, then, but I heard no sound. Certainly, I did not hear the howls from Neptune as the beast, burst from his prison, bounded down the stairs and flung himself upon the creature.

His furry form bore her back and obscured my vision; in an instant she was falling backward, away, into the sea that spawned her. Then, and only then, did I catch a glimpse of the final moment of animation in that which my consciousness had summoned. Lightning seared the sight inexorably upon my soul—the sight of the ultimate blasphemy I had created in my pride. The rose had wilted. . . .

The rose had wilted and become seaweed. And now, the golden one was gone and in its place was the bloated, swollen obscenity of a thing long-drowned and dead, risen from the slime and to that slime returning.

Only a moment, and then the waves overwhelmed it, bore it back into the blackness. Only a moment, and the door was slammed shut. Only a moment, and I raced up the iron stairs, Neptune yammering at my heels. Only a moment, and I reached the safety of this sanctuary.

Safety? There is no safety in the universe for me, no safety in a consciousness that could create such horror. And there is no safety here—the wrath of the waves increases with every moment, the anger of the sea and its creatures rises to an inevitable crescendo.

Mad or sane, it does not matter, for the end is the same

in either case. I know now that the lighthouse will shatter and fall. I am already shattered, and must fall with it.

There is time only to gather these notes, strap them securely in a cylinder and attach it to Neptune's collar. It may be that he can swim, or cling to a fragment of debris. It may be that a ship, passing by this toppling beacon, may stay and search the waters for a sign—and thus find and rescue the gallant beast.

That ship shall not find me. I go with the lighthouse and go willingly, down to the dark depths. Perhaps—is it but perverted poetry?—I shall join my Companion there forever. Perhaps . . .

The lighthouse is trembling. The beacon flickers above my head and I hear the rush of waters in their final onslaught. There is—yes—a wave, bearing down upon me. It is higher than the tower, it blots out the sky itself, everything. . . .

Scholars concede that there may very well exist a number of Edgar Allan Poe items published anonymously or under a pseudonym in forgotten and obscure papers or periodicals. New additions to the works of Poe are generally bits and pieces of literary criticism or inconsequential poetic doggerel that are finally validated as being from his pen.

Among the most interesting of the possibilities that scholars have roped off for perusal is a seventy-thousand-word Utopia titled "The Atlantis" which appeared in a monthly periodical, *The American Museum of Science, Literature and the Arts*, published in Baltimore, in the issues of September 1838 to June 1839 inclusive. The full title of the piece is "The Atlantis. A Southern World,—or a Wonderful Continent,—discovered in the great Southern Ocean, and supposed to be the Atlantis of Plato, or the Terra Australis Incognita of Dr. Swift, during a voyage conducted by Alonzo Pinzon, Commander of the American Metal Ship Astrea."

Despite its length, the work was never completed, probably because the magazine ceased publication with the June 1839 number. Or conceivably it was actually intended to be a permanent feature, to be used as a vehicle for promulgating the author's views on science, philosophy, politics, customs, religion, cults, and whatever else came into his mind.

Chapter 12 of Arthur Hobson Quinn's *Edgar Allan Poe* is devoted to itemizing the internal evidence that prompts scholars to believe that if Poe did not actually write the work in its entirety, he may have had a hand in revision because of the quantity of Poe-related subjects. Quinn reprints a portion of the work relating to "Rinosophia, or Nose-Ology," and contrasts it with similar lines in "Lionizing" (*Southern Literary Messenger*, May 1835), which are indeed close. At the time that "The Atlantis" was serialized, Poe was in the Baltimore area and a regular contributor to the *American Museum;* his works for the magazine included "Ligeia" (September 1838), "Psyche Zenobia" (November 1838), "The Scythe of Time" (November 1838), and "The Haunted Palace" (April 1839). His small production the years 1838 and 1839 could be rationalized if this novel-length piece was attributed to him.

Quinn attaches especial significance to the lengthy references to Martinus and Cornelius Scriblerus in the text, because he can establish that Poe was acquainted with the *Memoirs of Martin Scriblerus* co-authored by John Arbuthnot, Jonathan Swift, and Alexander Pope, for Poe used a quotation from that work in "Psyche Zenobia," published concurrently with "The Atlantis."

Some of the scientific discussions are shown to bear a relationship to the early portions of Poe's "Eureka." Animal magnetism, balloon voyages to the moon, craniology, and other subjects which Poe had a strong interest in are discussed in passing or at length.

Not mentioned, but certainly obvious to Quinn, was the fact that the nom de plume employed in writing the piece, Prospero, was also used as the name of the lead character, Prince Prospero, in "The Masque of the Red Death" (*Graham's Lady's and Gentleman's Magazine,* May 1842). Still further, the opening of the story, with its imaginative trip to the Antarctic in a magnetically powered ship capable of twenty knots an hour, along with its references to mesmerism, is in line with the Poe tradition. So are horseless carriages and a sky full of "floating balloons of all dimensions, that seemed to advance by voluntary effort toward every point of the compass."

There is another point in question. Despite the serious discussions contained in "The Atlantis," satiric humor pervades it all. For some reason, in all the scholarly tomes on Poe, one never seems to run across a chapter titled: "Edgar Allan Poe: Humorist." For humorist he undoubtedly was, at times a very clever one. From his earliest writing almost until the time of his death, he never ceased to pour out comic short stories and articles, some of them absolute slapstick. Perhaps because it does not fit in with a presentation of the onrushing tragedy of his life or the mood of his greatest works, there has been a tendency to push his humor aside rather than come to grips with the paradox of this obsession with satire and comedy. Yet its presence identifies Poe as much as does the dark spectral insight.

The first four chapters of "The Atlantis" are reprinted here, as far as is known for the first time since their original publication in 1839. They make up a remarkable sequence, important to the history of science fiction and the Utopia, whether they were written by Poe or not. The early chapter is straight adventure that might have come out of "The Narrative of A. Gordon Pym," a relation of pioneering into the unexplored Antarctic wastes with the latest scientific marvel in sea transportation. The collapse of all members of the ship as it passes through a transference zone into the realm of Saturnia, the lost city of the Antarctic, to be saved only by the unprecedented speed of the ship, was first-rate science fiction for its time.

The second chapter, "Our arrival at Saturnia" is Utopian writing in the classic tradition, describing the nomenclature and outward appearance of the newly discovered or lost land or city.

The third chapter, "My removal to a Hotel," finds the transition of the story from a basic Utopia to a serious fantasy in a Utopian setting, as it is discovered that apparently all the great men of history are reincarnated here when they die and that the author now has access to them.

Chapter 4, "My Meeting with Dr. Franklin, and the proceedings of the Philosophical Society," finds the author, on the advice of Benjamin Franklin, attending a scientific session at which Descartes, Galileo, Aristotle, Leibnitz, Halley, Bacon, and Maupertuis give their views on astronomy, space, time, the structure of the universe, and other matters of special interest.

There were fifteen chapters in all, covering the entire gamut of human existence, and when the fifteenth chapter closed, so had a discussion on religion, and Peter Prospero was left in Saturnia, apparently in a sort of durance vile forever. The quality of the writing is notable, and for those who wonder whatever became of the previously mentioned reference to Nose-ology and Mr. Scriblerus, they appeared in Chapter 14, published in the January 1839 issue of the publication, and were inserted into the text almost like extraneous essays. They may be found in Arthur Hobson Quinn's *Edgar Allan Poe*, as illustrative excerpts. For the space buffs, space travel was referred to in Chapter 13, where Prospero is shown a variety of inventions, including ". . . a balloon so constructed as to mount to any height, and even ascend to the moon."

All the foregoing would make a pretty convincing and exciting case for "The Atlantis" having been penned in whole or part by Edgar Allan Poe—except for one thing. The late authority on Edgar Allan Poe, professor Thomas Ollive Mabbott, was skeptical, and Arthur Hobson Quinn, having also departed this mortal coil, is no longer around either to defend or concede the point, though he probably is now frantically gesticulating from Saturnia.

Well, if Poe didn't write it, to whom did Professor Mabbott credit authorship?

He was very precise on that score. It was his opinion that "The Atlantis" was written by Nathan Covington Brooks, one of the editors of the *American Museum,* and a teacher of Latin and Greek in Baltimore. Brooks, he informed us, was a very close friend, admirer, and comrade of Edgar Allan Poe. They saw each other frequently, and Brooks would have read virtually every scrap of material written by Poe. What is more, they would have discussed the concepts between them. The admiration that Brooks had for Poe's ideas would have made it possible that he adopted many of them.

Mabbott had no conclusive documentary evidence, but was personally convinced that Brooks was responsible for the serialized philosophical discourse. This, of course, does not rule out Poe's contribution of ideas or dabbling in the essays, and even editing portions of the manuscript.

There you have it. Arthur Hobson Quinn and Professor Thomas Ollive Mabbott, two of the greatest Poe scholars of all time, leaned in different directions on the authorship of "The Atlantis." Read the chapters presented here, which accurately present the flavor of the work, and make your own decision as to which school of thought you incline toward.

The Atlantis

by Peter Prospero, L.L.D.; M.A.; P.S.

> *A Southern World,—or a Wonderful Continent,—dis-*
> *covered in the great Southern Ocean, and supposed*
> *to be the Atlantis of Plato, or the Terra Australis In-*
> *cognita of Dr. Swift, during a voyage conducted by*
> *Alonzo Pinzon, Commander of the American Metal*
> *Ship Astrea.*

> Salve, magna Parens frugum, Saturnia Tellus!
> Magna virum; tibi res antiquæ laudis et artis,
> Ingredior, sanctos ausus recludere fontes.
>
> VIRGIL.

CHAPTER I.

The origin of my enterprise.

As I am undertaking, gentle reader, to give thee an account, if not of a circumnavigation of the globe, at least of the most singular voyage, and most wonderful discovery ever made in the world, not excepting that of Columbus, it is but due courtesy, to gratify thy rational curiosity by informing thee of that process of thought and reasoning by which I was led to the conception of the bold and sublime enterprise. Know, then, that from my earliest years, my ruling passion has been a desire after knowledge, and my whole time has been sedulously devoted to study and reflection. I had the happiness to be born in the state of North Carolina, one of the southern divisions of our great republic, and to be descended from Anglo-Saxon ancestors. My parents, who were not without a relish of elegant literature, and a strong conviction of the immense advantages of education, allowed an unrestrained indulgence of my ardent propensity for reading. Whether, therefore, I was stationed in winter at the domestic fireside, or in summer under the shade of a tree, amidst the bustle of a schoolroom, or in the quiet seclusion of collegiate life, my book was always my most constant companion, and the best classical productions in Greek, Latin, English and French, were successively perused with rapture. In pursuit of science, I was not contented with that superficial knowledge which seems to satiate the desires and terminate the labors of too many votaries of literature, at the present day; but when I undertook the investigation of any particular branch, I endeavoured to penetrate to its lowest foundations, fathom all its depths and compass its most extended boundaries. Instead of wasting the powers of my understanding in attaining a partial acquaintance with every branch of science, and learning to talk volubly and write plausibly about every topic of polite learning, after that rapid glance at the whole circle which is comprised in a collegiate course, I aimed at a thorough mastery of the few to which I seemed to be most strongly prompted by natural inclination, and acquired habits of thinking and enjoyment. Through this process, I essayed to whet into the keenest edge of discernment, and address the native faculties of my mind, and communicate to them all the energy and perspicuity of which they were susceptible. And I avail myself of this opportunity to remark, that this appears to me to be the only method of study by which the minds of men can be successfully cultured and useful attainments made; and, on these accounts, is to be most earnestly recommended to all the cultivators of learning and aspirants after excellence in the elegant and useful arts.

During the prosecution of my studies and the perusal of ancient and modern authors, I had remarked, that no theologians or writers of history and antiquities, had ever been able to determine in what portion of our globe was situated the Ultima Thule of the classic authors, or the land of Ophir, from which large quantities of gold were imported into Palestine in the time of Solomon. Some supposed this valuable treasure to have been derived from the east, and others from the west, some from Spain, and others from Africa, some from Britain, and others from regions still more remote than England, in the north of Europe. In the *Timaeus* and other works of Plato, I found it stated as a fact, that when Pythagoras was in Egypt, he was told by her learned men of a large and populous island, denominated Atlantis, which lay in the Western Ocean, and had been inhabited by a great and powerful nation, long anterior to the commencement of Grecian history. When to these distinct and significant indications, denoting the existence of some wonderful community in the southern and western world, I added the typical, but satisfactory allusion to it in the authentic memoirs of the "Tale of a Tub," by Doctor Swift, in which he maintains that there lies in that direction an immense continent, designated as the "Terra Australis Incognita," which had been cantoned into various departments by Lord Peter, and advantageously sold to successive emigrants, all of whom were shipwrecked on their passage. I came to a definitive conclusion, that the voyages of Columbus and his rivals in navigation, had not completed the discoveries to be made in the Southern Hemisphere. It appeared evident to my mind, that some continent or large island, distinguished by wonderful peculiarities, and inhabited by a remarkable people, remained to be explored by the enterprise and perseverance of the inquisitive and skilful. By frequently revolving these reflections in my mind, a kind of presentiment was awakened, that I should become the projector and executor of a great undertaking by which a new world, more extraordinary than America, would be revealed to mankind, and those hitherto impassable barriers surmounted which preclude our access to the Southern and Northern Pole.

After first conceiving the hint upon this important subject, my imagination brooded over the enterprise until at length I became so inflamed with enthusiasm, that in the year 1835, I resolved no longer to procrastinate the period of its commencement. Accordingly, having an ample fortune at my disposal, I knew of no method by which I could more usefully devote it to the service of my fellow-men, than in making preparation for this voyage of discovery. The first question which recurred that was difficult of solution, related to the best means to be adopted in order to navigate successfully and safely, the Polar regions of the south. As I had seen all the expeditions to the north fitted out by British liberality for similar purposes, defeated, or limited in their success, by the extreme cold of those climates, I had concluded, that if ever the Polar seas were explored, it must be by steam ships, or some mode of navigation which is preferable to these. About this time was suggested the idea of constructing wheels which would move of themselves, and transport the largest carriages or boats by the influence of the magnet and its tendency to attract iron. I seized upon this suggestion with the utmost avidity, and after many experiments made with captain Pinzon, a lineal descendant of the celebrated companion of Columbus, and animated by the same spirit which displayed itself in that great navigator, we came to the conclusion, that a vessel might be propelled in this way, not only with more safety, but with greater velocity, then had ever before been witnessed upon the ocean. Captain Pinzon was now commissioned to select skilful workmen and a master mechanic, who should immediately commence the structure of our

magnetic ship, and after various delays, occasioned by difficulties in collecting the materials, procuring provisions and
seamen for the voyage, accumulating a small but select
library, and philosophical apparatus for our entertainment
upon the passage, we found ourselves upon the banks of
Trent River, near Newbern, in North Carolina, ready to
take our departure, upon the 4th of July, 1836. After cele-
brating this great anniversary of our independence with our
fellow-citizens, amidst the greatest hilarity, and partaking
of its festivity with a zest we had never before experienced,
we departed in the afternoon amidst the benedictions of
numerous friends and the acclamations of the multitude.
Seeming to proceed by magical influence, we soon passed,
at the rate of twenty miles an hour, through Pamlico sound
and Ocracoke bar into the Atlantic Ocean. Our ship, which
was about the size of the boats that ply their courses in the
Delaware and the Hudson, moved majestically through the
deep, and appeared to claim the homage which is due to
to the great genius of Fulton, to whose exertions are mankind indebted not only for the invention of the steamboat,
but for all those improvements in navigation and locomo-
tion which shall arise out of it. Proceeding at the rate of
fifteen or twenty, and when aided by winds and currents,
thirty miles an hour, we soon reached the extremity of the
United States, entered the gulf of Mexico, stopt for amusement at Havanna, thence proceeded along the coast of
South America, and soon found ourselves at the mouth of
the great river La Plata. Intending to avail ourselves of the
whole warmth afforded by the sun upon its return from
the equator towards the southern Tropic, we remained in the
delightful climate of Buenos Ayres, enjoying the hospitality
of the inhabitants and the admiration bestowed upon our
curious invention, until the beginning of October, at which
time we renewed our voyage with favourable auspices, and
under the most exulting hopes. From this period nothing
occurred which is worthy of record, until passing by Terra

del Fuego and Cape Horn, we had directed our course due south to the sixtieth degree of south latitude. Here our thermometer, which had hitherto denoted a temperate warmth, began rapidly to descend, and we were encountered by masses of floating ice which rendered our progess difficult and precarious. Before we reached the sixty-fifth degree of latitude, we saw at various distances those immense icebergs, which it required all our address and skill to avoid, which rendered some miles circuit necessary to compass them, and from the irresistible force of which, we were repeatedly involved in the greatest danger. In this conflict with icebergs, however, we found the full advantage of our new and voluntary mode of navigation. Being able to advance or recede at our pleasure, we eluded the attacks of these formidable enemies, and in spite of cold, storms and tempests, advanced triumphantly on our way, until in latitude seventy, when Fahrenheit's thermometer stood at 30° below zero, and we began to sink into despair, a series of phenomena were presented totally unknown to science and in the highest degree interesting to the philosophical observer. From a region of intense and intolerable cold and tempestuous weather, we were transported to a thick and murky atmosphere, in the gloomy and darkened state of which, we found respiration difficult, all our senses seemed disordered, and through the gloom every frightful and fantastic form floated that could be conceived as crude and monstrous. During our passage through this tract of ocean, all our usual prescriptions were suspended, and we sank into what appeared an incurable slumber, or deliquium. How long we continued in this anomalous state of being, it was impossible to calculate. But as the ship, from her peculiar construction, continued her course with the usual velocity, we soon found ourselves aroused from this lethargic and painful condition, and wafted into a region in which the air was not only respirable, but inconceivably soft and bland, and the light more sweet and serene than we had ever before beheld. The whole ocean and sky seemed now to beam with a smile as enrapturing as any idea we can form of heaven. From the facts which I have just stated, captain Pinzon and I agreed in the inference, that the reason why no navigators in these waters, have ever explored the country whose wonders I shall now unfold, is, either that they have been deterred from advancing through the icy regions before described, or that when they came into this air at first irrespirable by human organs, they have perished under its influence, inasmuch as the vessels in which they voyaged, not borne forward as ours by the new contrivance, have been arrested in their progress, and thus left them without the power of revival. Let captain Wilks, the commander of the squadron just despatched to these regions by the American government, and his assistant officers, who are to conduct this exploration of the South Seas, to whom we have communicated these facts, take warning from our experience, and be upon their guard against fatal disasters, when they shall pass beyond the latitude of seventy degrees south. Should they be able safely to pass over this irrespirable tract of ocean, all the wonders and glories of Saturnia, will be revealed to them.

CHAPTER II.

Our arrival at Saturnia.

No sooner had we been aroused from the state of unconsciousness, which was mentioned in our last chapter, than we seemed to be awakened into a new and more rapturous existence, and wafted into an elysian or Paradisal scene. When thoroughly revived from our temporary slumber, our minds and bodies had undergone a renovation, all the senses had become more acute and susceptible of pleasure, and all the perceptions of the understanding more clear,

satisfactory and enlivening. In this state of untried enjoyment, the vicissitudes of which had excited superstitious
alarms in some of our crew, and the most sanguine expectations in others, we continued our course due south, not
doubting that our labours would at length be crowned with
the most signal results. We had proceeded in this direction
but a few hours longer, when to our equal astonishment,
admiration and delight, we descried land, and soon found
that we were approaching the mouth of a noble river, like
the Hudson, through which vessels moving like our own and
magnificently constructed, were passing and repassing, at
once apprising us of our vicinity to a large capital. Upon
each side of this river, at its mouth, which appeared about
two miles wide, were stationed two superb light-houses to
guide mariners in the night, and in the stream were placed
luminous buoys extending several feet above the surface,
which prevented the navigator from deviating out of the
channel. Upon entering the river, we perceived on each
side a finely cultivated country, neat but commodious farm-
houses, magnificent dwellings, beautiful lawns and gardens
laid out in the chastest simplicity and most correct taste,
and altogether a country in which the allied arts of agricul-
ture, commerce and manufacture had exerted their utmost
skill in advancing it to the highest state of improvement and
perfection. While regaling ourselves with this sight, and con-
templating this delightful residence for man, what was our
emotion, when after plying our course about two miles farther within the land, we were ushered into a spacious bay,
and the vast panorama of the capital city and its environs,
its magnificent buildings, its hills, mountains, valleys and
superb monuments of art, were presented to our vision?
Vessels and boats of every size and various figures were glid-
ing in every direction through the bay and rivers, while the
wharves were thickly crowded with others loading and un-
loading—innumerable houses appeared to crown the sum-
mits of the hills and hang upon their declivities, the streets

were arranged with mathematical exactitude, of spacious dimensions and shaded with beautiful trees, at the same time that numerous streams intersected the city, all the parts of which were connected by durable and splendid bridges, that in their construction, indicated the highest progress in the arts. Over our heads were floating balloons of all dimensions, that seemed to advance by voluntary effort towards every point of the compass. As far as our sight extended, we saw the steeples of the churches, towers erected for various purposes, a college and observatory, more lofty than we had ever beheld, and whose tops appeared at the moment, to be lost amidst the clouds. Such a vast and sublime assemblage of objects, at once bursting upon our view, seemed to present to us the image of the New Jerusalem, as depicted in the Revelations, and threw me into an ecstasy of enjoyment, from which I did not recover until under the guidance of captain Pinzon. Our ship was safely fastened to the wharf of that town, to which we afterwards discovered the inhabitants had affixed the name of Saturnia, the capital city of the republic of Atlantis.

CHAPTER III.

My removal to a Hotel.

Nothing could exceed the astonishment which was excited by our arrival at Saturnia; the wharf was soon crowded with innumerable spectators, wondering by what contingency we could have escaped the perils of the deep, and have performed so unheard-of a voyage, and the news of this strange event spread rapidly to the remotest quarters of the town—I was equally surprised at the novelty of the objects now presented to my observation, the neatness and elegance of the place, as well as the decency, order and regularity with which every thing seemed to be conducted. The men and women presented the most comely and well-proportioned figures I had ever beheld and were remarkably well dressed; the wharves and houses, constructed of the best stone and marble, were truly magnificent, and the streets, promenades, arbours, parks and pleasure grounds, seemed to be laid out with all the taste and judgment which could be displayed in the workmanship of the most enlightened and scientific artisans and mechanics.—Not a vessel with sails floated within view, and the whole business of commerce and navigation is here conducted by vessels and boats which like our own, moved spontaneously through the waters. Here was more than realized, the bold declaration of Fitch, an ingenious mechanic of New-Jersey, who, above a half a century ago, predicted to the legislature of that state, that not only would our rivers be navigated by steam, but, that, finally, all commerce and trade between the different nations of the earth would be carried on by this method of communication. I cannot adequately describe the impressions made upon my mind by this singular and wonderful scene. I was rapt into a reverie, or rather an ecstasy of delight—the very air of the place appeared to be unusually pure and ethereal, the sun shone with a more serene splendour, and the heavens seemed to shed around us more select influences. Into what kind of country and climate, I inwardly ejaculated, have I been transported? To ascertain this, I was now impelled by irresistible curiosity, and my anticipation of the pleasure which awaited me, in this unexpected condition of being, arose to the highest pitch of enthusiasm.

My next step was to make efforts to disembark, and obtain an agreeable place of residence in the city. Calling for a porter, to bear my trunks and baggage to the most approved hotel, several men of this order immediately presented themselves, who, from the conversation which passed between them I learned were called by the names of Nero, Tiberius, Borgia, and Ravaillac,—what mean these appellations? I exclaimed with surprise. These are names to which

I have become familiarized in history, and nothing to the credit of the persons who bore them, but I never before had the honour of a personal acquaintance with those notorious gentlemen. Are those titles given you in derision, or by way of punishment for any offences you may have committed in this extraordinary world, into which I have been so unexpectedly introduced? These are the names we bore, replied they, holding down their heads, in our former state of being, that world from which, we presume, you have just arrived, and we are but too glad to exercise our present vocations, since we have just been released from very severe punishments to which we were condemned for the parts we performed in our former state of being. Is it possible, I rejoined, and pray, in what city and country am I now to consider myself; for, it seems to me, as if all that is passing before my eyes, are but disturbed visions of the night. Oh! sir, replied Nero, this is the city of Saturnia and country of Atlantis, the most outlandish and detestable abode that ever gentlemen were constrained to inhabit: all things are sadly altered since those glorious days when I and Tiberius were emperours in Rome. To distribute justice, as they call it, emperours, kings, popes, cardinals, lords, bishops, and all the great men of former times, are here condemned to the most ignominious punishments, and then compelled to labour on the highways or become porters, waiters, lackeys, carmen, and servants. Now, it might be right to deal in this manner with thieves, robbers, murderers, and villains, among the vile populace, but thus to humble, torment, and trample upon men of high rank and distinction, is intolerable. This singular conversation threw me into a train of profound study and rapt reflection; and I perceived that I had, indeed, reached a land of miracles. What inestimable advantages, thought I, would it be to mankind, did they know that besides that future state which is revealed in Scripture, they would have to pass through such a condition of being—such an intermediate dispensation of good and evil as they find here. In this frame of mind I followed Nero and Tiberius through several squares of the town, until we arrived at the hotel of which we were in quest. This was a magnificent building, constructed with remarkable simplicity and elegance; all the rooms and appurtenances of which were admirably adapted to the convenience and accommodation of travellers and guests. I took possession of one of the best furnished rooms, and determined as soon as possible to commence those inquiries in regard to the government, laws, institutions, manners, religion, science, literature, and arts, of this extraordinary people, of which a full account shall be given in the following chapters.

CHAPTER IV.

My meeting with Dr. Franklin, and the proceedings of the Philosophical Society.

After taking supper I retired to my room to obtain repose, and although from the agitation of my spirits, and extreme excitement of mind, I found some difficulty in composing myself to rest, yet at length I found in that temporary suspension of thought, which takes place in sleep, the relief and refreshment which my exhausted nature required. Upon waking in the morning, and being summoned to breakfast, it is impossible to describe my sensations when I discovered seated at the table by my side the old and valued friend of my father, Dr. Franklin, upon whose knees I had been oftentimes dandled in early life, in whose society I had been intimate, and for whose character I had always entertained unbounded veneration and sincere attachment. He soon recognized me; and after the warmest salutations, we entered into an interesting conversation, and he promised to introduce me to the acquaintance of the most celebrated men with whom the city of Saturnia abounds. Here, said he, are assembled the great and good of all ages and nations; they unite the labours of their genius in the structure of science, and the perfection of literature and the arts. Thus they improve the happiness of the human family—bringing with them the wisdom and learning they had accumulated during the limited term of their residence in the lower world, as we here denominate it, they have been adding to their stores of knowledge from age to age. At length, they have attained an elevation in science which is truly wonderful. Here, he continued, with increasing vehemence, here genius of all kinds meets a sure and ample reward—here every motive is furnished to stimulate the human mind into honourable and useful exertion. In this admirable republic you will discover no traces of an unequal distribution of good and evil, of rewards and punishments. Here the clouds that formerly hung over the ways of heaven are gradually dispersed, and its justice shines in its native lustre. Here, as far as human fallibility allows, rank, dignity, and station, are equally conferred upon talents and worth, and virtue becomes, in practice, the only true nobility. All vices are adequately punished, all errours and disorders rectified, and all virtues raised and rewarded. In short, he concluded, this is the state of things, after which in the former world, the philanthropist aspired, the patriot toiled, and the hero encountered sufferings and death, while its ideal image occupied the meditations of philosophers, the visions of poets, and the hopes of Christians. Franklin here appeared animated by an enthusiasm which I had never before seen in him, and I caught the infection from his lips. Our conversation became more and more frank, cordial, and interesting, and the interview terminated in his informing me, that as he knew my devotion to scientific and literary pursuits, he would call upon me in the evening, and begin the task of introducing me to the illustrious men of the republic, by taking me to the hall of the Philosophical Society, and giving me an opportunity of attending to their debates, and witnessing their proceedings. In order to the advancement of science in this city, said he, we have instituted societies whose labors are to be severally appropriated to the branches from which they receive their designation. Thus the Philosophical Society, of which I have just spoken, is exclusively occupied with the departments of natural philosophy and mathematics, the Metaphysical Society with the science of the mind, the Institute of Moral Philosophy with ethics, and the Literary Society with the cultivation of literature. There are also, for similar purposes, theological, medical, chemical, geological and botanical associations, as well as institutes of natural history and political economy, together with an academy of arts. I thanked him cordially for the information which he had been so good as to communicate, and expressed the pleasure I anticipated from our projected visit to the society in the evening.

After taking leave of Dr. Franklin for the time, I passed the morning in riding through the city in a vehicle like an omnibus, which by the same philosophical contrivance as that by which they propelled their vessels, seemed self-moving, and which advanced along the smooth pavement with admirable safety and velocity. I found the streets wide, and beautifully paved with smooth stones, and sidewalks of marble; the houses neat and magnificent, but built in a style of the greatest simplicity, and the inhabitants elegantly clad, but without useless or excessive decoration. When I had ascended the greatest elevations, I came to a square, in which was situated an observatory five hundred feet high, with which is connected the building in whose halls the several philosophical societies hold their sittings, while in the adjoining streets were neat and commodious dwellings, constructed in the several orders of architecture, for all the most celebrated philosophers of ancient and modern times. Here dwelt by each other's side, Newton, Locke, Bacon, Kepler, Gallileo, Gassindi, and the whole list of those who had cultivated natural philosophy, and in due order, came those who had distinguished themselves in the other branches of science. When I cast my eyes over this sublime scene, and beheld in these residences so many monuments reared to the greatest geniuses of the world and benefactors of their race, I could not convince myself that I was not dreaming. In passing forward through other parts of the city, we next beheld still more magnificent structures, erected as the residences of the President of the republic and the different officers of the Government, who were elevated to their present situations on account of their former talents, virtues, and public services. Tyrants and conquerors, and all who had proved themselves traitors to their country and enemies of the human race, those scourges of the nations, were condemned to the most ignominious punishments, while Cicero, Cato, Titus, and the Antonines, Alfred, Henry the Fourth of France, Washington, and several of our Presidents, with a long list of others, who had been raised to the chair of supreme magistracy. Of these state officers, however, we shall give a more detailed account in the sequel, confining our attention at first to the scientific and literary institutions.

At the appointed hour in the evening Dr. Franklin, according to promise, called in his carriage at my hotel, and took me to the meeting of the Philosophical Society. We were introduced into a large hall, brilliantly illuminated, in which was presented to me a scene which all attempts to describe would be unavailing, but which threw me into a tumult of delightful emotion. At the upper end of the hall upon an elevated seat, sat Newton, who presided this evening in his turn, although the same honour was shared in rotation with Kepler, Copernicus, Tycho Brahe, Gallileo, Des Cartes, La Place, Franklin, Rittenhouse, and all the most illustrious in this department of science. There was a large assemblage upon this occasion; and the gallery was filled with celebrated ladies, some of whom were honorary members, and were allowed the privilege of having their communications read to the society, when they had been previously examined and approved by a standing committee, appointed for that purpose. The secretary at this time was the great Huygins, the inventor of the clock, who, I was told, had filled this office after Archimedes, Pythagoras, Dr. Halley, La Grange, and others. The first production which was read was written by Des Cartes, and consisted of an inquiry into the cause of gravitation, and the motions of the heavenly bodies. The process of reasoning by which Des Cartes endeavored to reach a definite conclusion upon this topic, was in substance the following: He remarked that there was a sufficient ground for the opinion that, in every part of nature, whether found in the earth or heavens, there were the same agents exerting their forces, and the same primordial principles or materials upon which they operate. Thus the motions of the heavenly bodies are, in all probability, produced by the same agent as that by which the sap is made to rise in the tree, the air is set in motion, the fuel consumed in the grate, and the vicissitudes of the seasons are occasioned. Now, this universal agent he maintained to be the electric fluid, pervading the whole system of nature, and reaching to the very centre of the sun and planets, and constituting what Newton conjectured to be a thin elastic medium that might be the cause of gravity. In confirmation of this theory, he referred us to a new planetarium, which he had erected in one of the halls of the observatory, in which he had contrived within a brazen sphere of forty feet diameter, to exhibit all the movements of the planetary system produced by the action of the electric fluid collected in it.

After Des Cartes had finished the reading of his communication, I thought I could perceive in the silence of the members a rather ominous signal of incredulity and dissatisfaction with the principle propounded in it, and the experiment by which their truth was tested. In a few moments, however, a member dressed with unusual elegance, of a Grecian physiognomy, noble countenance, and penetrating eye, who, Dr. Franklin informed me, was Aristotle, arose and proposed to refer the subject to the consideration of a committee consisting of three members, appointed by the president, and exclusively devoted to this branch of science; and in consequence Newton nominated Gallileo, La Place, and Dr. Franklin.

The next contribution was a dissertation by Gallileo, in which he balanced the arguments in regard to the two theories concerning light, the one maintaining, that light emanates from the sun as its source, the other, that light as a medium, is diffused through universal nature, and that the sun is the exciting cause which sets its particles in action, and renders objects visible. To the latter of these opinions, Gallileo seemed disposed to adhere. To make report upon this topic, a committee of three were appointed, as chairman of which, at the suggestion of Dr. Halley, Newton was placed, while his two colleagues were Aristotle and Leibnitz. While this affair was on the tapis, Aristotle took occasion to remark, that his doctrine concerning light had been greatly misunderstood by some of his commentators and interpreters, they supposing that he had asserted this fluid to be a property of bodies, while he had strenuously maintained its distinct subsistence as a medium by the action of which upon the senses, objects are rendered visible. He allowed that a very serious objection to the doctrine of its emanation from the sun, is the inconceivable velocity with which under this scheme, it is presumed to travel from that luminary to the earth, and through all the regions of space.

A third piece was read by the great Leibnitz, the Newton of Germany, in which he proposed to ascertain upon philosophical principles whether the same laws of production, decay, and dissolution to which all animal and vegetable nature are liable upon this earth, are also applicable to the planetary system, and whether that system does not contain within itself the seeds of its own perpetual revivescence and renovation, insomuch that it can come to destruction only by the fiat of that Omnipotence who created it? In this treatise, Leibnitz held, that the system of nature maintains, at all times, an invariable identity, that the same materials are always comprised within its sphere, the same forces exerted, and the same laws prevalent. That while some of the minuter parts rise, decay and perish, or rather undergo a dissolution, the whole remains unchangeable and eternal, dissolvable only by Him who gave existence to it, and moreover, inasmuch as the immutable attributes of God would prevent him from utterly destroying so beautiful a system as the Solar, it never can and never will be destroyed. In vindicating this doctrine from what some might regard as its hostility to revelation, he maintained that the dogma of the gospel in relation to the great catastrophe of the world, does not imply the destruction, but some grand renovation, or transfiguration which the system is to undergo prior to the appearance of that new heaven and new earth which is to be the consummation of the present order of things. This treatise was referred to the examination of Bacon, Locke and M. Pascal.

After these treatises were disposed of, Dr. Halley read a short disquisition by Newton, in which he essayed to demonstrate the existence of God from the wise adjustments and select laws indicative of contrivance in the planetary system. This was referred to the consideration of Cicero, Paley and Sir Robert Boyle.

Lord Bacon, next, read a tract intended to prove the utter fallacy, and incompatibility with the true method of philosophizing, of all attempts to ascertain the mode in which the universe is formed, or the process by which it originated, and has continued to advance to its present state. He threw the whole assembly into repeated flashes of merriment, when he exposed to contempt and ridicule, the dancing atoms of Democritus and Epicurus, the whirling vortices of

Des Cartes and the still more whimsical theory of the Count de Buffon, who ascribed the formation of planets to the concussions of comets against the sun, and in their eccentric movements, striking off fragments from this orb. Nor did he treat with much less severity, the schemes of Burnet and his followers, and of those numerous philosophical romancers who imagine that they can trace the earth to an aqueous or incandescent state, and amidst the various forms of its fossil remains, both in the animal and vegetable kingdoms, presume to discover indications of progressive stages in improvement, during the successive generations of men and animals. Bacon maintained in this treatise, that upon no principles of the inductive philosophy, have we reason to conclude that the order of nature and its laws were ever materially different from what they are at present. The only method, said he, by which we could ever arrive at a knowledge of the process through which this world was elaborated, would be from analogy, or actual observation of the origin and progress of similar systems. And as this experience is impossible, there are no facts presented by which we can be led back to the conclusion, that the earth presented any specific form, or series of phenomena at its creation by the Almighty. He declared all cosmogonies, therefore, to be nothing better than the unsubstantial visions of ingenious men, or philosophical air bubbles. This work was committed to the scrutiny of Plato, Dr. Samuel Clarke and Bishop Butler.

The proceedings of this meeting, were concluded by the presentation to the society of a piece by Maupertius, in which this French philosopher, adhering to his old whimsies, endeavoured to show, that the most effectual expedient by which the theory of gravitation might be demonstrated, would be to dig a hole to the centre of the earth, and moreover, that the science of the mind may be most successfully cultivated by anatomical dissections of the heads of giants. The reading of this whimsical production, again threw the whole assemblage into an agreeable train of merriment and pleasantry, and in the midst of this comic sensation, the meeting was adjourned, after entrusting Maupertius' intellectual offspring to the scrutiny of Voltaire, Frederick of Prussia, and Archimedes.

Thus passed my second evening in the renowned city of Saturnia and in the republic of Atlantis. When I cast my eyes around upon this illustrious assembly, I felt like the Gauls upon approaching the Roman Senate, as if in a collection of divinities, and that, with infinite satisfaction, I could spend an eternity in such company.

POETRY ABOUT POE

H. P. Lovecraft's earlier works were most powerfully influenced by a reading of Poe. Residing most of his life in Providence, Rhode Island, Lovecraft frequently visited the Poe landmarks that were to be found there.

Though by nature somewhat of a recluse, H. P. Lovecraft was most expansive in correspondence and built up a wide group of friends with related interests, who sometimes visited him when in the area of Providence. It was on August 7, 1936, that H. P. Lovecraft paid host to two such guests: R. H. Barlow, a very close friend and youthful acolyte of his works, who wrote occasionally for the amateur magazines; and Adolphe de Castro, a confidant of Ambrose Bierce, who collaborated with that barbed-tongue iconoclast on "The Monk and the Hangman's Daughter" and had published in Lovecraft's prime market, *Weird Tales*, two stories that blended science with supernatural horror in the fashion of Lovecraft.

To climax the evening, the three repaired to St. John's Churchyard, athwart the former home of Sarah Helen Whitman—whom Edgar Allan Poe courted in 1847 and 1848—and among whose headstones he was said to have frequently strolled in meditation and contemplation.

The three sat down on a tomb in the graveyard and each wrote a rhymed acrostic to the memory of Edgar Allan Poe. With ungentlemanly haste, Adolphe de Castro sent his poem off to *Weird Tales*, where it was accepted and published in the May 1937 issue. H. P. Lovecraft and R. H. Barlow also dispatched their sonnets to *Weird Tales*, but had them returned because of de Castro's priority. Prompt submission of these poems to the *Science-Fantasy Correspondent*, a handsomely printed science fiction fan magazine of the day, resulted in the publication of the R. H. Barlow and H. P. Lovecraft verses in its March–April 1937 issue, actually beating de Castro into print. After Lovecraft's death, *Weird Tales* reprinted his poem in their May 1938 number.

Considering that all three pieces were hastily improvised in rather poor light, they are remarkably competent efforts. Quite evidently inspired by the concept of H. P. Lovecraft communicating with Poe through the device of phrasing lines inspired by the essence of his spirit in an old Providence graveyard, August W. Derleth, in a very successful dialogue in verse, "Providence: Two Gentlemen Meet at Midnight," published in the Autumn 1948 *Arkham Sampler,* arranges a meeting between the two, stressing their points of affinity.

EDGAR ALLAN POE

(An acrostic sonnet, written in a sequestered graveyard
where once Poe walked.)

By Adolphe de Castro

Enshrined within our hearts is e'er thy name,
Dear Bard, unjoyed by lasting happiness
Great love doth yield; but through thy pain and stress
A messenger, the ghostly Raven, comes,
Revealing horror stark and cold; he bore

A tear that flowed from eyes of lost Lenore,
Light-glinting, and the shade of her caress.
Lo, then, thy genius flamed with art that chills
A grim, ubiquitous malignity.
Night-gloomed and pulsing with portending ills
Pernicious yet delightful, brought to thee
On angel's wings, a gift that, loved and feared,
Enranked thee greatest monarch of the weird.

ST. JOHN'S CHURCHYARD

By R. H. Barlow

Endless, the darkly printed tombstones rise;
Dim evening sunset pours about them now,
Golden and pale, on path and grave and bough,
And furtively they stare with lifeless eyes,
Remembering ages lost beneath the years,
All silent now, with strife and love and tears
Like scattered leaves through which the autumn sighs.

Less than the leaves a century can grow
As tale and memory blend before the gaze;
No longer lost, these half-forgotten days . . .
Perhaps the shadows stir, perhaps they show
Outcast by life and death, the lonely form
Exiled, of Poe, the man of night and storm.

IN A SEQUESTERED CHURCHYARD WHERE ONCE POE WALKED

By H. P. Lovecraft

Eternal brood the shadows on this ground,
Dreaming of centuries that have gone before;
Great elms rise solemnly by slab and mound,
Arch'd high above a hidden world of yore.
Round all the scene a light of memory plays,
And dead leaves whisper of departed days,
Longing for sights and sounds that are no more.

Lonely and sad, a specter glides along
Aisles where of old his living footsteps fell;
No common glance discerns him, though his song
Peals down through time with a mysterious spell.
Only the few who sorcery's secret knew,
Espy amidst these tombs the shade of Poe.

PROVIDENCE: TWO GENTLEMEN MEET AT MIDNIGHT

By August W. Derleth

H.P.L.: Good evening, sir. We meet at last
along these streets both you and I have often passed.

E.A.P.: Indeed, we are not strangers, you and I,
for all the many times you passed me by
while you were still on that material plane
and pervious to cold and wind and rain.
I used to see you when you walked
past Helen's home, and one evening when you talked
till almost dawn with friends upon the stones
that mark more than a century of bones,
and wrote some verses with genteel comedy and some ado—
an acrostic, if I recall, a poem or two,
of which, sir—my respects—yours was quite the best.
Of your nocturnal wanderings, that evening marked a crest.

H.P.L.: Yes, I remember it—we celebrated one
who went before, who seemed of night rather than the sun.

E.A.P.: It is quite true that I
preferred the night owl's cry
to day's round. But this leaning toward the midnight air,
my friend, methinks we share.

H.P.L.: The night, sir, does for Providence and all things old
something that takes from them the chilling cold
of newness and the marks of what some poor, benighted men
incline to calling progress. Then,
too, there was for me the knowledge in this place
you would not choose a sunlit hour to show your face.

E.A.P.: True, there are some places that I would not go—
and they grow more in number; one year it is Brick Row
torn down, and on another a house I knew,
but there remain to such as us a few,
as always—Helen's home, and others on old Prospect Street,

Benefit and College Hill—these byways knew my feet
long ago, as once I knew familiar walls and floors
long since away. You, too, pause at once known doors;
there was a house on Angell Street you sought in vain
one night, and on Barnes, at number ten, and again
on College, number sixty-six—
old things, old places—nothing sticks
to us like these. I followed you another time; you went along
    the Seekonk where,
a child, you made obeisance to ancient gods of earth and air.
My friend, you see,
we share a common loyalty.

H.P.L.: How long ago that was! Since then, you knew,
        others took their place—Dagon, Yog-Sothoth, Cthulhu.

E.A.P.: A host of evil, as much the terrors of the mind
        as were those older, my own kind.

H.P.L.: All that is done, sir. But here all 'round
        still stands for us a kind of hallowed ground—
        hallowed in a way for each his own,
        and neither of us in this is quite alone.

E.A.P.: The night is young, my friend,
        and there are old, enchanting paths to wend.
        A walk down Benefit, past Helen's home, past that shunned
          house of old alarm
        once you celebrated . . . Let us forgo formality.
        Come, sir, my arm.

A VALENTINE'S DAY POEM TO EDGAR ALLAN POE

For Valentine's Day, 1846, less than a year from the end of her life from tuberculosis on January 30, 1847, Virginia Elizabeth Poe, then twenty-two years of age, wrote a poem to her husband. There is a sort of a supreme irony transcending the pathos that this girl, sick, dying, of limited education, should submit her love in a format in which her husband would come to be regarded as technically the supreme master of all American literature.

The poem was donated to the Enoch Pratt Free Library of Baltimore, Maryland, by distant cousins of Poe—Dr. Derick A. January of West Hartford, Connecticut, and Mrs. Worth B. Daniels of Washington. At the time of its receipt the director of Enoch Pratt, Richard Hart, released the verse for general newspaper publication and commented that it was "the most interesting and valuable Poe item received in the last twenty-five years."

Newspaper stories, distributed by Associated Press, intimated that the phrase "tattling of many tongues" referred to Poe's "flirtations" with other women. Its lines repeat the eternal hope of young love, that there exists somewhere the possibility of a romantic idyll, insulated from the activities of the world, and impregnable to outside influence.

UNTITLED VALENTINE POEM TO EDGAR ALLAN POE
FROM HIS WIFE, 1846

By Virginia Poe

> Ever with thee I wish to
> roam—
> Dearest, my life is thine.
> Give me a cottage for my
> home
> And a rich old cypress vine,

Removed from the world with
    its sin and care
And the tattling of many
    tongues.
Love alone shall guide when
    we are there—
Love shall heal my
    weakened lungs;
And O, the tranquil hours
    we'll spend,
Never wishing that others
    may see!
Perfect ease we'll enjoy with-
    out thinking to lend
Ourselves to the world and
    its glee—
Ever peaceful and blissful
    we'll be.

The only periodicals still published in the United States devoted to tales of horror, terror, and the supernatural at this writing are edited by Robert A. W. Lowndes as *Magazine of Horror* and *Startling Mystery Stories*. These publications are the prime regular source for tales in the mood of Poe ("The Oblong Box" by Edgar Allan Poe was reprinted in the January 1965 issue of *Magazine of Horror*) and one of the few markets for new writers who prefer to write in that vein.

Several decades ago, Robert Lowndes built a reputation as a poet of mood fantasy and accomplished the incredible feat of actually *selling* poetry on a regular basis to the newsstand fantasy pulp magazines *Famous Fantastic Mysteries* and *Fantastic Novels*. Most of it exalted the masters of the strange, A. Merritt and H. P. Lovecraft, but one was titled "To Edgar Allan Poe" * (appearing in the September 1940 issue of *Fantastic Novels*). It was particularly distinguished for two lines which captured the essence of Poe:

> And all thy wounded sensitivity
> Burst forth in strange, ethereal melody.

"Baltimore, October 3rd" was written especially for this book. It appropriately brings down the curtain on the sad, haunted life of Edgar Allan Poe.

*It had earlier appeared in an amateur magazine, *Fanta-Verse*, published as a one-shot for The First National Science Fiction Convention, May 1938, Newark, New Jersey.

Baltimore, October 3rd

By Robert A. W. Lowndes

And on Lombard Street, passing Couth & Sergeant's,
The rain light, but a chill penetrating,
Joe Walker came up toward me, running, his face
Red, and a wetness on it more than rain.
He stopped as a clock stops, stood there, looking
As if he'd told me something; eyes
Searching me, and the chill stabbing through. Joe
Reached out, grasping my arm, and still
No sounds, no words,
Nothing but silence and chill between us, grasping
My arm and drawing me into the tavern.

He pointed, and I saw Death,
                              Death sitting;
                                        Death
In an armchair, sitting, wearing a tattered hat,
And the clothing soiled . . . the golden bowl broken;
No blood, but life seeping out;
No moans, but words tumbling out,
                              disordered
Words I knew, words out of books I knew . . .
And the threadbare voice whose pattern had I not heard . . . ?
Where?
            And Walker said, "He's coming—the doctor's coming,
"I took him a note—Doctor Snodgrass—he's coming." One
In the crowd, the scurvy crowd from the Coop,
Where they kept the voters penned, feeding them liquor,
Went by us then, brushing the figure's hat, knocked it
Askew and I saw the eyes, the eyes now dull . . .
                                        Oh God,
God . . . Mr. Poe!

And I didn't want to go out that night, didn't
Want to stand in the lamplight and face them,

But I had promised, and they were old; Mother
Asked me first and I couldn't answer her then. I looked
Over her shoulder, beyond the light, where the shadow
Touched on the bookcase, touched diagonally, cutting
Across the copy of *Al Aaraaf* I had brought her,
And I wondered if the pages were still uncut.
The clear voice stilled, the voice
That had sung and spoken as none before in this land;
The eyes that harbored visions,
And visions beyond visions, glazed . . .
And I started to say, "Mr. Poe . . ." then the sound
Of my own voice drove away the words,
All of the words, all of the words I'd wanted
To tell them, fleeing now, out of my mind, the chill
Seeping in and the words I wanted to say to them
Gone.
        ". . . He's dying."

And I knew Mother would pray for him that night;
But Father's hand went up,
A little up from the arm of the chair; his head
Moving slowly, slowly from side to side. Then, the voice
Slowly, "Mr. Poe . . ."
                  Silence, another shake of the head . . .
". . . Drank too much."